RETRIBUTION

NOMAD BIKER ROMANCE SERIES

CHIAH WILDER

Copyright © 2019 by Chiah Wilder
Print Edition

Editing by Lisa Cullinan
Cover design by Cheeky Covers

All rights reserved. This book or any portion thereof may not be reproduced or used in any manner whatsoever without the express written permission of the author except for the use of brief quotations in a book review. Please purchase only authorized additions, and do not participate in or encourage piracy of copyrighted materials.

Your support of the author's rights is appreciated.

Disclaimer: This is a work of fiction. Names, characters, businesses, places, events and incidents are either the products of the author's imagination or used in a fictitious manner. Any resemblance to actual persons, living or dead, or actual events is purely coincidental.

I love hearing from my readers. You can email me at chiahwilder@gmail.com.

Make sure you sign up for my newsletter so you can keep up with my new releases, special sales, free short stories, and other treats only available to newsletter readers. When you sign up, you will receive a FREE hot and steamy novella. Sign up at: http://eepurl.com/bACCL1.

Visit me on facebook at facebook.com/AuthorChiahWilder

Insurgent MC Series:

Hawk's Property
Jax's Dilemma
Chas's Fervor
Axe's Fall
Banger's Ride
Jerry's Passion
Throttle's Seduction
Rock's Redemption
An Insurgent's Wedding
Outlaw Xmas
Wheelie's Challenge
Christmas Wish
Insurgents MC Romance Series: Insurgents Motorcycle Club Box Set (Books 1 – 4)
Insurgents MC Romance Series: Insurgents Motorcycle Club Box Set (Books 5 – 8)

Night Rebels MC Series:

STEEL
MUERTO
DIABLO
GOLDIE
PACO
SANGRE
ARMY

Nomad Biker Romance Series:

Forgiveness

Steamy Contemporary Romance:

My Sexy Boss

CHAPTER ONE

Dakota

"Come on, don't do this to me—not now. You can make it, just a few more miles," Dakota coaxed the Ford Explorer, gripping the wheel as if her life depended on it. "Well, okay, more than a few miles … but still …"

A strange cranking noise came from under the hood followed by a creak and a loud pop.

Dakota breathed out a long exhale and doubled down on the wheel, clamping her foot down on the gas pedal. She had just passed the sign for Philipsburg, Montana, and the SUV had to make it at least another twenty miles before they were home free. The whole damn day had been one from hell. Her knuckles turned white on the steering wheel, and the whole car gave a giant rattle, jolting her in her seat.

"Fuck," she said out loud as a sinking sensation whipped through her stomach.

Dakota knew with a sense of dread that there was no saving the situation. With a quick grumble, she pulled over to the shoulder.

"Please, with everything I've dealt with this past week, please just be fixable," she muttered under her breath.

The Explorer had been with Dakota since she'd first gotten her license at sixteen years old. Her dad had bought her the SUV from a buddy of his. It'd been far from new, had quite a few dents and scratches, but she'd fallen in love with it the day he parked the blue Explorer on their driveway.

For the most part, her beloved car had been more than reliable, but the irony that it had chosen this moment to crap out on her hit her over the head like a thousand-pound hammer. Everything in her life was breaking, so why the hell wouldn't the SUV follow suit? A new start. That's all she'd wanted, and look what she was getting for it.

Dakota pressed her lips together, jerked the key out of the ignition, and pocketed it. She closed her eyes and leaned back in the seat and swallowed past the lump in her throat. Blindly, she fumbled through her bag for the water bottle then took a giant swig. She was already overheating in the midday summer sun. AC was a nice little luxury that had been broken since her dad had bought the vehicle. She grabbed a tissue from her purse and wiped the sweat from her face as she stared out the windshield. *A miracle's not going to happen. I'm just delaying the inevitable.* Dakota yanked open the creaky door and shoved one foot onto the steaming pavement.

"Ugh." She tied her waist-length, dyed blonde hair up in a sloppy bun.

She winced as she stuck her hands under the burning hood and popped it, then looked down into the steaming wreckage of her engine. Yeah, there was no saving that mess. Dakota didn't really know what she was looking at, but anyone could clearly see that it wasn't good. The whole engine block smelled like burning oil—a thick and acrid odor. She slammed down the hood.

"Dammit!" she yelled. There sure as hell wasn't a way she could afford a tow truck, let alone a mechanic to check out the damage. She'd used the last half of her meager savings to buy gas a couple miles back, which was pretty damn pointless now.

There was no other option—it was time to stick out her thumb.

Dakota nabbed her bag out of the passenger seat, took a quick chug of water, and started to walk toward her final destination. The heat was already in her face as it sank into her skin in waves, and the air in front of her shimmered as she took slow, measured steps forward. The sun and humidity were relentless. There was little doubt it would only get worse, so walking the twenty or so miles into town? *Not an option.*

"Come on, universe, give me something good, will you?" Dakota murmured to herself as she stuck her thumb out and kept walking down the side of the nearly empty road. "Couldn't have happened on a highway, *nooo* … I had to take the damn back roads."

The idea of anyone stopping for a hitchhiker these days was insane. There was too much at stake and a majority of people didn't have the time or the heart to take a risk on someone who could be a psycho killer. Not that she fit the profile. A five-foot-five blonde with a slight, slim build could hardly take on anyone. The truth was that *she* would be prime bait for anyone trying to take advantage.

Dakota winced at the thoughts flying through her mind.

She rubbed her temple as her chest grew tight and she tried to take a deep breath. Nope, that wasn't happening. *Now isn't the time for a panic attack.* As a sweep of anxiety washed over her, she clenched her teeth and shut her eyes. *One breath. Two breaths. Three.* It was trite as hell, but sometimes it worked, especially if she was lucky and caught the symptoms quick enough. Thinking of all the events that had transpired to put her on the run *again* wasn't helping one bit.

"Focus, dammit." Dakota breathed in and out and tried to keep moving despite the epic heat wave and the threat of fight or flight that screamed in the back of her brain. She blinked a few times and studied the tarmac at her feet.

A loud rumble filled her ears then it died down to a deep growl.

"You need a ride?"

Dakota stumbled over her feet and glanced up. A metallic purple motorcycle blinded her under the afternoon sun.

"What the—" She took a few steps back. "Where did you come from?"

The rider grunted and shrugged one shoulder. He looked back toward the road, as if he was ready to get going again. What the hell was she supposed to do with this? Sure, she needed a break—but one who rode a motorcycle wasn't on the agenda. Dakota frowned and shielded the sun from her face as she looked him over.

The biker was clearly older than her twenty years, and he had an edge to him. A black bandana dotted with skulls covered his head and a small silver hoop in his right ear gleamed in the sunlight. Mirrored sunglasses with flame-style frames wrapped around his eyes and she could see her reflection in them, reminding her of the distortion mirrors at the carnival that used to come through her hometown of Pocatello, Idaho, when she was a kid. Dark blond scruff covered his strong jawline. He wore a sleeveless leather vest and blue jeans that fit tight over his corded thighs.

"You wanna a ride or not?" His voice was a low, gruff rub.

Dakota brushed away the stray hairs sticking to her sweaty face as she shifted from one foot to the other, her gaze still fixed on him.

A full sleeve of tattoos decorated the one arm she could see—and she was sure there was more ink on the parts of him that were clothed. A small tingle licked up the back of her neck. His tats ranged from skulls and a giant Grim Reaper to a few text-based pieces she couldn't make out that were slightly faded out. But either way, the biker had one hell of a canvas on him.

"You should've gotten better ink for those," she pointed toward his fading tats, still unable to make complete eye contact due to the sunglasses. "They went too shallow underneath the skin for the lines to take properly."

He jerked his head back but didn't say anything. Then he turned away from her and stared straight ahead, his foot twitching as if he couldn't wait to get back on the road. Everything about his vibe screamed impatience and confidence, and a funny feeling burrowed in her belly as she stood watching him. She figured any minute now he should ask her if she was getting on or not—but he just stared into the distance, bike rumbling, waiting for her to slide behind him. Dakota pressed her lips together and noted the huge fractured skull patch on the back of his leather vest.

Ah, hell. He's in a motorcycle club. She craned her neck and saw that he wore a patch that read "Nomad," on the bottom and "Steel Devils" on the top. She'd seen them ride through Pocatello and Idaho Falls enough times to recognize their patch. They'd ride in twos, their big Harleys breaking the sound barrier as they sped through the town. When she was young, she used to think that with all the black leather they wore, they looked like a swarm of flies buzzing past her hometown.

Fear mixed with intrigue, and she wasn't sure if getting on the back of his bike would be the smartest thing to do. Dakota had heard plenty of stories about the outlaw club over the years, and instead of even considering accepting a ride from him, she should be hightailing it out of there—the oppressive heat be damned. She glanced over her shoulder at the empty road and then back at the biker. She remembered the time when a few of the bikers had come into the tattoo parlor where she'd worked in Idaho Falls. Her boss had given them some new art, and now she wondered if this guy had been one of them. She squinted her eyes and stared at him, but she couldn't recall if he'd been at the Ink Stop before.

Dakota shook her head. She knew enough about the Steel Devils' reputation to stay the hell away. She'd had enough trouble with men for one lifetime, so there was no need to try her luck with anyone else who screamed "danger," and the biker on the idling Harley definitely fit that bill.

"You done ogling me, baby?" he rumbled out, looking back at her through his aviator sunglasses.

Dakota gasped. "I wasn't—"

"Yeah ... you were. Are you comin' or not?"

A loud horn ripped the answer straight from her lips. Her hand cramped where she was gripping her bag and she licked her lips. She tensed and moved to the side as a bright red Dodge Charger Daytona screeched to an abrupt stop right beside them.

"Fuckin' assholes," she thought she heard the biker mutter to himself.

The passenger side window rolled down and a preppy-looking college kid around her age stuck his head out with a huge grin plastered across his face. He looked like a golden retriever, all dopey and "aw shucks" like. Dakota raised an eyebrow, looking from the one stranger to the other with a mounting sense of *get me the hell out of here*.

"Hey, are you having car trouble again? Didn't we tell you last week to get that thing checked out? If you needed a ride, you should've called us—you know we wouldn't have minded." The stranger hit the side of the passenger door with his open palm and pointed with his thumb to the backseat. "Hop in and we'll get you back to town."

"Okay, thanks." Dakota picked up on what they were doing—giving her an out with the biker. "My cell lost power awhile ago, and the Explorer doesn't come with your top-of-the-line charger. You know how it goes," she said, playing along. She hiked up her bag. "Are you sure you have room in there?"

"Are you going to be stubborn again? We always have room for you." The guy's grin grew wider, his eyes a little bit rounder, slightly inclining his head toward the small backseat. "Get in or we'll be late for class again."

A ride with two college kids was probably a better bet than one with the rough, rugged and, most likely, dangerous biker guy.

Dakota smiled and started to walk toward the car. "Sure, thanks."

"I wouldn't go with them."

The words were so low that at first she didn't think she heard them right. "What?" She stopped in place and glanced over at the biker, who was still staring straight ahead on the idling motorcycle.

"Get on back. Those fuckers are bad news."

"Do you know them?"

"Don't have to—I know their *type*."

"Yeah, right. That's real convincing." She glanced at the two guys, who looked like they were still wet behind the ears, then back at the badass *biker* whose road name was probably "Menace" or something equally scary, and she shook her head. *This is a no brainer.*

Dakota turned away and didn't look back at him while she jerked open the back door of the Daytona, trying to ignore a song from the Chainsmokers blaring from the surround sound speakers. Cool air wrapped around her, and she figured listening to electronic music instead of her preferred hard rock was a small price to pay for air conditioning.

She leaned back against the cool leather seats and fixed her gaze straight ahead as the car sped down the road.

CHAPTER TWO

DAKOTA

LESS THAN FIFTEEN minutes later, Dakota regretted using her gut to define any of her life choices. Everything had started out fine, but it had quickly devolved into a frat party on wheels, and the two guys wouldn't listen to a damn thing she said. Her only hope was that she'd make it in one piece to town, and then she'd be rid of the misogynistic assholes.

"Hey, babe, we're taking you to our favorite bar to mix it up a little. You like shots?" "Golden retriever boy" looked at her from the passenger seat with another trademark wide grin. "What am I saying? I'm sure that a pretty girl like you loves to party. You would be kickass arm candy."

By now, Dakota had deduced that the jerk's smile wasn't brought on by any warm personality traits. It seemed to be the result of whatever drugs were free flowing through his system, because his pupils were as big as dinner plates, and he was talking a mile a minute.

"You're supermodel gorgeous. I'm sure you hear that all the time, don't you, babe?" the driver chimed in as he hung a right at full speed. The squealing tires echoed through the car and he laughed. "Tucker's going to shit a brick when he sees her at Duffy's with us."

There was little hope that the driver was in a more sober headspace. Neither of them had even given Dakota their names. Now it was only a matter of clinging to her sanity for the rest of the ride and hoping she had enough time to make a clean break for it before they tried to do anything stupid. Her internal alarms were already on blast, and she was ready to jet from the car as soon as the timing was right.

"You're going to love Duffy's," golden retriever boy said.

"Mmm ..." Dakota made a non-committal noise.

In the meantime, she perched on the edge of the seat and tried to be as polite as possible without making herself overly friendly. Since becoming a tattoo artist, she'd become a pro at innocent flirting and light conversation. A majority of her male customers at her old shop liked to think that she was free game just because she was a woman and she touched their bodies in a softer and more intimate way than her male counterparts.

Dakota swallowed past the knot in her throat, and her attention flew from watching Dumb and Dumber to staring out the window. The wheels in her mind whirred as she tried to figure out how to get out of the predicament she'd found herself in. More than once she'd cursed her bad decision of grabbing a ride with the clean-cut guys rather than the tough-looking biker. Licks of panic ran up her spine but she pushed them down, refusing to think about the past or what may happen with these two men. The last thing she needed was anxiety to cloud her mind.

"We're here, everyone out!" the grinning golden retriever shouted, as if there were a pack of people in the car. "Man, today is our lucky fucking day," he said, clasping his hand on his friend's shoulder.

As Dakota reached for the handle, the door popped open by itself and both guys waited outside in front of the car. *Just great! What a fabulous bunch of escorts.* She gritted her teeth, slid out of the car, and plastered on a fake-ass smile.

"Is this in the center of town?" she asked while trying to get her bearings.

"It's over that way." The driver of the Daytona pointed in the opposite direction from Duffy's. "You coming, gorgeous?"

He made the question irrelevant when his hand shifted to rest on her lower back, guiding her toward the metal front door of the bar. His crony took up a spot on the other side.

"So long as there's free beer in the deal, I'm in." She played along all the while measuring the seconds until she could stop playing stupid games and get the hell away from them. "Do they have anything low calorie?"

The men snickered and the driver's hand pressed firmer against her. Dakota figured she might as well act like how they were treating her and then they wouldn't be expecting her to bail. She had to be able to lose them sooner rather than later. One quick look around the dive bar they were currently strolling into made her think that she might actually be able to ditch these assholes. There were a lot of dark corners to hide in and then skitter out of when they weren't looking. With a nervous twist to her stomach, she let them guide her toward the bar.

"Don't worry, babe. We'll hook you up. Wouldn't want a delicate little thing like you to go thirsty."

Dakota leaned against the scratched up wooden counter and cased the place for all the nearest exits while the boys ordered their drinks at the bar. Being midafternoon on a Wednesday, the place wasn't too crowded, but there were more than a few stools filled at the bar by customers she supposed were the regulars. There was only one woman among them: she had wild gray hair, bright red lips with an unlit cigarette dangling between them, and sunken cheeks with deeply etched lines crisscrossing her pallid skin. The woman fixed her rheumy gaze on Dakota, occasionally dabbing at the corners of her eyes. Dakota resisted the urge to cringe and take a few steps backward.

"Here you go." The driver shoved a plastic cup into her hand, spilling sticky liquid all up her wrist.

"Shit," she muttered as she looked down into the red concoction. It had a cherry. No ice. She sniffed it and noted it was nothing a lightweight could stomach and certainly not before six at night.

Whatever it was, it sure as hell wasn't a beer. And Dakota had no intention on touching anything she hadn't watched the bartender pour. Her insides churned with fear, while on the outside she tried her best to play the cool hitchhiker, bubbly and moronic just like Tweedle Dee and Tweedle Dum expected from her.

"Good, huh?" Golden retriever boy nudged her as he and the other asshole crowded and herded her away from the bar and toward a table off in one of the corners.

Dammit, they aren't letting up.

"Yeah, it's fruity." Dakota faked a giggle before she put down the cup. "I need something with bubbles in it." The truth was her stomach was sour as hell and she needed a ginger ale to try and calm it down a bit.

"I'll get it for you," the driver said.

Dakota shook her head and started walking to the bar, knowing full well they'd follow her. "I'm good."

Sure enough, the two jerks were her shadow as she sidled up to the counter. The bartender gave her a quick once over.

"What would you like?"

"A ginger ale with extra ice."

"Don't you want a shot of something in it?" one of the idiots asked her.

She glanced over her shoulder and plastered another fake smile on her face. "Not now, but I'll get one next time."

"Here you go," the bartender said, putting the drink in front of her.

She took a long gulp, savoring the cool freshness as it slid down her parched throat. The bubbles from the carbonation tickled her nose and she rubbed it.

"How much do I owe you?" she asked.

"We got this, babe." The driver lifted his chin. "Put it on our tab, Lance."

The bar man grinned. "Sure. Have a good time, guys."

Dakota drained the glass and pushed away from the counter. "Which way is the little girl's room?"

"Oh, back there, doll-face. Don't worry, we'll hold down the fort while you touch up your makeup. Tucker just texted; he'll be here in a few. You want to look real good for him." The driver laughed and smacked her butt while golden retriever boy guffawed.

"I'll be back," she mumbled and then scurried to the bathroom. The whole way there she sensed their eyes on her behind. *Ugh, disgusting. I've got to get away from them.* Snippets from her past flashed through her mind, bombarding her thoughts with possible scenarios that could happen if she didn't get the hell out of there. Panic skittered over her, leaving her skin clammy and her temples pounding. *What am I going to do?* The way the assholes had talked to the bartender behind the bar, it seemed like this dump was a frequent stop for them. So there probably wouldn't be a lot of luck in enlisting the aid from the bartender, and the patrons in the bar didn't look like they'd raise one finger to help her. Once again, she was on her own.

Inside the windowless, dirty restroom, Dakota went through her bag, hoping an answer would materialize, out of nowhere. She still had her pocketknife, which she slipped into the front pocket of her jeans. That was a last resort, but one she wouldn't hesitate to throw into the mix.

Unlike the last time.

That would never happen again. Ever.

Dakota ran both hands through her hair and glanced at her reflection in the mirror. There were dark circles under her eyes, and she looked kind of crazed and a little bit manic. She closed her lids and blew out a short breath and then a series of longer, more measured ones as if she could yoga breathe her way out of this harsh, new nightmare she'd found herself in right now.

All the exits were in perfect line of sight from their damn table, and she doubted she could make a run for it without one or both of those jerks catching her. Considering her shitty luck for the most part, she'd probably run smack into this Tucker guy they kept yapping about.

"This day just keeps getting better and better for you, doesn't it?"

Dakota threw her stuff back in the bag and zipped it up, doing a quick knife check for accessibility and reaction time.

With no solid plan still in the works, Dakota glanced at the door and her breath hitched. There was no way she would put it past either of those idiots to barge into the women's restroom to find her. Icy-cold shivers ran up and down her spine. She had to get out of there fast before one or both of them came in and trapped her. Swallowing, she gathered the tattered edges of her courage and pushed the door open, then stepped into the tiny hallway that led back into the bar area.

"Sugar, you were gone an awfully long time. What did you do, fall in?" Golden retriever barked out a laugh as he cornered her, an empty cup clutched in one hand. "We were worried about you."

His fake concern was overridden by his sloppy alcohol breath and the fact that he kept pressing forward until her back was against one of the graffiti-covered walls. Dakota's heart drummed an erratic beat as fear pounded through her veins. No doubt, this was one of the worst case scenarios. She didn't take her eyes off him as her shaky fingers tried to slide down to where she kept the pocketknife.

"So you're playing hard to get. I like that—it makes it more fun." He took another short step forward until she barely had any breathing room and every inch of him was pressed up against her from the tips of her toes to her head. "Did you like the drink? It should be kicking in by now."

Dakota calculated ways to take him down. There weren't any.

"I didn't drink it, asshole."

"Yeah, you did—at the bar." He laughed dryly.

Nausea swept through her in a rush. Hot tingles charged down her skin followed by a cold sweat that left her head spinning. All at once, she couldn't tell up from down anymore. A dull roar of panic silenced all her other thoughts as his hands fell on her body, clamping on her arm that was moving toward the pocket with the knife.

Dakota jerked back on impulse—but there was nowhere to go from there. She couldn't utter a sound. Her whole body became paralyzed with old fear roaring back to the surface as heat swam up behind her shut eyelids and she froze under the weight of him.

"That's it, you want to be compliant for me, don't you?" he whispered, his breath hot and rancid against her ear. "You're a good little slut. Relax into me … uh-huh … that's it."

Before she could do or say anything else, his other hand moved up under her shirt as his lips sloppily eased down the column of her throat.

Her "no" died away to nothing as her future went on a collision course with her past.

CHAPTER THREE

COBRA

COBRA TILTED HIS head back as the whiskey slid down his throat. It wasn't fucking rocket science to tell when a woman didn't like something—and the pretty, curvy hitchhiker who'd almost hopped on the back of his bike wore a grimace that could crack glass. Cobra had a narrow view of the hallway from his table, and he'd been debating about getting out of his seat ever since he'd seen the fucking frat boy head toward the women's restroom.

But Cobra hadn't. He didn't want to be the one to break up a good time if they were just meeting up for a little kinky public fun. But judging by the hitchhiker's expression at the moment, it didn't look like she wanted the fucker plastered across her body. Standing up, Cobra's blood burned through his veins as he stalked across the bar.

Yeah, there was no damn way he was letting that fucker grope her. Not even for a motherfucking second. It wasn't like Cobra had a hero complex, but he knew a bad time when it popped in front of his eyes, and what was playing out less than a foot in front of him wasn't right in any sense of the word.

Without saying a thing, Cobra snuck up on the fucker. When the girl locked eyes with him, expression wide and vulnerable with surprise, he put a finger to his lips and drew a finger across his throat, pointing to the asshole pinning her to the wall. She gave a barely imperceptible nod and flinched at something the motherfucker was doing along her neck.

"I got you," he mouthed, hoping she could read lips in the muddy darkness.

A low growl barely leaked out from between Cobra's lips. One minute his hands were fisted at his sides, the next, his fingers were tangled in the back of the asshole's hair, arching his neck back as the sonofabitch cried out in surprise and pain. Cobra's other hand grabbed the jerk's wrist, yanking his arm backward until the biker felt the bone barely shifting from the joint.

Motherfucker was howling like a puppy—all but begging Cobra to leave him alone like a bully on the playground, not a grown-ass man getting his rocks off on an unwilling woman. He whimpered and Cobra tugged up a little harder, face-planting the asshole into the wall. He yelled in agony and pinwheeled his free arm. Meanwhile, Cobra saw the hitchhiker skitter out from under her attacker.

A thin smile tugged at Cobra's lips as he watched her waste no time in dashing into the bar area. A groan snapped his attention back to the jerk in his grasp.

"If you touch another girl who doesn't want it, I'll find you, fucker. Got me?" Cobra breathed against the guy's cheek, using his leverage to force him down on his knees as the guy made small, pained noises. "Answer me."

"Sure, yeah, I won't do it again," he panted, his upper body weaving where Cobra still kept him upright. "I'm wasted. I didn't know what I was doing."

"Bullshit!" A fist to the pathetic loser's jaw brought out another yelp.

"Okay. Please, it hurts."

Cobra grunted without much sympathy and tossed the douchebag aside like a piece of trash. Thankfully, it looked like he'd kept everything quiet enough so that the other people in the joint wouldn't take his confrontation as an invite to put the smackdown on anything that moved in the bar. An all-out brawl fest wasn't on his schedule for that day. Cobra planted his feet wide apart and watched the sniveling pussy as he crawled toward the corner wiping the blood from his nose and mouth with the hem of his shirt.

Now that *that* was done and over with, Cobra wouldn't feel right with himself until he checked on the hitchhiker. If she was still even there. Cobra turned around and walked out from the small hallway, and his eyes flicked to the exit farthest away from the bathrooms where he watched her purple backpack duck out of sight before the door closed without any noise.

Cobra scrubbed a fist over his face. He should've been more forceful when he'd noticed the assholes were playing like they knew her, but he didn't want her to feel pressured from him, especially since she'd seemed afraid of him even though she kept checking him out. She'd thought she was being clever by sneaking peeks at him, but he saw every single glance and the way she reacted to it. It was pretty damn sweet.

Snapping back to the present, Cobra got his ass in gear and hightailed it outside the bar before the cute hitchhiker found another ride. He threw his hand up as the sun shone in his eyes and dug in his pocket for his sunglasses. The parking lot only had a few cars and a couple of rice burners in it—pretty much like it was when he'd pulled in. He hadn't planned on stopping at Duffy's for a shot, but when he saw the assholes' Daytona, a bad feeling had hit him in the gut, so he decided to check things out. Cobra didn't have many regrets, but letting the woman go off with those sonsofbitches had been damn high on his short list. At least he'd been given the chance to correct it.

"Where the fuck are you?" he muttered under his breath as he walked around.

On the far side of the building, he spotted her leaning against the wall with her head in one of her hands. Cobra hesitated, then stood in place and watched her. He had to play this one right or else he'd spook the hell out of her, and that's the last thing he wanted. She already had hesitations about him, and he didn't want her to think he was coming over to finish what the dumb fuck had started inside the bar.

Without trying to conceal his footsteps, the gravel crunched under his boots as he walked toward her. Dakota's head jerked up from where she stared at the pavement, then she glared at him as if she'd already expected trouble and was ready to meet it. Cobra watched her fingertips linger along the pocket where he figured she was carrying a weapon. *Smart girl.* He held out both his palms in the air, indicating that he had nothing to hide, and kept his distance.

"You doing okay?" he asked, low and quiet so he didn't frighten her.

"Why do you care? Did you come back here to finish what that asshole started?" She jerked her head in the direction of the bar. "Did you decide you want a piece of me while the getting is good?"

Cobra flinched and took a quick step backward, shaking his head. For a split second it angered him that she would think that of him, but then she didn't know him. Disgust made his lips curl from the mere thought of her accusation.

"Forcing a chick doesn't get me off."

"Doesn't stop everyone from trying it." She coughed and wiped a hand across her forehead, her hand still resting on her pocket.

"Not me—that's not my scene. You got a knife in there?" Cobra pointed at her hand.

"Yeah, so don't try any shit with me." Her chin lifted in defiance.

He almost broke out laughing, but he didn't think she'd see the humor in it, so he just nodded and crossed his arms across his chest.

"It's fuckin' hot out here, and you don't look so good." A thin layer of perspiration misted over her pallid skin, and she looked like she was going to faint.

She stood up a little straighter, gripping her bag as if she was ready to bolt. "Thanks for the save back there."

The apology was begrudging, like she still didn't trust him. That was fine because he wasn't trying to win any Good Samaritan of the Year award.

"Maybe you should go back inside and get a glass of water. I'll go with you to make sure no one messes with you."

She waved her hand in the air. "I'm good." She swayed on her feet and Cobra hesitated to move toward her, trapped between his instinct and the twisted reality of their situation. Instead, he cleared his throat, unable to shift his focus from her.

"Really," her voice was hoarse and her chest rose up and down too fast, "I'm fine."

Bullshit. He took a few steps closer.

"Did you drink anything?"

"Do you think I'm stupid? No, I didn't touch anything they gave me."

"Are you dizzy? World doing a one-eighty?"

"Probably sunstroke." She wouldn't meet his stare and she swung around her backpack, grabbing a bottle of water from inside and taking a few desperate swigs. "I just need some air conditioning."

"Uh-huh," Cobra said, scanning her wavering body language. "That's probably it."

The hitchhiker was a stubborn one, that was for damn sure. She was pale as a sheet of paper and wavering like there was a wind machine behind her head. Judging by her shaking hands and rapidly blinking eyes, he gave her less than five minutes before she crashed to the ground.

"Really, dude, I don't need your help anymore. You can—"

Before she could finish the sentence, Cobra shot forward to catch her as she fainted into his arms. Fuck, she barely weighed anything. He could feel her ribcage through her shirt as he maneuvered her into his strong arms. Picking her up like a child, she slumped against his chest as her head lolled back. He cradled her neck with his hand and glanced down into her relaxed face.

"Damn, you're young," he said in a low voice. "What the fuck have I gotten myself into?"

There was no way Cobra was going to leave her like that, but he couldn't very well throw her on his bike and hope to hell he could hold her in place long enough for her to sleep off whatever made her feel like shit. He scanned the road's skyline for the nearest motel in the area.

It wasn't the greatest option, considering what just went down with the girl—but he didn't have anything else on the back burner. With a quick readjustment of her weight in his arms, he looked down into her serene face and started walking to the nearest source of air conditioning that wasn't connected to Duffy's.

Mountain View motel was not one of the nicer ones in town, but it was the nearest one to Duffy's, so Cobra pushed open the door and entered the small lobby. A teenager, looking at his phone, barely acknowledged Cobra when he strode up to the desk. As soon as he kicked the base of the counter, the teen jerked his head up, his eyes widening when he saw Cobra and the unconscious woman in his arms.

"I need a room."

"Uh ... I'm going to need to see your driver's license." The young man's eyes darted from the woman to Cobra and back to the woman.

Cobra jerked his chin at the hitchhiker. "She's sick."

The fresh-faced kid pursed his lips together.

"Don't act like you don't see worse things around this fuckin' dump." Cobra balanced the woman on his hip and took out a wad of bills and handed the teen three twenty-dollar bills. "That's for you giving me the key to a room right now."

The teen grabbed the crisp bills and shoved them in his pocket. "The room's fifty a night and that's with tax. How many nights you going to stay?" He glanced at the woman again.

"Don't know, but at least a couple for sure." Cobra handed him a hundred-dollar bill.

The teenager placed the bill in a drawer then slid a room key Cobra's way. "The manager will probably check up on you."

"I don't think so." Cobra stared fixedly at him until he squirmed then turned away.

"I'm just saying 'cause he sometimes does that."

"Just make sure he doesn't." Cobra shifted the girl in his arms again. "There's some shit that happens around here, right?" There was no way drug dealing and some paid fucking didn't go on around this dump.

The kid's face screwed up tight and his shoulders folded onto themselves. "Yeah," he squeaked out, unable to make eye contact. "Way more than I would like, though you aren't the usual … customer."

"I bet I'm not." Cobra's intuition tingled. He was positive that the young woman in his arms had been drugged, and that meant there was some dealing taking place in Steel Devils' territory. He'd find out what the hell was going on, but for now, he nudged open the door with the toe of his boots and stepped out into the sticky heat.

When Cobra arrived at their room, he turned the lock then stepped in. He placed her on the mismatched blanket covering the full-size bed and took a seat at the rickety table with a sigh, finally relaxing for what seemed like the first time in a long-ass while. His stomach rumbled as he ran a hand through his hair. *What're the odds of her waking up and freaking out while I go get some chow? Fuck.*

Cobra walked over to the bed and looked down at her. The cool air from the AC blew strands of blonde hair across her face. Thin eyebrows arched over almond-shaped eyes that he remembered were brown but not dark. They were more like the color whiskey would be if sunlight shone through it. Her lashes were dark and looked like they were heavy with mascara. Her features were delicate and she had a rosebud mouth and the cutest button nose. His eyes skimmed down to the rise and fall of her chest and a pair of small, perky tits. *Fuck.* He shifted his gaze away but not before he caught a glimpse of the curve of her hip.

"She's too fuckin' young," he said as he lifted the other side of the blanket and covered her.

Cobra grabbed the room key off the table and glanced over at her again. He'd make sure she was okay, and then he'd send her on her way. Staying away was the smartest thing for him to do right now because his body was reacting in a way that was pissing him the hell off. The last thing he needed was to shack up with a woman who looked like she was barely eighteen.

Closing the door quietly behind him, he slipped the key in his pocket and started walking back to Duffy's to retrieve his bike.

CHAPTER FOUR

Dakota

"What the ..." Dakota shot up from the cool covers while the room spun, and she quickly shrank back down again.

A low moan came out of her dry mouth. Christ, she felt like she'd been hit with a baseball bat a couple of times, wrung through a washing machine, and left out to bake in the sun. As bits and pieces of the afternoon came back, she curled up into a ball on her side. Dakota blinked a few times. How had she gone from the bar to—

"Where the hell am I?" she croaked, trying to thrust all her energy down into her hands so she could scramble up and figure out where she was now.

A ping of distrust went off in the back of her brain. Yeah, this wasn't good. Not. At. All. Despite the fact that her joints and muscles seemed to ache everywhere, she pried herself off the bed and managed to make it over to the scratched up table and chair set in the corner. A quick internal inventory later, and she didn't think whoever had brought her here had any time to do what they wanted to her, considering she still had on all of her clothes.

When a throbbing headache stabbed in the back of her brain, it took everything inside her not to scream. It was all too much. The whole damn day, all of it from start to finish had been a complete and total bust. If this was a signal as to how the rest of her life would go from here on out, then there wasn't anywhere she could run where her shitty luck wouldn't follow.

Dakota ran her fingers through her hair, wincing as they tugged through the tangles. She glanced back at the bed and saw her backpack on the nightstand. Just as she was ready to walk over and make sure nothing was taken from it, she heard running water. Adrenaline licked through her as she grasped the arm of the chair. When the water shut off, her eyes snapped to the closed door to the left of the bed. The bathroom. She inhaled and exhaled quickly. There were a couple of options as to who could be behind door number one, and Dakota struggled with the idea of even bothering to find out. If she was smart, she would get the hell out of there before the guy came out and forced her to stay.

Her fingers tightened on the laminated armrest, and she wobbled in place while trying to stop the world from getting on a giant roller coaster of sensory overload. Dakota moved the dusty curtains and peeked outside. It was dark. *I've been out for a while. How the fuck did I wind up here?*

Then the bathroom door burst open and Dakota whirled around and gasped. In the door jamb was the good-looking biker. His hand went to the towel around his waist and he didn't say a word.

They stared at each other across the small space. Despite her mental, physical, and emotional upheaval, something pulled tight down the line of her body as she blinked a few times and quickly shook her head. But that only made the vertigo worse and she whimpered and hung her head.

"Fuck, stop breaking yourself." He was next to her in what seemed like less than a second, his still damp hand supporting her elbows as she hunched over the chair feeling like she was going to faint all over again. "Follow me."

Dakota was useless as he led her back to the bed and set her up so she was lying on a mound of pillows while he clung to that awfully small towel. The biker made taking care of her seem like it was second nature, like they weren't strangers. Drops of water from his damp hair settled across her clothing and sank into her skin.

"Why did you bring me here? What the hell happened?"

Despite the fact that they kept eye contact, he said nothing. His emotions remained completely in check and his face gave nothing away—a blank slate. The least he could do was give her the rundown while she was pathetic and reeling. Instead, he threw a fast food bag in her lap, then strode back into the bathroom and shut the door.

"When you come out of there, I expect answers, biker boy," she said.

Silence from behind the door.

"You have to come out some time."

More silence.

Images of his finely chiseled chest with a smattering of hair covering it burned into her brain. Dakota shut her eyes and clenched her jaw. Yeah, like sheer stubbornness could clear away the stab of arousal that coursed beneath her skin. *This is a crock of shit. So he has a good body. No reason to get all hot and bothered by it.* With a sigh, she dug one hand through the crinkly paper bag and pulled out a wrapped burger. Food didn't sound great with the stomachache, but maybe it would clear up whatever fog bogged down her head.

She took a tentative bite and then a few more while her eyes stayed glued on the door. Finally it opened, and his gaze ran over her, taking in the crumpled wrapper in her lap and the soggy, cold fries being shoved in her mouth.

"Good."

That was it? Dakota cocked her head, and while chewing on the fries, she was pleased to note that whatever worked its way into her system was currently on the move, now that she had food in her stomach. She supposed it must be similar to a hangover.

"Start talking," she said. Another handful of fries went into her mouth as she shifted on the bed.

Two could play at this game. He wanted to be all dark and brooding and a man of mystery? Well, he would serve up what she wanted to know whether he liked it or not because she wasn't going to let up until he started talking. Even if he was a man of little words, he owed her some answers. She wasn't above asking nicely, but so far that didn't seem to be a tactic that would get her anywhere with him.

"Whaddaya want to know?"

The biker lounged against the dresser across from the bed and shoved his hands deep into his jeans' pockets. His jaw jutted out when she didn't answer right away.

"Tell me everything." She threw the burger wrapper into the plastic bin across the room and was way too stoked when the wadded up ball went around the rim before sinking into the trashcan. "I don't have forever, you know."

"Oh, you got somewhere to be now?" He snorted as if the idea was nuts.

"Why would that be so unbelievable?" Dakota curled her legs to her chest, and the quick movement made her head swim as she closed her eyes to try and shut out the disorientation. "You don't know anything about me."

"I know enough."

His ominous answer drew her eyes open, and she was drawn like a magnet to his serious, unreadable expression.

"Tell me. Please."

There was a crack in his façade. Cobra blinked, then his eyes widened a little bit and he shifted from one foot to the other all the while never taking his eyes off her. She could tell by the way he held himself that he hadn't expected her to ask so nicely, and something about it caught him off guard. *Interesting.* Dakota made a mental note and crossed her arms over her chest with a small sigh.

"You're not gonna like it."

Dakota made a small finger motion for him to get the hell on with it. He was obviously older than she, and out of all the shit he'd seen in life, she doubted tonight had been the worst or even close, so why he was so tightlipped was something she couldn't understand. Maybe it was a secret club thing. He didn't want to betray his brothers and reveal too much to the outsider, even though she couldn't figure out why a motorcycle club would have anything to do with those two assholes.

"You got yourself into a fuck-ton of trouble by taking that ride today. After putting you to bed, I did some work and found out those bastards drugged you using a liquid method that's popular on the streets."

"But I didn't drink whatever it was they gave me," she said.

"Didn't you have a soda?"

She shook her head slightly then cocked it to one side. "Yeah, but I got it from the bartender. Wait … how did you know I had a ginger ale?"

"I've got a gift of getting people to open up to me." A sinister smile whispered across his lips.

"What tactics do you use to get the information?" Her insides quivered and she placed her hands across her stomach.

"Whatever it takes. Anyway, the bartender slipped you some Liquid X."

"What the hell's that?"

"GHB—the date rape drug."

Her hand flew to her mouth as she gasped. "The *bartender*? Why the hell would he do that?"

"He gets a kickback from the assholes who gave you a ride."

"I can't believe how stupid I was."

"Don't beat yourself up. How the fuck could you know the former bartender was part of the scheme?"

"Former?"

"I had a heart-to-heart with Duffy. He didn't know the SOB was doing that shit in his place."

"You know the owner?"

"Yeah. I met him at Sturgis a couple of years ago. You're just lucky you didn't drink any booze with that shit in it, otherwise you'd *still* be out."

Dakota rested her head on her knees and took a deep breath. "Who the fuck sells this stuff to guys like them?"

"There's big money in it, and where the dough is, you'll have a drove of people lining up to get a piece of it."

"That's a pretty general answer. Care to elaborate?"

"I don't think you'd benefit from getting involved, so I wasn't planning on it."

She sat back and stared at him.

"You're serious?"

"The less you know about this shit, the better off you are."

"So, what *can* you tell me?"

He scratched the stubble on his jaw and his eyes narrowed, as if he was trying to decide if she could really handle anything he was about to reveal or whether she was too fragile. Dakota met him head on and didn't look away.

"I found the assholes who did it and it's handled." He shrugged. "They won't screw with you again."

That's it. He'd taken care of it, which could be anything from roughing them up to burying the bodies.

"And I'm just supposed to be satisfied with that response? They were taken care of and that's the end of it? I just go on with my life now?"

The muscle in his jaw throbbed. "Yeah … or you could stay here with me."

CHAPTER FIVE

DAKOTA

DAKOTA STARED AT him for a minute then shook her head. "You've got to be kidding me." She swung her legs out onto the side of the bed and shot daggers at him.

"No, not like that—"

"Yeah, sure," she grumbled, beyond sick of being a chew toy for men to salivate over like a piece of used-up property. "Save me to get in good, and then throw out the real payment for your help. So noble of you."

"I didn't fuckin' mean it—"

"Oh, stop lying to yourself and own up to it. You're a grown-ass man who wants to get laid after doing a good deed," Dakota mouthed off, not letting him get a word in edgewise because she knew the name of the game, and she also knew none of his sex could be trusted in the slightest. She was an idiot for staying this long with him.

Another on a long list of mistakes that she would be paying for until she was dead and buried. A shiver coursed down her spine and she tried to blink back the heavy veil of tears that were clouding her vision.

"Thanks, but no thanks."

She leapt to her feet and marched toward the door. No sooner had she moved less than a foot when his huge barrel chest blocked her vision.

"Get the hell out of my way!" Tears tracked down her cheeks and she swiped them away.

"Fuck, I'm an ass."

"No argument here." Dakota tried to sidestep as he put himself in her way again. "Let. Me. Go."

"Go where?"

The words sank home for the first time since she'd left Idaho Falls. There hadn't really been a plan in place, at least nothing concrete or executable. It had been a matter of moving—and moving fast. She had to get away from *him*. That was the only plan. It was a knee-jerk reaction built on fear, panic, and desperation. But now that she was here and so much had already happened in less than twenty-four hours, her lack of a plan suddenly seemed juvenile and naïve—a dumb course of action as she tried to get her life back on track.

"You got a game plan?" His question, asked without judgement, seared into her brain.

"What does that matter? You think your idea is the way to go? I shack up here with you and you take care of me in some kind of *sugar daddy* situation?" Unable to stand still while he remained blocking the only exit in the room, she started pacing back and forth. "I won't sell myself for a bed or give myself away like some stupid trophy. I don't know what you're used to in your MC with all those biker bitches throwing themselves at you, but that's not how I operate, okay?"

"Fine with me, but if you'd shut the fuck up and listen to me for a second, you'd find out that wasn't what I meant at all."

Dakota stopped in the middle of the room, mad at the way his low, gruff timbre made a fine layer of goosebumps slip over her skin. She chewed the inside of her cheek, unable to meet his eyes.

"Okay, then talk."

There was nothing but silence between them for what seemed like an eternity, and she wanted to laugh at the absurdity of the situation.

"First off, you shouldn't be going anywhere when neither of us has a clue of the possible long-term side effects of the drug in your system. Second, you got nowhere to go—no home base, and I don't relish the idea of thinking about you on the streets getting harassed again or going hungry or some shit—"

"I'm not your responsibility—"

"Listen up, short stuff."

Dakota clamped her mouth shut even as a retort bubbled up to the surface of her mind.

"You're feisty and I can appreciate that, but you asked me to make my case, and now you're shitting all over it before I can finish, does that seem fair?"

"No," she replied weakly with a sigh.

"Okay, so knock it the fuck off. I wouldn't be going to all this damn trouble if I just wanted easy tail. I can get that anytime, anywhere."

Yeah ... I believe that. She glanced at his tight gray T-shirt and rock-hard biceps then looked away. There wasn't any woman on this earth who would say no to a man who looked as fine as he did—*except for me, right now. Ugh ... my life's such a damn mess.*

"I'm sorry."

"Better." The biker rolled his shoulders and licked his lips. "I'm treating you the same way I would any other broad that was in trouble. I don't want jack shit out of it. The truth is that I just couldn't deal with my conscience if I let something happen to you down the road when I could've prevented it. So, until we know for sure that you're gonna be okay and you got a plan, I'm offering you a place to crash with protection. Nothing more. I'll sleep on the floor."

"Nothing in exchange?"

"That's what I said, and just so you know—I don't like repeating myself."

"I'll try and remember that. So, is this the part where we swap names?"

"Are you gonna give me your real one?"

Dakota scoffed and crossed her arms, observing the biker with a slight bit of side eye; he was looking at her watching him. The intensity pulsing between them was palpable. Tingles skittered across her body, making the hairs on the back of her neck stand on end.

"Dakota. That's my name. What's yours?"

"Leo, but I go by Cobra. Stick to Cobra."

"Got it, Snake." Dakota grinned when he glowered, then she slid back onto the bed.

"How old are you?" he asked.

"What difference does that make?"

Cobra let out a strained sigh. "I don't need any trouble if you're a minor."

The corners of her mouth twitched up. "I'm legal, so you don't have to worry about it."

His lips parted, and he stared at her.

She rolled her eyes. "I'm twenty-one. Satisfied?"

"Bullshit."

"I am. I can't help it if I look younger than my age. You can check my ID in my backpack."

Not thinking he'd really do it, surprise etched on her face when he walked over and began rummaging through it. Cobra held up her driver's license. "If you paid more than ten bucks for this shit, you got gypped. Where's your real one?"

The surface lines on her forehead deepened. "Do you always think you know everything?"

"Yep." He poked around in her backpack for a few more seconds, then pulled out a small vinyl card holder and unzipped it.

"Hey! I didn't say you could do that." Her hand swatted at the air.

"You said to look for your ID. Fake shit doesn't count."

Dakota pursed her lips as she watched Cobra's green eyes scan over her actual driver's license.

"So you're twenty. That's good to know. I figured you were around eighteen," he muttered.

"Since we're sharing so much … how old are you?" A frown creased her brow.

"Thirty." He shoved the card holder into her backpack.

Dakota paused to let a smirk run across her face. Then she said, "You look older."

"Whatever." Cobra leaned back and rocked on the heel of his boots.

For a moment or two, silence stretched between them. She fidgeted with the lose threads on the blanket and then realized what she was doing and willed her hands to stop. Clearing her throat, she pushed the cover away from her and looked up. "So I'm assuming you want financial help in paying for this lovely room. I'm pretty sure this isn't a free ride."

"Do you have any prospects for jobs? Maybe a waitress?"

"I'm a tattoo artist." Dakota darted her gaze around the room then back to him. "I've got an interview with a new shop manager in town."

Cobra shifted and cleared his throat. "I can give you a ride."

"Considering my car crapped out on me, that would be great. Do you live here?"

"For now."

"You're not one for divulging information, are you?"

No answer.

"Is this where you've been staying?"

"Nah. I just got the place today."

"Where were you before, or should I ask who was the lucky woman?" She laughed but he didn't join in.

"I was camping. In the summers, I like to live outdoors." His eyes never wavered from her face.

"So what do you do?"

"For now, I work outside." Ready to ask another question, she opened her mouth, but he held up his hand. "Enough."

"Just one more. Please?"

That tenderness she'd seen earlier when she asked nicely came back and he nodded.

"Do you still do stuff with your MC?"

The softness disappeared in less than a heartbeat and it was replaced by asperity. Cobra didn't utter a word.

A brick wall might as well have been erected in the middle of the room. Dakota blew out a breath and closed her eyes as shades of red swam behind her eyelids. If he wanted to keep his secrets, that was fine with her, especially since she was carrying around her own as well. She leaned back against the headboard and her lids fluttered open.

"When should I expect that you'll be gone then? In case I need a ride or I have somewhere I need to be …"

"I freelance. I'll be in and out." Cobra cracked his knuckles and kept his gaze locked on hers.

"Okay, I got it."

A loud ring came from Cobra's pocket and his shoulders tightened before he reached into his jeans and pulled out his cell. He glanced at the screen. "I gotta take this outside."

The door flew open, and he stalked out of the room. As it shut with a loud bang, Dakota jumped but then relaxed back into the bed. She heard his deep voice but the words were inaudible even though she strained her ears. Giving up, she pulled the sheets up and under her chin. *Okay, so staying with a stranger isn't the worst mistake I've ever made, and Cobra seems nice enough. Good intentions and all that, right?* All she had to do was keep a good head on her shoulders and she had this—it would be a piece of cake.

Just because Cobra was with the Steel Devils didn't make him a bad person. He'd saved her from those assholes at the bar and from a fate that made her cringe just thinking about it. That meant something. The worst thing she could do was decide Cobra was persona non grata because of his club's supposed actions.

No, what she needed to do was get a better understanding of his character outside of the MC and what his Nomad patch meant in the grand scheme of things. That was assuming she could get him to tell her anything.

All of this is going to take time.

It seemed strange to think that after so many years, time may actually be on her side. That there was an end to the fast-paced chaos that had been her life since high school.

Stop running.

Stop hiding.

Maybe.

But not yet.

CHAPTER SIX

COBRA

COBRA STOOD IN front of the motel dumpster because it had the best vantage point of the place. Nothing could be left to chance, even if he was back in Steel Devils' territory and the brothers had the place on lock down. His attention hovered over the parking lot as he clamped the phone to his ear.

Cobra heard a rustling then breathing with laughter faint in the background. "Yeah?" he said.

"Fuck, dude. How're things?" He heard the familiar baritone of the Steel Devils' president.

"Not too bad."

"Where the fuck are you?" Grinder asked.

"Philipsburg."

"How long you been there?"

"Couple of months."

"And you've waited this long to call. Fuck, man." The connection crackled. "You talkin' outside?"

"Yeah," Cobra replied.

"The connection's shitty."

"Yeah."

"We're havin' a party on Saturday. Satan's Legions are gonna be there. When's the last time you saw any of them?"

"Sturgis, I think."

"Fuck ... has it been that long?" Grinder asked.

"Yeah."

"So get your ass to Missoula and party with us."

Cobra swallowed and his mouth went down into a frown. He'd been pushing away from the MC for a while now—going nomad and making his own way in the world—but now with whatever the hell was happening with this drug situation, he had to drag in the other guys for a little gab session.

No point in wasting time on small talk.

"Can't make it. You've got outside sellers in your territory, Prez. I knocked a few heads together earlier today. I caught them trying to date rape a girl at Duffy's and they were using Liquid X. The pussies gave up their source after a couple of blows. The head honcho is a dude who goes by the name of Big Pat. Ring any bells?"

"Fucking hell," Grinder breathed out.

Cobra could just imagine him lighting a hand rolled joint and taking a long drag.

"You're sure that was the sonofabitch's name?" Grinder asked.

"Yeah. I wouldn't forget such a fuckin' lame moniker."

There was breathing on the line, and then Grinder said, "Thanks for letting me know, bro. It's been like chasing fuckin' rats around a maze, trying to herd these new fuckers who keep cropping up. We got a handle on it in Missoula, but some of the other towns in the area are so damn vulnerable. There's no fuckin' way we're gonna let this asshole sell on our turf. We ran the fucker outta Lolo, and now he's set up shop in Philipsburg?"

"You've gotten soft, Grinder. You shoulda exterminated him."

The president's raspy chuckle seeped through the line. "We need you back, dude. You're the only enforcer this club's ever had who never batted an eye when he took someone out."

"I'm just surprised you let the fucker go." A brown spider scurried across the pavement, crossing in front of Cobra, and he squashed it with the toe of his boot.

"That wasn't our fuckin' plan, but the SOB's brother-in-law was the motherfuckin' sheriff, and we decided we didn't need to start up shit with the damn badges."

Cobra took a deep breath then let it out. "You've got it under control in Missoula, though?"

"Yeah. In Frenchtown too. Brute's been workin' a lotta hours with Iron and some of the other brothers, managing the dealers we got out on the streets. One of the fuckers double-crossed us last week, so we had to make an example of him. We're pretty much on solid ground except for this fuckin' snag."

Grinder swore again and he heard a loud noise over the line, as if the guy had thrown something heavy at the wall.

Cobra didn't say a word.

"I'm so fuckin' pissed! You think those pussies you roughed up will get back on the circuit?"

"Don't know. I drove 'em into the ground, but stupid is as stupid does." Cobra rubbed the back of his neck and sighed as he gave the parking lot another quick scan. "Big Pat sounds like he doesn't much care who he's recruiting ... not a lot of sense in that one. Sounds like he's just a greedy fucker with shit for brains."

Grinder grunted in agreement and he heard another loud inhale from across the phone line.

"I'll call church and do some recon in the area. See if we can track back any final sources and set up some bait to nab the fucker."

This time it was Cobra's turn to grunt and he hoped the phone call was winding down to an end point. Talking for too long made him antsy—it's why he preferred taking to the open road with nothing but the wind as his companion. Solitary time wasn't taken seriously anymore. Too often people wanted to party and shove themselves into social situations because they couldn't deal with being alone. Hell ... they didn't fucking like their own company.

But Cobra lived through enough shit to know what he wanted out of life and how to get it without wasting his time chasing after other people. His expectations were pretty damn simple: a place to lay his head at night, a warm woman to share his bed sometimes, a few shots of booze, and the open road at his fingertips. Everything else? Fucking damn it all.

"We done?" Cobra asked.

"We're solid. Just keep me in the loop if you hear anything. The club will come up with a game plan to get rid of this fucker once and for all. It's good to hear from you, bro."

"Likewise."

Cobra broke the connection with a click of a button then headed back to the motel room.

He hadn't planned on keeping the cutie around, but Dakota needed help and he wasn't one to turn a blind eye when someone was in trouble. Fuck only knew what the bastards would've done to her if their plan had gone off without a hitch. Too many possibilities flashed across the front of his brain until he winced and paused outside the closed door to their room.

Regardless of how it could have played out, she was here with him now, and he was actually glad that she'd agreed to stay with him. He'd have to be careful not to fuck it up and make her feel unsafe with him. Dakota would run for the hills for sure, leaving him with a mark on his conscience that wouldn't heal too easily. He had to be on his best behavior, and based on the way she'd given him so much sass just a while before, he knew the situation would be challenging. She didn't even know him, and she was in his face—all indignant and fucking cute. *Easy, dude. Damn.* He had to admit that the sweet young woman had spunk, but he also suspected that a lot of her bravado was put on to hide her vulnerability. He appreciated the way Dakota held her own, and he figured it was what kept her alive in a world that was insistent on killing the human spirit.

Still, it meant she was absolutely going to push Cobra's fucking buttons, rip apart his boundaries, and throw his life into a tailspin for the next week or so until she could afford a place and get back on her feet. To go from constant silence to girlie chatter every second of the day? Yeah, that was going to be new and different. All he had to do was keep her at an emotional distance. That shouldn't be too hard since he'd been doing it with people for most of his life, but there was something fragile and damn sexy about the hitchhiker that stoked the fires deep inside him.

Forget that shit. She's off-limits. Better to find a whore to relieve the itch if it got too bad. *Shit.*

The knock on the door was louder than Cobra had intended. He felt like a jackass knocking for permission to enter his own room, but he didn't want to walk in on her changing. Yeah ... that would throw his "best behavior" plan right down the crapper.

"Come in." Her voice was soft, like fingers caressing his skin.

Fuck!

He opened the door and saw Dakota perched on the bed going through her backpack.

"We good?" she asked, not lifting her head up.

"Yeah." He peeled off his cut and turned it inside out before gently folding it.

"Do you have a time you like to go to bed that I should know about since I'm kind of invading on your space here?"

A smile tilted up from his lips. Cobra would hardly consider this dump worthy of being declared his fucking space. But whatever, the sweetheart was being considerate.

"You're probably still tired." He walked over to the mini fridge and took out one of the beers he'd brought back after roughing up the two shitheads, and popped the top before bringing the can to his lips.

Dakota shrugged one shoulder and kept digging, becoming more frantic.

"You'll need more sleep tonight. Your body's still recovering."

He couldn't deny the prickle of curiosity that peaked his interest while he watched her turn over her backpack and dump out the rest of the contents on the bed.

"While you're doing whatever the fuck you're doing, I'm gonna go to the front desk."

She didn't seem to acknowledge him, which was fine since none of this was his problem, at least not up to a point.

"You don't need to knock when you come back. I'll be in the shower," she said.

A flash bang image of her naked and dripping wet shot through his thoughts, and it was a damn nice image at that. With a quick jerk of his hand, he opened the door hard enough that it banged against the wall, and then he walked out, forcing himself not to look back at her.

Cobra strode across the gravel parking lot, his boots kicking up a cloud of dust with each step. There were plenty of broads out in the world, and he didn't need the one in his room. Fuck, he didn't need one at all, but sometimes he ended up shacking up with a woman in various towns and cities across the country. He'd stay as little as a few days to several months with different women, but he never fell for any of them. The problem was they'd always fall in love with him, and that's what usually broke up the union, then he'd pack up his stuff and hit the road.

It wasn't like Cobra had anything against love, it was more that he just didn't believe in it for himself. And the fact that he'd never fallen for any of the women who'd littered his life over the years told him that the whole falling-in-love crap was a crock of shit.

Cobra stopped and looked at the salmon-colored hues streaking the sky and his mind drifted to Sylvia. He hadn't heard from his sister in almost six months. Sylvia always called him when she needed money, and he usually wired her some. He hadn't seen her since he'd left L.A. at sixteen years old. Then the image of *his* face assaulted his mind.

His father had been a stern and strict disciplinarian, and Cobra had the scars to prove it. A Marine, his father had run the house like a fucking bootcamp. The only respite he and his brother and sister had was when their dad had been deployed overseas.

Cobra reached into his pocket and took out a joint then lit it. The only sanity in their home was their mother. He blew out a stream of smoke. *And where the fuck are you, Mom?* He snorted and kicked the stones on the ground.

Thinking about his parents brought home the fact that love was a damn myth. He'd loved his mother and she left him, and when he was young he'd loved his father who then hurt him. No ... trusting and loving someone equaled pain and heartbreak, so he kept everyone at a distance. That's the way he liked it.

Another long inhale and a slow, steady exhale. But ... Dakota? Cobra wouldn't mind having some fun with her, but she was fucking off limits for him. He didn't see her as a hit-it-and-quit-it kind of girl, and he wasn't down to screw her and then have a stage five clinger on his hands.

Yeah, fuck no, if he needed to get some pussy, he'd give Jenny a call—she still had the hots for him. He'd met Jenny a couple of years before when he'd come through Philipsburg for the motorcycle rally. She was a single mom and worked as a stripper over at the Satin Dolls. They'd seemed to hit it off, so she asked him to move in with her and he did. Four months later, he was packing his stuff while she watched him, her cheeks streaked with tears. Jenny hadn't believed him when he told her he didn't love her, so he had to move on. Cobra liked Jenny a lot and hated to hurt her, but he'd told her from the start that what they had was temporary.

A few months after that, Cobra had been in Chicago when Jenny called telling him she missed him and was willing to accept them as friends with benefits. From that point on, he'd send some money to help her and her daughter out, and whenever he'd pass through the town, he'd give her a jingle, but he never shacked up with Jenny because he knew history would repeat itself.

The image of Dakota in the shower pushed out other thoughts in his head. Damn, that girl was a pretty little thing. He chuckled when he recalled how pissed she got when he refused to answer any more questions. Yeah … a woman like that could get under his skin and drive him insane. Make him think crazy shit too, like wanting to feel her writhing under his body as he thrust into her.

Fuck.

He tossed the spent joint on the ground and stubbed it out then walked quickly to the motel office. The frigid blast of air wrapped around Cobra as he strode over to the front desk. The same pain-in-the-ass teenager stood behind the counter. The kid eyed him up and down as if the teen hadn't seen Cobra before. The kid's eyes narrowed in suspicion and his fingers hovered under the counter, probably near an emergency button that would call the badges.

Cobra was used to the treatment; it came with the territory of having a patch on his back. Nomad or not, people were easily spooked over shit they didn't understand.

"Do you got any extra pillows and a blanket back there?"

"Uh, lemme see …" The kid trailed off, not moving an inch from where he was standing.

Cobra coughed into his fist and widened his stance. A clear I-don't-have-all-fucking-day signal. The teen scurried away, disappearing down the hall. Cobra thrummed his fingers on the counter, trying to keep the rising anger inside him at bay. He wanted to get back to the room, take a short nap, and then get out on the streets to gather intel for the club. He was in a better position to find shit out than his brothers, who were a couple of hours away. He also wanted to swing back to Duffy's to make sure those shitheads didn't get any funny ideas again.

"Here." The desk attendant shoved over a thin blanket and a lumpy pillow without a cover on it. "That's all we had in the supply closet. Things are tight tonight. I guess no one wants to be lonely." A stupid grin cracked the teenager's face.

Cobra stared at him until the grin disappeared, then he gathered up the blanket and pillow and pushed away from the counter.

"Thanks," he said, opening the front door.

"How's that lady doing?" the kid asked.

"Fine."

The door slammed before the desk attendant could ask any more questions, and Cobra headed back to the room. He wondered if Dakota was finished showering, but he threw the thought out of his head because he didn't need to be thinking about *that* right before he got to the room. Cobra didn't know much about his pretty roommate, but even after having known her for less than twenty-four hours, he knew one thing for damn sure—she was running from something or someone.

Cobra had spent the majority of his life doing the same damn thing, so it took one runner to know another one. As long as Dakota didn't involve him past the point where they were at now with each other, everything would be all right between them.

There was being a gentleman, and then there was being an idiot. Whatever secrets she wanted to keep hidden could stay that way but she needed to respect his as well. It would be a delicate dance, but he knew the steps.

As long as he didn't trip and fall into her bed in the middle of the night, they would be golden.

He opened the door and walked into the room.

CHAPTER SEVEN

DAKOTA

DAKOTA WOKE UP in a cold sweat, her heart pounding out of her rib cage while trying to grab a breath big enough so she could stop panicking. A shudder rushed down her spine and she licked her lips as her attention shifted in the half-darkness toward the mound of blankets on the floor. Cobra was breathing deeply; he obviously hadn't moved much since they'd both gone to bed. Relief sank into her bones.

When he'd lain down on the floor with his pillow and blanket, she hadn't been too sure his good behavior would stick—at least not the whole night. It'd taken her a solid two or three hours before she'd plummeted from weariness into a deep sleep.

Now she caught her breath and tried to put her thoughts into some kind of order.

Logic was still far away, but panic was receding as she sat up and immersed herself back into the surroundings. With every crack in the paint she counted, the memories fled deeper into her mind. The less on the surface, the more she could ignore the shadows that'd been haunting her from the past.

I need to get out of here.

Without thinking, Dakota nabbed the door key Cobra had left on the dresser and swung the backpack on her shoulder. Still in her blue jeans and a tank top, she maneuvered carefully over the sleeping biker toward the door then tiptoed around him. Each measured step seemed like it took an eternity.

Less than a heartbeat away from putting her hand around the doorknob, fingers gripped her ankle and pulled back hard enough that she nearly tripped. A small shriek escaped her lips, and she covered her mouth with one hand. All the small hairs on the back of her neck stood on end.

"Where're you going?" Cobra's slow, sleepy words nearly knocked the wind out of her lungs.

"Why does it matter to you? Shit, you didn't have to scare me like that."

She shook her ankle, but his fingers tightened to a slight pinch on her flesh. Dakota held her breath.

"It matters." He released his grip and rubbed a hand over his face. "Wait for me. I'll come with you."

"I don't need an escort, Cobra. I'm a big girl. I can do things by myself. Next thing you know, you'll be giving me a curfew too."

Dakota clutched her bag tighter as she turned the knob on the door.

"I'll be back in a little bit."

"You got a cell?"

"No." Dakota stopped the line of questioning and pulled open the door. "Don't worry, I can handle myself."

She watched a ripple of unease flow across his expression before he shoved a hand through his hair and exhaled a big breath.

"Be careful. Don't go back to Duffy's."

"Give me some credit for not being a total dumbass," she muttered and headed out into the abrupt morning sunlight. Powerful rays flooded over the parking lot, and the gravel shimmered as it caught the sunlight. The metallic clatter of pots and pans filtered from a nearby open window, and a chorus of birds broke the drone of semi-trucks barreling down the road.

With slightly shaking hands and adrenaline still coursing through her veins, Dakota pulled her hair up into a ponytail and mentally worked out her game plan. She had about twenty bucks stashed away from her last paycheck at the tattoo shop in Idaho Falls and maybe another four or five dollars in change at the bottom of the backpack. Not even close enough to get a new cell phone or grab a cab anywhere.

It looked like she was walking it again, but at least it would give her time to think and reflect, hopefully on the things of her choosing and not on the demons that always tried to gnaw at her brain. Not sensing a need to pick a particular direction, Dakota just started walking. If she was going to work here for the foreseeable future, it made sense that she get the lay of the land.

While the burning sun beat down on her back, relentless and wicked, she traced a path to the nearest tattoo shop on the downtown strip. The general rule was that tattoo parlors weren't too hard to find based on proximity to bars, strip clubs, and general downtown fun times and madness. By the time she reached the modest shop, she probably didn't look her best, but she could still draw a straight line if they demanded a line test on the spot.

The little bell on the front door dinged as Dakota pushed into the shop.

"How can I help you?" The man behind the counter was already halfway out behind the desk before she was inside the place. "Are you here to schedule an appointment?"

His attentiveness was a good sign. The fact that he wore a smile on his face was even better. Not something she was super used to after working at her last shop. Her last boss catered to a rough set of clientele, but it paid the bills and she hadn't worked up the courage to go anywhere else at the time.

"Hi, it's nice to meet you. I was wondering if you had any artist openings? I'm new to town and I could use a gig."

The man cleared his throat. "Oh, well …" To his credit, he didn't look her up and down at all, which had basically summed up her qualifications for the shop in Idaho Falls. "As a matter of fact, we just had a freelance slot open up for an artist. It's a ninety-day stint, but after the trial run we'd have you sign a full-time contract, if that sounds like something that would interest you?"

The man leaned against the reception counter with his arms and legs crossed, his head tilted as his brown eyes seemed to be assessing her, but not in a creepy way.

"Sure, that sounds pretty perfect, actually … I have my portfolio …" Dakota reached into the backpack and pulled out a binder of past sketches and references from other shops she'd worked at for the past two years. "Can we do an interview today?"

The guy chuckled and licked his lips. "Man, we could do with a little of your eagerness around here. I like that." He took her binder and started flipping through it. "Have a seat on the couch and we'll get started. It already looks like you're better at black and white portrait pieces than our last artist …"

At that point everything became a fuzzy blur of nerves and apprehension as her world boiled down to winning over her possibly, new boss and being grateful that the universe had been so kind to throw this opportunity in her lap. The truth was that Dakota had come to town without any prospects. There hadn't been any interview at all. She'd lied to Cobra so she wouldn't seem quite so pathetic.

But now, everything was working out way better than she could have ever hoped for since her car had broken down. If life would unfold a little bit better every single day, maybe she could take her first real breath in years without looking over her shoulder. For a solid hour and a half, the fear she lived with in her gut a majority of the time, faded away.

For once, she felt peace.

"Well, everything's in order here, and I'm impressed with your work and your attention to detail. Nothing's lining up that's telling me not to hire you on a trial basis, Dakota. If I can get you a contract today, when can you start? We've got a few appointments overbooked with the rest of the shop and spreading them around would give me a lot of good will."

"I can start tomorrow. Does that work?"

The man nodded. "Great," He handed the binder back and scratched the back of his neck. "Let me get that contract for you so you can go over everything and let me know if you have any questions."

Dakota nodded and watched the guy head back into the shop. Everything seemed on the up and up here. The place was clean, well-lit, and the manager genuinely seemed to care about the staff and talent he brought into the place. It was like winning the lottery for tattoo places, and she tried to suppress a huge grin, not wanting him to think she was too eager.

"Oh, fuck, I'm sorry," The man handed her a stapled contract and a pen. "I didn't even give you my damn name. I'm Bucky. It's nice to meet you."

He stuck out a calloused hand and she shook it.

"I'll be behind the counter making some follow-up calls, and that'll give you time to look over everything and let me know if you have any questions." Bucky tugged on his green band T-shirt, stuck his hands in his pockets then walked behind the large counter. "A few of our artists should be showing up in an hour or so for their first appointments if you want to do a meet and greet, otherwise I'll figure out a staff meeting tomorrow so we can get you introduced to everyone. Sound good?"

Dakota nodded, read over the contract, and signed on all the dotted lines before handing it back. She also handed in her book, so she could advertise to the new clientele. Bucky shook her hand again.

"I really wasn't expecting you today, but I'm glad you showed up. Payout is every other Friday, starting with this week. Are you good with that?"

She nodded, heart in her throat, as she thought that maybe her luck was too good to be true. For a beat, they stood across from each other, both of them silent. All of a sudden a chill skated over her skin and her heart began to beat out of her chest. Dakota knew she needed to get the hell out of there before she totally lost it and ended up on the floor in a trembling heap. Then Bucky would realize he'd made a grave error in judgement.

"I'll see you tomorrow." Dakota waved and rushed out of the shop, clutching the backpack to her chest while her brain spun with all the things she had to do before tomorrow to get ready for her new job.

She felt like an idiot and a newbie, but for a few minutes she stood on the sidewalk outside the tattoo parlor, soaking in warmth from the sun and trying to push down her nerves. *That worked out great. My luck's changing.* But she figured the universe owed her one after having dealt with a broken-down car and getting drugged by a bunch of frat boy Neanderthals.

Dakota blew out a long, slow breath. No. She wasn't going to focus on that right now. Those thoughts were too close to the surface of everything else that had happened lately and she didn't want to deal with it.

At that moment, a sharp whistle split the air. She jerked her head up to gaze toward the startling sound. Across the street, Cobra was perched on his motorcycle, the metallic purple and chrome blinding under the strong summer sunlight. A helmet dangled in one of his hands.

"What the hell?" Dakota breathed out, her eyebrows drawing in with confusion. "What're you doing here? Following me? You know that's kind of creepy, right?"

Cobra's expression was blank, but he inclined his head for her to come over.

"You've got to be kidding me. I told you I can handle this on my own, I don't need a well-meaning bodyguard—"

"Breakfast?" His gruff, one-word shout from across the street made her stomach rumble in automatic recognition. "We'll talk then."

Dakota hesitated, unsure of how much longer she could remain impartial to him if they kept acting all buddy-buddy together.

"Get over here."

She stayed rooted to the spot.

"I'm paying."

With those magic words uttered, Dakota didn't waste any time heading across the road. Cobra handed her the helmet.

"You ever ride on a bike?"

"I'm good, just hold on and pray, right? That's how this works?"

He snorted, and she could've sworn she heard a little bit of laughter.

If Dakota wasn't careful, she'd end up being the one who crossed the boundary.

CHAPTER EIGHT

COBRA

"YOUR MENUS ARE at the table, pick a seat, and let me know if you have any questions. Tina will eventually come around to take your order."

Cobra put his hand on the small of Dakota's back and guided her across the yellow linoleum floor, past the slew of customers perched on stools around the lunch counter, and back to a corner booth near the window.

The Scotchman was one of Cobra's favorite diners in a three-hundred mile radius. A cross-section of the area's population buzzed around at all hours, coming together under the shared enjoyment of greasy breakfasts served twenty-four seven, burgers fried on an age-old griddle and, of course, decadent slices of pie.

Most of the waitresses referred to the diners as "Hon" and were short on charm, but the hash browns made the long wait worth it. Cobra dreamed about them and took every opportunity when he was in town to break out an excuse to make a stop for them.

Dakota slid across the vinyl seat and sat across from him. He faced the front of the diner so he could see who came in. He always sat at a back table or booth in most restaurants; it'd become a habit from years in the MC and then in prison. Cobra had learned to always watch his back and know what the fuck was going on.

"Any recommendations?" Dakota turned over the sticky, plastic-coated menu. "Or will it all kill me?"

"Everything's good. Pick what you want."

"Careful on the orders. I tend to take them pretty literally, and yeah, I'm skinny, but your girl can eat. I once won a pie-eating contest by a mile and went back for seconds."

There was no stopping the small smile that crossed his face. Cobra wondered if Dakota had any idea that she'd referenced herself as being his girl. By the look on her face, he doubted it. She was talking a mile a minute. It was adorable as fucking hell, and it made his life way easier, because he wasn't the king of conversation on a good day.

Nah, he was better with his fists than with his tongue.

But Dakota? She was more animated than she'd been the day before—full of piss and vinegar, giving him a rundown of her giant breakfast order. Everything from pancakes to a muffin and a western omelet with extra cheese.

"You want hash browns too. Trust me."

Her eyes lit up, and he chuckled. The pretty one practically glowed as she analyzed and planned while he tried to figure out where the fuck she was going to pack it all away.

"So, you're a regular here?"

"What tipped you off?" he asked, looking around the diner to catch the eye of any of the waitresses who were either bored or playing on their phones.

He snapped and Tess scurried over to their table.

"Hey, Cobra, how are you?" The curly-haired waitress smiled then glanced over at Dakota then back at him.

"Been good. You?"

Her smile faded a bit. "Oh, it's just the same old, same old."

"Yeah." He handed her the menus.

"You guys ready to order?"

Cobra lifted his chin at Dakota who beamed then began to recite her gargantuan order.

After Tess sauntered away, Cobra was left with a woman across from him who was talking at full speed about her job interview. Never in his life had he been in the company of someone so animated, let alone *listened to* someone who didn't take a fucking breath while talking. He blinked and wondered if she was this outgoing with everyone; there was no damn way she reserved this as special treatment for him.

By the time their food arrived, he figured he didn't have to say jack shit through the entire meal.

"Tell me about you," Dakota said.

The question left him blindsided mid-chew. Cobra damn near choked, and he took a quick sip of orange juice as he met her eyes over the pile of food set in front of them.

"What about it?" he replied.

"I didn't say *it*, I said *you*." Dakota shifted her fork in her hand before skewering a large bite of pancakes. "You're a him, not an it."

"Observant."

"One liners don't make a conversation, Cobra." She stuck the bite in her mouth and chewed rapidly. "If I'm going to bunk with you for the next week until I get on my feet, then you're going to learn how to make small talk or at least act like something other than an AI."

"AI?" He put down his fork and sat back in the booth, resting one arm along the back of it. "Is that a fuckin' insult?"

"Artificial intelligence. You act like a robot."

He grunted and looked down at his plate. Not the worst thing he'd ever been called—far from it, but the kitten had claws. Everything about her was loud, demanding, and it seemed like she was on a mission to keep him in check. *What the fuck did I pick up on the side of the road?*

"What do you want from me?" He breathed out, somewhat indulgent to her whims. "Because you're just gonna badger me until you get it."

"You're a quick study." She winked at him and reached across the table for the blueberry muffin.

A sly little pussy cat. She challenged him in a way he hadn't been in a long time. It was both interesting and irritating as all hell. She ruffled his feathers and he never knew what would come out of her mouth.

"That didn't answer much," he commented, going back to the hash browns on his plate.

"I'm getting you to talk more, aren't I?"

"By cheating, sure." He finished chewing and caught her eyes with a glance. "No one likes a cheater."

"I don't know that I care if you like me or not." She smiled wickedly.

"If I'm your meal ticket, darlin', you want me to like you."

"What I want to know is who I'll be sharing space with for the foreseeable future. You seem like a nice enough guy, but you could be a closet serial killer. Maybe you like to take your time with your victims."

"Wouldn't I be luring you into liking me then if that were my game?"

Dakota frowned and he knew he had her there.

"Okay then … what does *NOMAD* mean?" she asked.

Cobra leaned back, resigned to answering her questions. He could probably feed her little bits and pieces. Nothing serious, but enough for her to be satisfied.

"A nomad's a guy who does his own thing within an MC. I still have an affiliation with the Steel Devils, and I like to hang out with my brothers, but I'm not under any obligation. Happy?"

"Pleased as punch." She shot a sarcastic smile in his direction. "Now, your turn."

"Huh?"

"Ask me one. That's how we do this social thing, we ask each other questions."

"If I'd known helping you out came with speed dating, I would have fuckin' skipped it. Just be happy with your damn breakfast, and let's call it a day."

"So you don't have any burning questions you're dying to throw my way? There's nothing itching in the back of your skull that's crying out to be answered?" Dakota broke off a piece of muffin and popped it in her mouth.

"It's sure as hell flattering that you think so much about what I want to know. I don't usually get that much attention, sweetheart."

He'd caught Dakota off guard, and her cocky expression faltered a bit around the edges as her shoulders folded in on themselves. Fuck, now he felt a little bit bad. But only a little. She would recover well enough.

"That's not what I meant." Dakota kicked his shin under the table.

Fuck, could she get any more adorable? They might as well have been back in fucking middle school.

"What can I do to get you to act like a normal human being?" She teased, taking a sip from her coffee cup. "Work with me here."

"I'm not a *get to know you* kind of guy, sweetheart."

"So adapt."

She wasn't giving up. He had to respect that kind of attitude.

Cobra stretched out his legs, pushed back against the seat cushion, and captured her gaze.

This was going to be a long breakfast.

CHAPTER NINE

DAKOTA

"Whatʼre you going to do while you're in town?" Dakota tried another angle, unwilling to give up that easily. "Do you have a schedule I should know about in case you're not in the room, so I don't worry too much?"

Cobra scoffed and pushed away his plate, half his food still on it. "It's been a long time since anyone tried to keep tabs on me. You're not being very subtle about it."

"Who says I'm trying to be subtle at all. Can we cut the back and forth and actually have a conversation?"

"Fine, why the move to Philipsburg, sweetheart?"

He turned the tables and she blinked, mouth opened in a wide *O*. That was a valid question—she couldn't deny it. Dakota took a long sip from her water glass and dabbed her lips with a napkin as she eyed him over the table. Obviously, she didn't know him well enough to trust him too much but there had to be some kind of give somewhere while navigating each other and living in close quarters together. She didn't have to give Cobra her entire back story, but maybe just a little of it.

Dakota swallowed past the tightness in her throat and pulled her hair back draping it over her other shoulder with a small sigh. Where to even begin?

"I didn't have a great experience at my old job, and I needed a new start. Not much was happening in the city, and ... uh ... people thought they could do things that were less than appropriate." She took another gulp of water.

"Because you were a female," Cobra spoke slowly, almost a question without it being a question.

"Yeah, something like that. I had to get out of there. I needed a fresh start."

Cobra grunted and stirred a spoon through his oatmeal.

"Anyone ever tell you, you eat like an old man?"

Cobra cocked his head to the side. "Healthy isn't old, sweetheart. And the way you keep sneaking glances at me like you want to eat me whole? I can't be too old, right?"

Dakota nearly choked on her bite of food and lurched in her seat. Sonofabitch, he'd noticed, though she guessed she hadn't been as subtle as she should have been or tried to be—and she wanted to smack her forehead against the countertop. She'd been behaving like a fifteen-year-old with a crush. Dakota's attention went everywhere but on him as her mind churned with possible reactions and smartass comments. Instead, Dakota shoved piles of food in her mouth so she could keep herself occupied before she said something else stupid as hell.

"What? Cat got your tongue? Not so rough and sarcastic now, huh?" Cobra leaned back in his seat with his arms crossed, although his face didn't twitch an expression. He was so damn hard to read. "Don't get so bent outta shape—I've done my share of looking too." He winked at her.

Dakota wasn't one to blush but, all of a sudden, a rush of heat flashed through her, and she grabbed her water glass and ran it all over her face. Cobra's smile was infuriating and she had to hold herself back from throwing the water at him. She hated that he knew what he said bothered her, and she hated it even more that it *did* cause a reaction inside her.

"Okay, I'll tell you something. It's only fair. There was a time I never played fair, but not so much now."

"Interesting." Perspiration beaded under her hairline.

Silence and the slow chatter of the rest of the customers in the diner stretched between them while she watched Cobra linger over his breakfast, waiting for him to talk.

He looked up. "I was an enforcer in the MC way back when. The reputation I had still follows me. Anyway, after a stint in prison, I didn't want to go back to doing that, and I didn't wanna land back in the fuckin' pen. I needed some time to myself to get my head screwed on right, so I became a nomad."

"Very. Interesting."

"Is it?" Cobra's eyes didn't waver from hers.

"Of course. So what did you do as an … enforcer?" Goosebumps swept up her arms and legs just uttering the word. It seemed dangerous, vicious, and ruthless.

"I can protect you, no problem. Leave it at that."

"I don't need your protection, Cobra."

He scoffed and sat back in the booth with a knowing look that Dakota wanted to wipe right off his smug face.

"I've survived this long. It's really not that funny."

"You're way too stubborn for someone I just saved less than forty-eight hours ago, sweetheart. You may not *need* me to save you, but it works a lot better when I do."

She balled her fingers into fists as she digested his words and tried her best not to explode at him in public, especially when what he said was actually true.

"Are you done?" Dakota glanced at his half-finished food and eyed all of her clean plates. In her defense, she hadn't eaten so much since she'd high-tailed it out of Idaho Falls.

"I'll get boxes," he said.

"You want to take the leftovers with us?"

"Sure. Why not?"

Cobra got up and Dakota watched him, ogling his ass as he took all that strong and tall muscle behind the counter and grabbed some

Styrofoam containers. No one even batted an eyelash at the gesture. Clearly, he did come here often, which gave her pause given the fact that he made his lifestyle seem, well, nomadic. Wasn't that the point?

Ugh, why the hell was she even investing this much thought into it in the first place? They were ships passing in the night. They'd probably be sharing space for a week or two, at most, before she was able to find her own place and get back on her feet. So there was no need for all of ... this. *But damn, if he isn't sexy with his hard body and dreamy green eyes. And those tats. Fuck ... I want to look at them real close.* Her breath came quickly through her parted lips with almost a hissing sound. *I need to stop thinking about him. We'll be out of each other's lives in no time. I don't need to get to know him.* At least, not super in-depth. They didn't need to bare each other's souls or something.

And judging by the way her body reacted to Cobra, even a tentative friendship was out of the question. Besides, once she got a place of her own, Dakota didn't even know if she'd see him again, or if she even wanted to.

Cobra had been in prison and she could only imagine what landed him there. He'd been an enforcer in a notorious motorcycle club. He was also much older than anyone she'd ever gone out with before. Dakota wrung her hands. There were so many factors in the equation, and all of them spelled danger with a capital *D*. After spending so many years running scared, she craved tranquility, so she wasn't in the market for a good-looking biker who exuded raw sex and danger.

Dakota scraped the scramble eggs off the plate and into one of the boxes Cobra handed her.

"When do you start at the tattoo parlor?"

The change of subject was a clear shift and she paused to push away her thoughts and come back into the moment.

"Tomorrow."

"Do you want a ride to work?" Cobra licked his thumb after sticking it in some of the food going in the boxes, and for a moment she just stared at it before it popped out of his mouth. "Did you hear me?"

Crap, I need to get a grip.

"Uh, yeah, that would be really nice. Thanks."

"Yeah."

Dakota didn't follow up with any more conversation because now that he was revealing some things, she was suddenly very aware of being in way over her head. Dakota felt oddly closer to Cobra than she had earlier that morning, and she didn't like it one bit. Even though he didn't live his life by society's rules, she wasn't as wary of him as she'd been when he offered her a ride. When she thought back to the people she'd known an awful lot about, she wanted to puke. They were fake and hiding behind a mask of respectability. And the worst was Taylor: how he'd hurt her without even one iota of regret. *Don't think about that asshole. Don't. Please ... don't go there.*

"You flinched," Cobra's voice chased the shadows away. "You good?" He stood off to her side of the booth with the bag of leftovers in one hand.

Dakota smiled and grasped his hand. "Yeah, I'm good." His skin was warm and cool at the same time—if that was even possible. She wanted to bring it to her face and feel the roughness of his skin against her cheek.

"Fuck, darlin'," he mumbled.

Her eyes snapped to his and something about the way his gaze moved over her face made her stomach dip. Maybe it was how his touch sent sparks through her, but suddenly Dakota was *very* conscious of him, very aware of the raw power of his masculinity.

"Did you wanna slice of coconut cream pie to take with you, hon?" Tess asked, breaking the moment Cobra and Dakota shared.

"Yeah. Thanks."

Tess glanced over at Dakota. "You want a piece too?"

She slid her hand off of his and look past him. "Do you have any blueberry?"

"We sure do, hon."

"That's what I'll have."

"Gotcha. Be back in a minute." Tess rushed away.

Dakota slid out of the booth then brought her hands above her head and stretched. From her peripheral view she saw Cobra watching her movements.

"Here you go." Tess handed a plastic bag to Cobra. "I'll see you"—she pressed her pink-tipped finger into his chest—"later, hon." She threw him a quick smile then hurried off.

"You ready to go?" Cobra asked, his voice sounding gruffer than usual.

Grabbing the two boxes from him, she nodded. As they walked toward the cashier, his hand grazed hers and sent a line of awareness from the tips of her fingers all the way up her shoulder as her temples buzzed from the contact.

I don't even know him. But look what happened when I trusted a man I did know. This is just crazy. But the thought of Cobra's strong arms around her, keeping her safe and protected, sounded like the best plan in the world at that moment. A voice in the back of her head kept telling her that she should run hard and fast in the opposite direction, but there was a gentleness she saw behind Cobra's rough and tough armor he wore all of the time. *But I thought Taylor was sweet and loving. And I got in the car with those two clean-cut guys. I'm far from a good judge of character. I should just move on to another town. Disappear.*

Instead, Dakota slid on the back of his bike and wrapped her arms around his deliciously muscled torso reveling in the heat of him. She hoped he didn't notice that her fingers were shaking as she tried to get herself together again. As adamant as she'd been about getting to know him, the closer they got to each other, the harder it would be to resist the pull that drew her to him. The mystery that oozed from every dangerous pore of his body captivated her.

Dakota knew she was flirting with danger, but there was something about Cobra that made her want to stick around and get to know him better, even though her logic screamed against it.

CHAPTER TEN

COBRA

FOR THE PAST few days Cobra had spent far too much time thinking about Dakota. He tried to ignore the attraction and his desire, but it was impossible, and it irked him but also drew him like a magnet at the same time. The pull was off the damn charts.

Dakota pressed closer against his back as he steered the bike around a curve. Her arms wrapped firmly around his midsection and the feel of her firm breasts crushed against him made his dick jerk.

Cobra clenched his jaw then twisted the throttle back, and the bike lurched forward. Dakota's hands slipped down and landed right on his growing erection. He gripped the motorcycle's handlebars so tightly his knuckles were white.

For a man who prided himself on control, Dakota made him want to throw it out the damn window, snatch her up into his arms, and convince her to allow him to taste every inch of her body for hours on end, knowing he would never get sick of exploring her smooth, pale skin. A low growl vibrated through his chest. Her fingers pressed lightly against his bulge and his heart hammered beneath his breastbone like he was a fucking teenager cutting class to make out behind the bleachers. It was damn surprising and irritating as hell that he would be so interested in a woman this quickly beyond anything other than a quick roll between the sheets.

But there was something about Dakota, something rare and different.

I sound like a fuckin' pussy. Cobra snorted as his lips thinned in frustration. He didn't know anything about her except she was having car trouble and he'd stuck his fucking nose where it didn't belong—*twice*, to save her pretty, fiery little ass. Now, here they were with her strapped onto him like plastic wrap and his head all tied up in knots like some kind of pathetic asshole.

Another curve around Sapphire Mountain, and a few strands of Dakota's hair blew in the wind and wrapped around his arm. They were soft like silk threads and glistened in the sunlight. The only thing he knew was that like him, she had her share of secrets and some determined demons who kept trying to scratch their way to the surface. That was obvious, but he wasn't sure if he wanted to know what hers were for fear that he'd be pulled in even more. The more time they spent together, the more he fought to keep his distance before his feelings got out of control. The fact that Cobra was even thinking about feelings pissed him off in a big way. *She's just a fuckin' chick. That's all.* But deep down he knew the storm brewing inside him wasn't so clear-cut and simple.

By the time Cobra pulled into the motel's lot, he tried to shove all notions of her into the back of his brain.

He was thinking way too damn much. It wasn't fucking healthy.

"Thank you."

Her sweet voice startled him, and he turned toward her and held out his hand to help her off the bike.

"What're you thanking me for?" The feel of her hand in his felt nice. *Fuck!*

"The beautiful ride. I loved it." She leaned against him.

Cobra let go of her hand and took a step away. "I'm glad you enjoyed it. There are so many kickass roads in this part of the country that are awesome for bikers. Next time, I'll take you to Georgetown Lake."

Dakota shielded her eyes with her hand as she looked at him. "I love the water—it's so calming yet energizing. When I was a kid, a group of us used to spend the summers at Monkey Rock. It's a swimming hole in Pocatello."

"Did you go there with your parents?"

"Sometimes, but most of the time they were too busy to go with us kids. My dad's a long-distance truck driver and my mom works at Ridley's—it's a grocery store. I usually went with my friends."

"Do you have any brothers or sisters?" Cobra surprised himself because he rarely asked questions or was interested in a person's backstory.

"I have a sister who's four years older than me. She's married with kids. I also have two younger brothers, and then my brother Luke who's two years older than me. We were real close. I used to hang out with him and …" Her voice trailed off as she looked away from Cobra. A dark shadow crossed her face, erasing all traces of her cheeriness. "… his friends." She stared vacantly into the distance.

I touched on something.

A car door slammed and Dakota jumped; fear etched her face.

"It's just someone banging a door shut," he said and grasped her hand in his.

She giggled. "I guess I'm a bit jumpy."

"Why's that?"

Dakota shrugged then shook her head. "Do you like rom-coms?" she asked, changing the subject.

Cobra decided to let it go and play along with her. "What the fuck are you talking about?" He let go of her hand.

She laughed. "Romantic comedies. You know—movies."

"I don't really watch movies, and if I do, they're either horror, sci-fi, or action."

"Then today's the day you venture out of your comfort zone. I saw that *Moonstruck* is on one of the channels. I can pay for it since I just got my first paycheck today. It's not much but, hey, I've only been working for two days."

"Don't worry about that."

"I want to—it's my treat. I bought microwave popcorn at the convenience store. Are you in?"

The light had come back into her eyes, and Cobra wanted to keep it there for as long as he could.

"Let's do it," he said and walked in front of her toward the motel room. He opened the door and stepped back as she slid past him, catching the scent of pine and cool, clean air on her clothes. She ambled over to the air conditioning and pushed some buttons.

"That feels good," she said, lifting her arms up and leaning closer to the blasting air.

"You wanna do this now?"

Dakota looked over her shoulder. "Yes. Is that good with you?"

Cobra grunted and grasped the edge of the dresser while he kicked off his boots.

"You can pick the next movie we watch, okay?" She padded over and sat down on the edge of the bed swinging her feet and looking at the TV.

"You want a soda?"

"Sure."

He walked over and handed her a can of 7-Up, then popped the top of his beer and took a big gulp.

Her face scrunched as her gaze followed his movements.

"What?" he asked.

"How come you never ask if I want a beer?"

"'Cause you're not twenty-one yet." Another gulp.

A laugh ripped from her chest. "I can't believe you just said that. I mean, you don't really live by society's rules, you know."

Cobra narrowed his eyes. "Do you wanna a beer?"

"No, thanks. I don't like the taste."

"Fuck, woman, you're exasperating." He drained the can, crushed it in his hand then tossed it into the trash can.

"Nice shot." Dakota giggled.

Cobra made a small noise and took a few steps closer and their eyes caught—this time she kept his gaze and held it. He grabbed the remote from the nightstand. "Here. Get the fuckin' thing set up while I go change, then we'll watch it."

"Are you sure you don't have anything better to do?"

Her voice was so soft, he almost didn't hear her. He blinked a few times, his back already turned to the bed and took a deep breath, closing his eyes. Damn, she sounded so vulnerable, sweet, and uncertain. Very different from the Dakota who usually smarted off to him with her sharp-as-a-knife tongue. This new side to her was playing havoc with his usually stable frame of mind ... and his dick.

Cobra forced his shoulder muscles to release as he continued into the bathroom, grabbing a new shirt and pair of jeans from his bag outside the door.

"When we get hungry, I'll order Chinese or pizza. You got a preference, let me know."

"Okay."

Her answer was just as small, but more certain. Cobra shut the door, leaned his head against it, and blew out a small breath. She was getting to him and he didn't like it one fucking bit. Not at all. He fisted his hands through his hair and paced in the small confines of the bathroom.

A cold shower needed to happen, fucking stat: a non-verbal timeout to reset his shit and re-sort his thoughts before he went out there and did something stupid and regrettable. Dakota seemed to have enough shit going on without him adding to it. If he took them a step further, what the hell was next—would he confide in her? Open himself up to her? *No fucking way*—that wasn't the way he rolled.

"Cobra?"

He was mostly undressed when her knock made him pause, and his whole body went on high alert. The water was already turned on as he unlocked the door and jerked it back the barest crack. A slight blush crept up into her cheeks.

"What's up?"

"Can I use the bathroom before you hop in the shower?"

Cobra nodded and shimmied to the side then opened the door wider so Dakota could get inside the cramped space.

"It's all yours. Sorry, I didn't ask."

"No worries." She slid into the bathroom.

His hand still rested on the doorknob as she stood there staring at him. Her attention seemed to burn a hole through his skin.

"You've got more tattoos," she breathed out, licking her lips.

"Yeah," he spoke gruffly, clearing his suddenly tight throat as he avoided her open stare on his nearly naked body. His cock twitched beneath his boxer briefs and his jaw hardened as he willed himself to get a damn grip so she could do what she came in for. "I've had a lot of work done at various times."

"I knew you had some but I haven't seen them all up close like this."

When Dakota took a step forward, awe washed across her face, and he wondered if she even knew what she had done. Instinct seemed to draw her closer to him. Her eyes traced all the tats that ran from his chest, to his shoulders, and down his arms. Art was Cobra's form of expression and an outlet: a part of him that he could control while he was doing time—and when he was free again.

"You like them?" Cobra stood a little straighter and pulled his shoulders back, allowing her to explore him where normally there was scrutiny and dirty looks from judgmental assholes. "You don't think I'm some kinda thug?"

"No, I *know* you're a thug." She laughed, clearly giving him shit as she zoomed in on the intricate tattoo that started at his stomach and folded around his ribcage. "But your ink doesn't make you who you are, Cobra. Your body is incredible. Like a living, breathing story on your skin. When I was a kid, I saw a man at the swimming pool who was a walking painting. I mean every area of his body—except his face—was covered in pictures that moved when he did. I was fascinated by him, and it stayed with me for years. Even though your body isn't as illustrated as that, it's exquisite."

Cobra scoffed, trying to pretend that her warm breath across his chest wasn't making him all kinds of hard while she stood less than an inch away him. She still had her eyes glued on his upper body, and he hoped she kept them there, otherwise there was no way he could conceal what was tenting in his boxers.

He grabbed the towel on the sink's counter behind him and held it in front of him, hoping that did the trick. "They aren't all fucking Monets, you know." He inhaled sharply as Dakota gripped one of his arms, holding it out under the fluorescent light.

"The gradients are still interesting. I can tell they aren't all from the same artist."

Cobra made a non-committal noise and shifted from foot to foot. Her touch burned into his skin as she turned his arm around and over exploring the designs. But he supposed with every second he was on good behavior, it showed her that he wasn't like all those other assholes and douches who only wanted what was between her legs and nothing else.

Dakota was learning to trust him, which was good, but there was only one small problem—at that moment he had a hard-on from hell. *Fuckin' perfect timing.*

Cobra stepped back. "Didn't you want me outta here?"

"Oh … yeah." She dropped his arm and stood up, leaning against the bathroom counter. "That would be good."

He nodded then ducked out the door before Dakota could see what he had rocking in his boxers just from the touch of her soft hands on his skin. *Fuck!* He glared down at his cock as if it were the enemy.

Even if Dakota wanted to fuck him, Cobra would wait for her to approach him, or at least give him stronger signs than her hands on his arms as she admired his ink. *Fuck … my MC brothers would have a heyday with this shit.* And he wouldn't blame them. He was acting like a goddamn infatuated schoolboy chasing after the pretty girl in class. *Dammit to hell!*

Cobra shook his head and crossed his arms, doing everything in his power to ignore the lust ripping through his system. *She's just new and shiny.* The shit would fade … it always did in the end. *Been there done that.* All the pretty girls blurred into one big collage. For Cobra, there was always a detachment, but with Dakota something was different.

"Get out of your own head, you moron," he murmured under his breath.

"Okay, we're all clear. Sorry about that."

Dakota's voice caught his attention and his head jerked up from where he'd been staring at a smudged stain in the carpet.

Cobra pushed away from the wall. "No problem. I'll be out soon."

"Great. When you get out, you can tell me what some of those symbols mean and who the artists are. I may want to use some of their designs." Dakota grinned and threw herself onto the bed on her back.

"So you're using me as a living art gallery?"

"What? You don't like being used?" She teased, putting her hands behind her head.

His lips went into a grim line and he forced back a frown. What he didn't want was her hands exploring his body unless she wanted to take it to the next level.

"I've got to get in the shower."

Images of her fingers and her tongue tracing the outlines of his tats made him rush into the bathroom.

He locked the door, slipped off his boxers, then turned the water to cold.

CHAPTER ELEVEN

DAKOTA

THE SOUND OF rushing water seeped from under the bathroom door as Dakota looked up at the ceiling and tried to repress the sense of warmth spreading in her chest. It'd been there ever since Cobra had slept on the floor that first night and she'd woken up unharmed. She had her doubts, but the biker seemed to have been keeping his word.

Cobra made her feel peaceful and safe and protected—she hadn't felt that way with anyone in a long time.

It didn't escape her that she hardly knew him, and the fact that Cobra had earned a small bit of trust in such a small amount of time had her head spinning a million miles an hour. By the way he acted, Dakota thought that maybe Cobra was feeling a bit secure around her too. For the past several days, her constant attraction to him had been at the forefront of her brain, and it angered her like hell. She always swore she wouldn't be one of those silly girls who got bowled over by their need to get laid, but she knew in a scared, small corner of herself that wasn't what the attraction she had to him was all about. There was something about Cobra besides his rugged good looks and mighty fine body with all the artwork that mesmerized her.

Maybe it was that Cobra had plenty of chances to hit on her and he didn't. At first Dakota flirted with him to bait him, but later, she did it because she liked him and wouldn't have minded if he tried to kiss her. But he never once acted out. Cobra was a perfect gentleman. Dakota giggled out loud and clamped her hand over her mouth. It was endearing as hell, but a part of her wished his rougher side would come out and play. *What am I thinking? I can't get involved with him. But why* hasn't *he tried to kiss me?* Annoyance pricked at her. From the way he looked at her to his hard-on in the bathroom just a few minutes earlier, it was obvious he was attracted to her. She'd have to be blind not to notice the way he stared when he thought she wasn't looking, or the way his body reacted whenever she touched him.

So what are you waiting for? Maybe he thought she was too young, but that was ridiculous. Age was so damn arbitrary, and she wasn't one of those giggly airheads who annoyed her when they came into the tattoo shop. Cobra and she seemed to have a lot in common, and he was actually going to sit through a romantic comedy just because she wanted to see it. *He's such a sweetie.* A carnal tingle skittered down her spine.

If there was anything wrong with their situation, it wasn't the attraction level, that was for damn sure, which should've made everything else far more difficult. Dakota took a deep breath and grabbed for the remote. Once the TV was on, it was easier to ignore her roaring thoughts, her sudden explosion of sexual need clashing with darker things: the memories and pain she hadn't acknowledged in a long time—that didn't have any place in this new life.

A fresh new start was why Dakota had come here in the first place. It was only fair that she press the reset button on everything else too. So, sleeping with the first available guy, even if he was playing hard to get, wasn't going to help the situation.

Dakota closed her eyes, lulled by the channel surfing, until an image appeared of Cobra hovering over her with his biceps bulging and his tats dancing as he crushed his lips to hers while pushing deep into her. She squirmed on the bed cover. *Enough. He's going to be blowing out of this town and that'll be it. Isn't that what he said a nomad was—no roots?*

"You look deep in thought." His rough voice sent a hot shiver through her.

Dakota glanced at the bathroom doorway and her gaze traced the small patches of glistening water on his upper chest and torso. His eyes flicked away from her as he walked over to the other side of the bed. Her pulse throbbed at every delicate point in her body as she wiggled over a bit to make more room for him. Cobra's weight made the mattress creak in objection.

"Almost makes me fuckin' glad I took the floor," he said, settling onto the bed.

There was no way not to notice all the space he left between their bodies. It was a small bed, but Cobra managed to keep things super PG. Part of her was grateful, almost relieved, but another part of her roared in protest and whined for her to outline the planes of his abs with her tongue.

Stop it right now.

"Are you, uh …" She hesitated and looked at the screen.

"Am I what?" he asked.

Dakota fidgeted a bit, but determination … and audacity pushed her forward. "Uh … are you like this with all women?"

"What?"

He turned toward her, resting on his elbow, the side of his face pressed into his palm. A crease of confusion knitted his brows. Dakota squirmed a bit then faced him. Her hand brushed his thigh. She chewed on her inside cheek then raised her eyes to his. He looked deep into them as he reached down and grasped her hand. His touch only covered her fingers and part of her wrist, but she felt it in her whole body. Dakota was surprised that the sizzle between them didn't spark through the air like the lightning bugs that had circled her grandmother's porch during one of the many trips to Georgia her family had taken when she was young.

Dakota inhaled a deep breath and then let it go. "Do you always keep yourself so closely guarded when you're around other women? So respectful, or …"

She let the last of her question hang in the air, unspoken between them, and she almost hoped he wouldn't pick up the thread. She shifted her gaze from his face to the television screen.

Cobra let go of her hand. "I get plenty of ass when and how I want it, sweetheart." He shifted, making the bed move against the box spring.

"I'm sure you do," she mumbled.

"I don't need to take what's not being offered up, and it doesn't give my ego a little boost to fuck a woman who isn't fucking me back. If a woman wants me in her bed, I won't play games, and she's going to know exactly what she's getting from the experience, so putting on a front just to get some ass isn't what I do. If you call that being guarded or respectful, that's on you."

Dakota glanced sideways at him then turned her head and their gazes locked. His stare was intense, as if challenging her to prove him wrong.

"I can appreciate that," she whispered, brushing a stray hair from her face.

Cobra's lips tipped up into a small half-smile, his eyes burning.

She dragged her gaze away and averted it back to the screen. She couldn't believe she'd asked him that. *What the hell did I hope to accomplish? Was I giving him the go to have his way with me. I'm so fucked up about all this.*

"Cher's in the movie?"

His question broke in on her musings. "Uh … yeah, she is. She's great in it. It's a very funny movie."

"What's it about?"

Dakota gave him a quick rundown, and he just stared at the screen as he listened. "You're strictly a romantic comedy guy, I can see that." She grinned.

"Like I said, I don't watch movies much. I'm more of a book person." Cobra plumped up the pillow with his fist, put it behind his head and lay back, stretching out beside her.

"You're not at all—"

"What you thought when you saw me?" He finished her sentence without a critical or condescending tone to his voice, and she relaxed back against the headboard. "All people have secrets, but I don't want who I am and what I'm about to be one of them. But judgement swings both ways. Some of the worst people I've ever met have looked the best on paper."

Dakota flinched and curled her hand tighter around the remote. There was no doubt about it: she knew *that* very well.

DAKOTA WOKE UP with a start. Her heart beat fast and there was a buzzing in her brain. Soft light trickled in through the curtains, and she rubbed the sleep out of her eyes. Sitting up, she looked over at the floor and saw it was empty.

The mattress creaked and Dakota looked to her left and saw Cobra curled up on the other side of the bed snoring lightly. She slid back down and carefully rolled onto her side and looked at him. His features were much softer in sleep, the lines that grew taut around his eyes were smooth. He looked peaceful. At that moment, she wanted nothing more than to curl up into the curve of his body. Dakota reached out to sweep a wisp of hair off his forehead, but she stopped midair, remembering he was in an outlaw MC and would probably jerk awake in a heartbeat. She didn't want that—she loved watching him so unabashedly.

They must've crashed after they'd eaten the pizza he ordered. They had spent the majority of the night debating gender roles in movies from the classics to the present day. Once she'd started talking about it, Cobra became interested in it, and his knowledge on the subject didn't come from watching the movies, but from the numerous books he'd read about film, psychology, and social interests.

The man was an anomaly: quiet, well-read, introspective, and gentle. He was more than muscle and brawn for the MC; he was steady and critical in every aspect and choice he made during their interactions.

Even though their discussion the night before was heated at times, he didn't take it to the next level or throw things like some of the men she'd known. Cobra just ended the disagreement with the clichéd phrase, "We agree to disagree." A smile tugged at the corners of her mouth. Dakota couldn't picture him as an enforcer for an outlaw club.

Maybe that had been his past, but it wasn't the man who was sleeping beside her at that moment. Her Cobra—tingles skated through her at the thought that he was *hers*—probably evolved from the things in his past. Dakota wasn't a naïve idiot, and she hardly thought he was a choirboy, but a part of her believed that once he'd landed in prison something changed inside him and he wanted to break away. Cobra had hinted as much to her, and the fact that he was living a nomad life reinforced Dakota's belief that he was tired of the violent MC life.

She sighed. The truth was, none of it was her business. They were just temporary roommates and didn't owe each other a heartfelt rendition of the stories of their lives.

Unable to sit still any longer, Dakota slid out of the bed. They had both crashed so hard the night before that neither of them were under the covers, and she still wore her clothes from the previous day. She stretched and tipped her head from side to side.

"You're up." Cobra's voice cracked with sleep, and she nearly jumped out of her skin.

Dakota turned around just as he sat up. "Damn," she cried out. "Do you always have to do that?"

"What?" He yawned, and she heard joints popping as he got up and walked around the end of the bed to stand right in front of her blocking her way to the bathroom. "It's not my fault you're so skittish, sweetheart."

Dakota shrugged and started unbuttoning her jeans ready to give him a full show if he didn't move away quick enough. He wanted to play games? Oh, she could stick her hand in the ring without getting burned. She got her pants halfway down her ass before he glared, took a step back and walked to the other side of the room and faced the wall.

"What the fuck are you doin.?" he said.

"Changing."

"Take it to the bathroom."

Dakota smirked to herself and kept taking off her clothes, doing everything possible to make as much noise so he knew exactly what was going on the whole time. She took her time with every single piece, then, with nothing on but her underwear, she stalked toward her bag that was catty corner in the room next to where he faced the window.

"Why should I have too? You made your intentions clear with me. We're friends and friends share space, so we can be innocent with each other if it means nothing, right?"

She swore he growled, a low trickle of sound that chased goosebumps up and down her arms. But she wasn't about to back down now.

"You've been nothing but good to me, so why should I walk around afraid of what you're going to see by accident when I know for a fact that you're not going to turn your head and invade my privacy?"

"You're so fuckin' sure of that, sweetheart?" Cobra said, low and even, each word measured with tension that practically vibrated from his body. He was ramrod straight as his chest moved up and down with his quick breaths.

The sharp trill of his cellphone snapped them both out of the moment, and she watched as he fumbled on the table for the device.

"What?" he yelled.

CHAPTER TWELVE

DAKOTA

COBRA TURNED AWAY from her and leaned against the wall with the phone in one hand and the other holding the curtain apart.

"... yeah, we can take care of it ... no ... fuck yes, I heard that bullshit ..." His gaze fixed on the parking lot.

Dakota strained to hear his conversation as she got dressed, aware of his low, hushed tones but questioning why he didn't just take the call outside the room like all the other times. As she threw on a clean tank top, he started pacing across the room. One hand flew down his face and he made a noise of annoyance.

"... any kind of pull back from those assholes?"

Whatever they said on the other line must not have shocked him because he grunted and threw himself into the worn chair at the table.

"Tonight?" His stare suddenly flicked to Dakota and back down to the table. "Yeah, I can do tonight."

He clicked off and, with a groan, chucked the cell halfway across the table then leaned back in the chair so his head hung backward.

"When do you start for the day?" he asked.

"I need to be there by ten." Dakota crossed her arms and watched him as she measured his reactions. "I have no idea how long that gives me."

"You've got about an hour." He pulled out a joint and lit it.

"What're you doing tonight?" There was no way to keep the questions out of her voice. "I heard you on the phone."

His head shot up and his eyes narrowed and he put both booted feet up on the table with a loud *thud.*

"That's because I didn't try to hide it. Let me know when you get off tonight. If I don't pick up, leave a message—I'll get it. No matter what, I'll be there to pick you up at the end of your shift."

"What if I want to walk home? You're not my official babysitter, Cobra."

"Walk home?" He said the words as if he didn't comprehend their meaning. "Sweetheart, if you think about walking home in the dark in this neighborhood without me ..." He stopped talking, but he shook himself in the chair. "Just don't fuckin' do it. Wait for me."

"You can't order me around purely because you helped me out one time. That's not how this is supposed to go between us." Dakota protested, pushing away from the wall as a surprising amount of anger rolled through her chest making it hard to breath. "You don't get to take away my choices."

"No, but friends don't allow friends to make dumbass choices, and walking alone is a risky, stupid move that could get you in a fuck ton of trouble, that I'll then have to clean up ... as your damn *friend.*"

Dakota felt every muscle in her body tighten on reflex and instinct, fighting a one-sided battle against common sense that had triggered something deep down beneath her cells. She couldn't even name the feeling. A rare burst of emotion that made her want to lash out at him even while she knew he was only looking out for her best interest, no matter how bossy he was being in the moment.

"You look like you want to chop off my head, sweetheart," Cobra spoke evenly taking his boots off the table and moving slowly to get up from the chair. "Do I need to take myself elsewhere until you're done with ... whatever this is here?" He motioned to her whole body, frowning. "I'm not fucking opposed to leaving you alone in the motel, I just don't want you out there—"

"Can you go get us breakfast? I need to eat if I'm going to have a steady hand for work. I also have to clean up."

His eyes widened and his mouth hung slack for a beat before his jaw snapped shut. Cobra stuck his hands in his pockets with a frown. She could sense the weight of his stare on her all the way across the room. Prickles of tension moved across her scalp as she met his eyes and refused to look away from him.

"This isn't over, Dakota."

"It is for me." She walked toward the bathroom. "After I get my next paycheck, I'll get out of your hair and we can both go back to living our lives without a problem. You get that, right? Moving from place to place and not settling down is your style, so you don't really need me, do you?"

"I'm getting donuts." He marched out of the room and slammed the door shut behind him.

AFTER DAKOTA CHOKED down a glazed donut, Cobra took her to work and she slipped off the bike and stood on the street chewing the dry skin around her thumb. Neither one of them broke the silence between them. A lingering sense of unfinished business buzzed through her brain. *Why the hell am I being such a bitch to him? Am I mad because he ignored me when I changed my clothes. What do I want from him ... from me?*

Maybe she wanted to unload all her secrets on Cobra to finally free herself from their chains that fettered her. Would he understand? Maybe. Did Dakota want to take the chance? Several days ago she would've said "hell no," but now she wasn't so sure.

"I've got to go," she whispered.

Cobra grunted, his fingers gripping the handlebars, his gaze staring straight ahead.

"See you." She crossed the street and heard the screech of cams as he sped away. A queasy feeling churned in her stomach and she didn't think it was because of the donuts.

I'm so fucked up.

Dakota opened the door to the shop and walked in.

Nervous energy kept her adrenaline high as she worked on a slew of customers. As far as tattoo parlors went, Bucky's place was all right. Of course every shop had quirks and ways of doing things, scheduling customers, and cliques. Dakota managed it all while also navigating the unspoken misogyny that rippled through the shop when she noticed she was the only woman working there. Although it wasn't unusual, she was hoping for more progressiveness in this town. Bucky was cool with her, but Kai—one of the artists, seemed to resent her because she had already started getting referrals. Most of the time she was so busy working that she forgot he was even there, but sometimes Kai could really get under her skin. For the most part, Dakota ignored his envious ass.

Hours later, Dakota waved goodbye to her last customer. Stretching her arms high above her head, she reached for the ceiling.

"That feels so good," she said to no one in particular. She glanced at the reception desk.

"You're eyeing the phone like it's going to walk up and bite you. Do you need to use it?" Paul, the shop's manager asked.

She nodded and he shoved it in her direction.

"You don't have to ask, so long as I'm not on it, you can use it any time."

"Thanks," Dakota let go of a breath she hadn't known she'd been holding and picked up the cradle. "I forgot to charge my cell, and I don't have a car yet."

"Got it." Paul nodded then turned his back to give her some privacy.

So far, he and Bucky were the only two who didn't seem to act like tight-lipped dicks whenever a girl was around them. The rest of the artists gabbed among themselves like little old ladies at bingo any time there was a free second, and Dakota had become the official errand girl when she wasn't with a clients. Even though it irked her, she was the new artist on the block, so she did a lot of the grunt work. At least she had a job.

The phone rang and she waited for Cobra's delicious, low timbre to come over the line and make her knees go slightly weak. Just in case he answered, she rested her elbows against the counter.

The phone picked up.

"Hey, I'm ready," she said softly.

"I'm outside," he replied.

Dakota hung up the phone and looked out the front window and saw him sitting astride his purple Harley. She wondered how long he'd been waiting. Dakota hadn't told him when her shift would finish, so Cobra could've been out there for a while. When she came walking up to him, he lifted his chin at her and switched on the engine.

"When did you get here?" Dakota screamed in his ear as they roared off toward the motel.

"I haven't been waiting too long," His voice rumbled up into her arms. "I've got a thing I gotta go to tonight. You'll be okay on your own?"

"I'll be fine."

He nodded and that was the end of it until they were back in the room.

"You sure?"

"About what?" Dakota used the mirror next to the TV to apply a pinkish nude lipstick that had been hanging around in her backpack since she'd left Idaho Falls. "Are you talking about tonight while you do your thing?"

"Yeah."

She spun around and saw him leaning against the closed door as if he couldn't get out of there fast enough.

"I don't plan on doing anything crazy, so rest assured, bodyguard." Dakota smiled and stared up into his eyes noticing the hesitation in them. "After the day I had at work, I just want a quiet, easy night. No worries."

"If you say so."

"Oh, did you check on my SUV?" Cobra had arranged to have a guy he knew from work tow it to his brother-in-law's shop.

He tapped the side of his head as if trying to jog his memory. "Yeah, I did. The guy said it'll cost $1,250 to fix."

Dakota staggered back. "What the fuck? I can't believe it."

"He's not trying to rip you off. You're in a small town and parts are hard to come by. He said that it's the labor that's expensive. Normally, we could go to a salvage place and try to find the parts, but there aren't any around here. The problem is with the engine."

Dakota sank down on the edge of the bed. "What the hell am I going to do? I don't have that kind of money."

"Kelly Blue Book gives $343 for trade-in. Skip said he'll give you five-hundred bucks for it."

"Can I think about it?"

"Yeah, sure, it's your car." Cobra dug in his pocket and held something out toward her. "If you need me, my number is already preprogrammed."

Dakota took the burner phone and turned it over, examining it. It was a strange thing to give her since they weren't planning on staying in each other's lives much longer. Suspicion niggled at the back of her mind. *He's letting me stay for free with him, he takes me and picks me up from work, he buys most of the food, and now he's giving me a burner phone? What does he* really *expect from me?* It seemed like the true wolf in him was finally coming out.

"Thanks," she mumbled, gazing in his direction.

Cobra stiffened against the door and his lips pulled down into a frown as his stance widened.

"Look, I just noticed you haven't been using your cell and figured you don't wanna talk to someone, but you need a phone. I didn't want you to feel like you had to stay here all the time because you had no way of reaching out for help. I'm not here a lot of the time."

Dakota stared down at the phone in her hand and didn't say anything.

"Fuck, if you don't want it, I don't care." An audible sigh. "Yeah, I do. You're keeping it because you may need it."

"I'm fine with it. Thank you," she said in a soft voice as she put the burner in her back pocket then glanced up at him.

"It's got about four hours of minutes on it." He rubbed the back of his neck and pushed away from the door. "More than enough to last you the week."

She nodded and reached over to snag the remote off the nightstand, then turned on the television but muted the sound.

"What the fuck did I do?" Cobra crossed the space between them in two long steps and Dakota averted her gaze down to the carpet.

She kept her eyes glued downward and she shook her head.

Cobra placed two fingers under her chin and as he lifted her face to look at him, he scanned for some kind of clue in her expression. "Fuck, talk to me. I can't walk out that door without knowing what the hell I did to put that look on your face, Dakota."

She pressed her lips together and closed her eyes. "I guess I don't understand why you're being like this ..." she trailed off, still clutching the TV remote in one hand.

"Whaddaya mean?"

The pad of his thumb rubbed against her cheek, and sparks of electricity raced across her skin. The scent of his skin, leather, and soap combined tugged at her senses and she shivered, sucking in a sharp breath.

"Are you going to tell me?" he said in a low voice.

Dakota shifted on the bed then looked up at him. "You've done so much for me these past several days, and what have you gotten in return?"

"Oh fuck, darlin', no ..." Cobra dropped his hand. "That's not what this is about at all."

"Protection comes with a price and no good deed—"

"That's not what I'm doing here. Fuck it! You think I'm helping you out and watching over you just so I can get into your pants. Give me some goddamn credit, sweetheart."

"But I see the way you look at me." Dakota gave a half-shrug. "I know our situation isn't ideal."

Cobra stepped back. "I'm not gonna say I don't find you attractive 'cause I'd just be lying. I'm a man, so of course I'm gonna fuckin' look at a pretty woman, but I don't want anything from you. I'm helping you because I want to." He scrubbed his face then pounded his fist in the palm of his hand. "Sleeping in the bed together last night was a big mistake. I'll make sure it doesn't happen again."

A knot in her stomach twisted and one of her legs bounced up and down.

Cobra glanced down at his phone. "I gotta get going."

Dakota stood up and gripped the edge of the nightstand to steady herself. "Cobra, I'm sorry," she said to his retreating back.

The door closed then she heard the rumble of his bike and the tires squeal as she hurried to the window. Her chest tight, she watched until the red taillights disappeared down the road, and the faint sound of the thunderous engine faded into silence.

CHAPTER THIRTEEN

COBRA

THE MOSSY, EARTHY smell of the lakeshore filled Cobra's nostrils as he sped along the Anaconda-Pintler Route on his journey to Missoula. He'd purposely avoided the interstate, preferring the quiet of the wide-open country road. The rush of cool wind swirled around him as he passed through forested mountains, then twisted and turned down through the canyon. Old mining relics, lush greenery, and wildflowers dotted the landscape. Continuing surges of adrenaline buzzed through Cobra and he let all the shit from the motel room evaporate in the air. Riding was his way of meditating and throwing away life's bullshit. When he was on his Harley, he was one with the environment, and he felt alive in its purest form. Without the ride, there wouldn't be any purpose to life.

During the three years Cobra had spent in the pen, the only thing that made him swear he'd never go back was how damn hard it was not being on a bike. The first and most important thing he'd missed was his Harley-Davidson—hands down.

When Cobra reached the Missoula city limits, he twisted the throttle and took a sharp turn down a small road. It'd been over a year and a half since he'd been around these parts, not to mention the clubhouse as well. The last time he was in Philipsburg, he didn't want anyone to know he was back in Steel Devils' territory, but this time around he wanted to see his brothers, and the shit about the off-limits dealing going on in Philipsburg was the impetus which took him on the road leading to the club.

Cobra high-fived Razor who manned the gates at the entrance to the club's compound. He killed the engine and jumped off the bike then took out his phone to see if Dakota had called, but she hadn't. A slow burn smoldered inside him whenever he thought of Dakota's distrust in him. It had shocked him because he thought they'd gotten beyond all that, but apparently not. "If I wanted to fuck her, we would've done it by now," he muttered as he put his phone back in his jeans pocket. There was no way she wouldn't have been willing. She accused him of checking her out, well, her sassy little ass had been ogling him plenty. "Hypocrite." Cobra shoved his hands in his front pockets and walked slowly toward the front door.

Offering her a place to stay had been one big fucking mistake. Everything about it from the very beginning had been an overcomplicated, impulsive blunder. Cobra paused and looked up at the darkening sky brushed with lavender and indigo clouds and the occasional glitter of a faraway star. He blew out a deep breath then clenched his jaw. At the end of the week he'd get her the hell out of there, and then go back to the Sapphire Mountains and pitch a tent. Yeah, they'd go their separate ways, and all the bullshit would stop. Dakota could keep the fucking phone and do whatever the hell she pleased. He'd be finished. *Done and outta the damn town once the MC resolves the disrespect that's going on there.*

Hell, she could do her thing, and he could go back to being responsible for just one person—*himself.* Cobra took a deep breath and let it out slowly before walking into the clubhouse.

Ink spotted him right away. The dude was still uglier than a monkey's armpit, and his mouth hung down like he was seeing a ghost.

"Fuck, bro, whaddaya think ... that I'm dead and have come back to haunt your sorry ass?" Cobra said as he strode over to him.

"Cobra ... it's been too fuckin' long," Ink said, pulling him in for a bear hug.

"Spending too much time in solitary made you a goddamn hermit," Hulk joked as he clasped Cobra on the shoulder. "How're you doin', dude?"

"Good." Cobra rubbed Hulk's rounded belly. "I see that you're being taken care of."

"Fuck you." Hulk laughed and placed both hands on his stomach and shook it like a bowl full of jelly.

Cobra guffawed and smacked him on the back. "I heard you got a new bike. I gotta see it."

"Whose been talking about me?" Hulk's eyes narrowed.

"Me," Grinder answered as he came over.

Hulk's eyes widened and a group of members who'd sauntered over broke out in laughter. A large grin broke across Hulk's face before he joined in and did the same.

"Glad you're back," Grinder said to Cobra.

"Me too." He waved his hand around the large room. "I've missed this."

A tall, skinny man who didn't look to be more than twenty came over with a bottle of beer and a double shot of whiskey. Cobra lifted his chin at the dude and took the drinks from him, and the young man slinked away.

"How many prospects you got?"

"Three," Grinder said, bringing the beer bottle to his mouth.

"And seven club whores," Pee Wee added. "One of thems got such sweet big tits. I remember you like 'em big." He chortled.

"Remember how we used to fuck in the hot tub?" Ink asked.

"Yeah," Cobra replied.

"You hooking up with some big-titted honey in Philispburg?" Pee Wee asked.

Dakota wearing a yellow tank top that covered her small, perky breasts flashed through his mind.

"Nah." He took a drink of beer.

"Then Shania's the one for you, brother," Grinder said, putting an arm around him.

Cobra nodded then scanned the room for Breaker. When he was an active member, Breaker and he used to cause all kinds of trouble in the bars in Missoula. They had a blast shutting the smart-assed mouths of snot-nosed punks who thought they could take the two bikers on. The jerks always found out they couldn't.

"Where's Breaker?" he asked.

Boulder shook his head. "He's in Omaha—his mom died."

A jolt of sadness shot through Cobra. "Fuck, that's tough. I didn't know she was sick." He remembered visiting Marjorie many times with and without Breaker. When Cobra had gone nomad, he'd make it a point to go through Omaha if he was in the area to stop in and see how she was doing. He'd always take her to a steakhouse, and she'd talk about it for days to Breaker. Cobra chuckled to himself when he recalled the time Breaker called him and told him to quit taking his mom to expensive steakhouses because it made him look bad. Cobra had joked that he couldn't help it if Breaker's idea of fine dining was Burger King.

Damn. I really liked Marjorie. She was a good sport. Breaker was so close to his mother that Cobra knew her death must be tearing him up something awful. For a split second he wondered if his mother was still alive, then he pushed the thought from his mind.

"Did you hear me?" Boulder asked, dragging Cobra out of his reflections.

"No, sorry, dude. I'm still reeling from learning about Marjorie."

"Yeah. According to what Breaker told us, she had a massive heart attack. Julia found her when she went over the next day to drop off her kids. Can you imagine that?"

"Damn. Julia was real close to her mom, just like Breaker," Hulk said.

"She was a damn fine woman," Cobra said.

A few minutes of silence fell among the members as they empathized with the loss one of their brothers suffered.

Grinder cleared his throat. "We can continue the welcome home shit after church. Let's get going." He looked at the vice president. "Round everyone up."

Sparky nodded then walked away.

Fifteen minutes later, Cobra sat on one of the folding chairs in the meeting room, and it felt as if he'd never left. The room was stuffy and hot, and the swamp cooler was a poor substitute for air conditioning. Cobra wiped the back of his neck, then reached over and opened a window. Despite the ventilation, the dank odor of sweat filled the room.

Grinder hit the gavel on the table and the scant rumble of conversation stopped; all eyes were on their president.

"We're gonna make this short tonight since it's hot as fuck in here and smells like ass."

The membership chortled. "As you know, Cobra stumbled onto some shit in Philipsburg that we gotta put a stop to." The brothers raised their voices, swearing and promising the offenders would die in evil ways. Grinder held up his hands. "There's time afterwards to trash the motherfuckers, but right now Cobra's gonna tell us what he knows, and we're gonna figure out how to take Big Pat down."

The members whooped, whistled, and pounded their fists on the table.

Cobra pushed the chair back and rose to his feet, waiting for the racket to die down. The gavel crashed down again on the table, and the guys looked back at the front of the room.

Cobra lifted his foot onto the edge of the chair and leaned forward. "Big Pat's the one who's distributing the drugs in the area. He picks real dipshits to do his dirty work—frat boys, teens, even strippers. He pays them ten percent of what they get and he takes the rest. The fucker's dealing meth, GHB, and weed."

"Asshole's been warned before," Iron said.

Cobra jerked his head at the member who leaned against the wall.

He'd just come in a few minutes before and Cobra hadn't seen him. Besides Breaker, Iron and Brute were some of the other brothers he was especially close to.

"We should've killed his fuckin' ass when he did shit in Lolo. Good to see you, brother." Iron raised his fist and Cobra returned the gesture.

"Iron's right," Hulk grumbled.

"We discussed this when we found out the fucker's relation was a damn badge," Sparky said.

"And we voted on it." Grinder leaned back and crossed his arms.

"I didn't vote for shit. I was against it." Iron kicked his foot back against the wall.

"We know, and that's in the damn past. We're talking about what to do *now*, so unless you got something helpful to add, shut the fuck up." Grinder glowered.

Cobra straightened up. "As I was saying, I don't think this Big Pat asshole has got a hardcore, organized business going. He should be pretty easy to take down. I'm gonna find one of the guys who slipped Dak—uh … this girl some GHB and make him tell me where this dealer lives. I haven't been able to find the douchebag, but I'm still looking."

"And when we find him, he's fuckin' history," Iron said, his eyes narrowed at Grinder and Sparky.

The rest of the members voiced their agreement with Iron, and the president slammed down the gavel once again.

"This time we'll take the asshole out. Cobra will let us know when we can send some brothers up to help him out," Grinder said.

"When the time comes, I want Iron and Brute to be among the brothers heading my way," Cobra added.

Grinder nodded.

"By the way, where the fuck is Brute?" Cobra looked around the room.

"He's had a date with the crapper since yesterday," Iron said as several members laughed. "Food poisoning. He's gonna be sorry he missed you, man."

"Yeah. Tell him I'll see him soon. I wanna get this wrapped up before long 'cause I'm planning to move on," Cobra said.

"Where to?" Ink asked.

"Not sure yet," Cobra replied.

"We didn't adjourn church yet, so keep the fucking chitchat for later," Grinder interjected.

"You got anything more?" Sparky looked at Cobra who shook his head. "Then I think that wraps it up."

"Church is done." The sound of the gavel bounced off the walls. "Go party."

Loud whoops and yells mingled with the rush of footsteps as the members filed out of the room. Cobra walked over to Iron and hugged him hard.

"It's good to see you, bro," Iron said.

"Yeah. It's been too long."

The two men walked into the main room, talking and reminiscing.

"You gonna crash here tonight?" Iron asked.

Dakota alone in the motel room filled Cobra's mind. "Nah, I gotta get back."

Iron chuckled and handed him a beer. "You got pussy waiting for you?"

Cobra shook his head. "It's not that. I just got some shit to do." He clinked bottles with Iron then tipped the bottle back.

"Bullshit. I know that look."

Cobra didn't answer, and for the next hour, he shot the shit with friends he hadn't seen in a long time. At one point, he was tempted to take up with the big-titted new girl and crash in one of the rooms, but the thought of Dakota by herself and vulnerable while he wet his dick didn't sit too well with him, so he pushed away from the bar.

"Gotta get going. We'll be in touch." He looked at Iron.

"You going so soon?" Ink asked.

"Got stuff to do." Cobra fished out the keys to his bike from his pocket.

"Like what?" Ink challenged.

"He's got some prime pussy, and he doesn't want to share," Hulk said.

"Unlike some of you, I gotta work to feed my belly and keep my bike running." Cobra waved his hand in the air as he walked toward the door.

"Have fun with your sweet piece," Iron yelled out.

Shaking his head, Cobra walked out into the night.

WHEN HE PULLED up to the motel complex, there were no lights on in their room, and he figured Dakota had zonked out early. She'd told him it was a long day at work, and it was already past eleven o'clock at night, so Cobra didn't think anything of it when he inserted the key in the lock and turned the knob. The door creaked a bit when he cracked it open and he walked in, careful not to wake her. Standing by the entrance, he waited until his eyes adjusted to the dimness, then he looked over at the bed and his gaze widened. Dakota wasn't there.

"What the fuck?" he said out loud.

Cobra flipped on a light switch near the door, and a golden glow bathed the room. He walked over to the bed and stared down at the covers. The remote was in the middle, and a box of Chinese takeout sat on the nightstand along with a half full bottle of water. Cobra scanned the area for a note but didn't see anything. His jaw tightened and he rolled his shoulders five or six times to work out the kinks.

"Not your problem, brother. She's a big girl—stubborn and irritating as fuckin' hell, but a big girl. Just watch some TV and crash."

Despite the pep talk, a small fission of fear worked his stomach into knots. Cobra closed his eyes and breathed out a long exhale before he rolled his shoulders again. Taking a quick walk around the place wouldn't kill anyone, and if he found her, he could say he was out for a bit of fresh air or some other bullshit. Without thinking too much about it, Cobra jammed the key back into his pocket and let the motel room door slam shut.

Moonlight splashed across the parking lot, and a light shone from the office, creating an elongated rectangle on the grass. Surprised that the manager was still on duty at that hour, Cobra strode over and turned the knob. The door swung open and he walked inside. No one was there. He turned around to leave, but muted voices in the distance caught his attention. Slowly he sauntered over to a closed door near the desk. Cobra grasped the knob and before he could turn it, the door burst open, and he jumped back to avoid being clobbered in the face. Jake, the manager, cried out and an older, heavy-set man stopped in his tracks for a second then spun around and retreated back into the room, the door closing behind him.

"The office is closed," Jake said, wiping his forehead with a tissue.

"The front door was opened," Cobra replied as he stared at the wiry man.

"I forgot to lock it."

My gut's telling me something's not right.

"Whaddaya need?" Jake crumpled the tissue and tossed it in the trash can. "Even though I'm off duty, I can still help you out. A manager's job is never done, and I don't mind anyway because I like to help out the customers." A toothy smile spread across his face.

The manager rubbed Cobra the wrong way. Jake was a fast-talking slicker who reeked of insincerity.

"Where's your pretty girlfriend?" Jake propped his elbows on the desk and leaned forward.

Cobra ground his teeth and his nostrils flared.

The manager seemed to have caught on that trouble was brewing because he straightened up and took a few steps backward.

"I've gotta get going, so if you don't need nothing, then I'll be locking the door now." Jake clutched a pen and kept twirling it around in his hand.

"Who you got back there?" Cobra jerked his head toward the closed door.

"What?" Jake's face blanched.

"You heard me." Cobra leaned over the reception counter.

"A buddy of mine came by and we're catching up." Jake inched toward the door.

Cobra didn't believe him for one minute, but he didn't get the vibe that Dakota was back there. It didn't go unnoticed by him the way the slimy manager stared at her or tried to talk to her whenever he got the chance. To Dakota's credit, she ignored the douchebag, but she'd brought it up one time to Cobra that Jake gave her the creeps.

"I really do have to lock up." The manager stared at Cobra, a nasty snuffling noise came from his nose as his chest rose and fell.

"I'm gonna say this once—stop ogling Dakota. Don't look at her. Don't talk to her. Don't get near her again. You got it? Next time I'll come in swinging, and you won't like the mess I'll make of you."

Jake nodded, his left eyelid twitching like crazy. "Gotcha. I didn't mean no harm. I was jus' being friendly, but she's not too friendly anyways, so okay … yeah … I gotcha. Yep."

Cobra gave him one of his cold, detached death stares that he'd used when he was an enforcer for the MC, loving how the asshole's lips and chin trembled. After a couple of minutes, Cobra grew tired of watching the pussy's face turn ashen while his body shook like a damn leaf.

"Just remember what I said, 'cause I don't like repeating myself."

"Yeah … sure," Jake stuttered.

Cobra turned around and walked out of the office, chuckling when—within five seconds—the lock clicked behind him and the lights went out.

If he wasn't looking for Dakota, Cobra would've hidden in the shadows to get a better look at the dude who'd been in a big hurry to conceal himself. There was something about the older guy that raised a red flag for him. He'd have time to think about it later, and ask the surly teen on the day shift what he knew about the dude.

Around the corner, Cobra saw a tall fence wrapped around an area. Soft white lighting illuminated tall treetops rustling gently in the breeze, carrying the faint smell of chlorine. He walked over to the area and continued toward a chain-link gate, noticing the pool water lapping at the tiled edges. Lights embedded in the sides of the pool gave off an almost eerie glow, and he saw Dakota swimming across the blue water.

Cobra opened the gate and walked into the pool area, avoiding a lounge chair that was haphazardly placed in front of the entrance. Dakota was oblivious to him as she stood up in the shallow part of the water, the wet T-shirt clinging to her body. Cobra was mesmerized by her as his mouth went dry and his heart raced. A rush of arousal streaked through him and landed on his growing dick.

Fuck! He knew he should yank his eyes away, but he couldn't—he was captivated by her.

Dakota reached up high above her head, and when her T-shirt rose up and revealed the underside of her butt, he about lost it. Cobra held his gaze as the water rippled beneath her and the shadows from the tree branches moved across her face. Then reason poked through his sexual fog, and for a split second, every muscle in his body froze before anger set in.

"Are you fuckin' crazy?" he said, walking to the edge of the pool.

She turned around and her face washed blank with confusion, like her brain cogs couldn't turn fast enough to register that the snarling voice belonged to Cobra.

"You're out here alone in the pool wearing *that*? What the fuck, Dakota?" Cobra glanced around and saw a towel from the room draped over one of the iron chairs and he marched over and snatched it up.

A taut face replaced the blank one from seconds before, and she shook her hair as droplets of water flew everywhere.

"I'm fine," she said, wading to the pool stairs. "Water relaxes me."

"You should've taken a fuckin' bath." He held open the towel.

"I needed a swim. Don't be mad."

Dakota scrambled out of the water then slowly walked toward him. The T-shirt molded over her swaying hips and her pert breasts like a second skin. A groan rose in his throat when he noticed that her nipples were hard against the wet top. Cobra gripped the towel tighter, adrenaline pumping through him. Thoughts of Dakota naked in his bed, writhing beneath him as his thumbs teased those taut nipples filled his mind. He needed to get her out of that T-shirt and into her fuzzy nightshirt, then tuck her safely in bed while he took another cold shower.

She stopped a few inches from him and cocked her head. "Did you have a good time tonight?"

Cobra flicked his attention from her tits to her face and then back to her tits. "How long have you been out here?"

"Just about twenty minutes. I ordered some Chinese food and watched a movie, then all of a sudden I got so restless and antsy—like I was going to climb the walls or jump out of my skin. So I decided to go for a swim after I noticed the pool yesterday. Imagine, this place having such a nice pool."

"You're shivering," he said in a low voice as he held the towel higher. "Come on over here."

"Only if you promise you're not mad at me," she whispered.

His gaze roamed her body and his temperature rose. What was it about Dakota that turned him on and made him so fucking mixed up? He shifted his weight from one foot to the other. "I'm not mad," he rasped.

A tiny smile tugged at the corners of her kissable mouth.

"Come here," he said in a low voice.

Dakota licked her lips then walked to him, and when he laid the towel on her shoulders, she shrugged it off then looked up at him from beneath her lashes. In the soft lights reflecting from the pool, she was beautiful. Cobra snagged his arm around her waist and yanked her closer to him. He could feel her tits pressing against his chest, the hard nipples pushing into his skin, and it hit him like a taser straight to his cock.

"Fuck, darlin'," he muttered. He should end this here and now, but he just wanted one taste of her sweet lips, then he'd push her away and they'd go back to the room and pretend this never happened.

Dakota stood on her tiptoes and wrapped her arms around his neck. Cobra's leg slipped between hers as his hands slid down her back, grasped her ass cheeks, and jerked her closer to him.

"You're such a hot temptation," he said nuzzling his face in her damp hair. It smelled like oranges, chlorine, and the night air.

"Hmm …" A little sigh came from her sweet lips, and it drove him damn near crazy.

"If we keep holding each other like this, I'm gonna forget all about being on good behavior." His lips skimmed through her hair.

She tilted her head back and locked her eyes on his.

"Being good is so damn overrated," she whispered. With those lips parted, Dakota's mouth looked much too tempting to resist.

The heat of her touch burned through him, and the need for her was off the fucking charts. "Dakota," he rasped, wrapping her hair around his hand and pulling firmly on it.

Her breathy little moans landed on his throbbing dick.

Fuck it.

Cobra yanked her hair even more until she winced. "There's you, baby … and there's me. Then, there's this dark, nasty craving in between. I'm aiming to close the gap." He crushed his mouth on hers, then his tongue pushed inside her open lips.

CHAPTER FOURTEEN

DAKOTA

DAKOTA KISSED COBRA back, her tongue slipping inside his mouth to the hot sweetness there, and he pushed in deeper, a low growl rumbling deep in his throat. Heat flared through her as she slid her hands up his chest and around his neck. Cobra wrapped his arm around her waist, yanking her hard against him, and the fusion of their bodies filled her with such desire and need that she clawed at his shoulders and nibbled his bottom lip.

"Fuck, sweetheart," he gritted, biting kisses down her neck while his fingers gripped her ass, pushing her further into him.

Dakota tangled her fingers in his hair and pulled his face closer to hers, urging the kiss to deepen. She loved the twisted dance of their tongues, the hard edge of his teeth on her lower lip.

Cobra lifted his head, his breath uneven as he dragged in air. "You're driving me fuckin' wild, darlin'." His lips skimmed hers then moved over her jaw, peppering it with light, tingly kisses before he swept his mouth back on her and kissed her deeper, harder, rougher.

Never had Dakota been kissed this way—it was incendiary.

His lips slid across hers. "You're playing with fire, little one." His voice was harsh and grating as it smothered against her mouth.

"Maybe I want to," she whispered.

Cobra wrapped strands of her hair around his hand and yanked her head back, then he leaned down and kissed the pulsing hollow at the base of her throat. The touch of his lips on her sensitive skin sent shivers of desire racing through her veins.

Dakota rubbed against the hardness in his jeans, and a low hum emitted from his chest. She felt the body heat radiating from him as she slipped her fingers under his T-shirt and ran them over the ridges of his sculpted muscles. Dakota glanced up at him with wide eyes, slightly breathless while she pressed tight against him.

"Don't you want me?" she whispered, locking eyes with him.

"What the fuck do you think?" he rasped.

Cobra brought his mouth down over hers, taking her breath out of her body. One small touch lit a fire. One of his hands remained pressed against her lower back while the other entwined underneath her damp hair at the base of her neck, anchoring her lips to his mouth.

Her hips ground against the front of his jeans as his teeth nibbled on her lips, ear, and neck. Dakota moaned and rubbed against him faster, like a cat in heat.

Cobra reared back, moonlight casting shadows in the hollows of his jaw. Her fingers rested along his shoulders before they dug into the heavy weight of the muscle there, and he grunted lightly as his facial expression completely shut down.

"Are you sure about this? I mean—"

"I want it ... I want *you*, Cobra."

He snatched her wrist from his shoulder and dragged her to the motel room without a single word. Cobra fumbled with the key then kicked open the door, slamming it shut with the sole of his boots. He dropped her arm and cornered her against the wall, a wolfish, intense stare pinning her as surely as if it were his body.

"You want this. You want me. You're sure? Even with the ramifications?"

Dakota allowed the weight of his question to settle underneath her skin. Her lips still stung from where his kisses had bruised them, and she could still sense his hand tightening at the base of her skull despite the fact that he was standing less than three inches in front of her. His face went feral as his gaze locked onto her breasts, and he stared at her as if he wanted to devour her.

She was going to give him that chance.

"I'm sure," she said, looking him in the eye.

Dakota tipped up her chin and trailed her fingers between her breasts, the damp T-shirt still clinging to her like a second skin. "This doesn't change our friendship," she whispered, lightly squeezing her nipples until they pebbled hard against the thin fabric. She watched Cobra's eyes widen, his mouth pulling back into a possessive, cocky smile that made her blood overheat with need.

"Fuck," he muttered under his breath as he came close to her.

Cobra swiveled his hips against her and shoved her leg around his waist. While he held her, caging her against the smooth, cool wall, their noses touched, and she fought to get every inch of him.

Every time Dakota moved forward for a kiss, his head tilted backward. A teasing little dance that made the currents of desire spark all the way down to the throbbing ache between her legs. Through the harsh fabric of his jeans, his hard cock pressed against her quivering sex.

"Cobra," she pleaded.

He laughed, a strong, masculine sound that made her insides turn to mush. Dakota shivered and tipped her head back as she worked her hips against him. Cobra stroked the side of her face, his fingers slowly working their way down her body. She held on when he lifted the hem of her T-shirt and touched the bare skin of her belly. The coolness from the air conditioner danced across her flesh. Goosebumps scattered across her arms, and she reached out for him.

"Not yet, sweetheart." He pushed her hand away, and raised her shirt a bit more. "I wanna take my time revealing your sexy body." Cobra bent down and swirled his tongue in her belly button, tugging the T-shirt higher as he kissed his way up to her breasts.

Dakota whisked the shirt over her head, and Cobra suck in a sharp, audible breath.

"Fuck, you're gorgeous."

He grabbed both breasts and pushed them together then kissed the tops of them. Dakota gasped and splayed her hands flat against the wall. He raised his head and stared intensely at her as he inhaled deeply and growled as he exhaled.

A passionate cry fell from her throat in a gasping, tearing sound of need. "Cobra, please."

He gripped her wrists in his hand and pinned her arms above her head.

"Keep them there," he whispered against her ear.

His warm breath trickled down her neck as his mouth sucked and his teeth nibbled, biting along the hypersensitive line of her flesh. Her lids fluttered closed, and she let everything fall away.

A pause fell between them and Dakota opened her eyes and saw his fiery gaze slide over her like one long stroke of his hands over the length of her body. A sly smile tugged at the corners of his mouth as he reached out and took her aching nipples between his fingers, pinching, twisting, and tugging on them. A sweet pain pulled at her clit.

She couldn't keep track of him. One minute he was biting a line along her collarbone, making her tremble and arch against him; the next, his warm, teasing mouth was locked around and flicking her nipple with short strokes of his tongue. Dakota fought not to cry out too loud while he molded her body with his hands and lips, his tongue and his teeth.

Then she heard the click of metal as Cobra unthreaded his belt out from between the loops. He took a step backward and snapped the belt before letting it fall to the carpet beneath their feet. He crooked his finger in her direction.

"Undo my pants, sweetheart."

Dakota walked over, drawn to him like a magnet to carbon steel. When his hand landed on her shoulder and pressed down, she didn't hesitate, knowing exactly what Cobra wanted as she lowered to her knees and undid his button.

"Good girl," he said in a low, deep voice.

She smiled up at him, enjoying how big and protective he felt hovering over her while she worked at his jeans, all the while knowing with an aching sense of urgency what she would find when he was out of them. Anticipation rang through her temples and her fingers became more insistent, tripping over themselves as his fingers gently threaded through her hair.

Without being told, Dakota reached into his jeans and drew out his thick, hard cock. Cobra hissed and widened his stance. She stroked once, up and down, admiring the soft yet firm feel of him beneath her fingers. Dakota swallowed and lowered her mouth around him with a slow, teasing slide. His fingers tightened on the top of her head as a whispered curse escaped his lips. His hips tensed, and she placed her hands on either side of them to anchor herself in place.

"Fuck, darlin'," Cobra rasped.

Dakota felt his muscles strain against her fingers as she eased up along his shaft and slid back down, establishing a rhythm that was both deep and slow. As her tongue flicked the ridge under the smooth crown, he shuddered, and a ragged exhale slipped through his lips.

"Keep doing that."

"You like that, don't you?" She laved wet strokes up and down as she squeezed the base of his dick.

"Yeah, that feels so fuckin' good." Cobra buried his fingers in her hair, digging into her scalp.

When she cupped his balls and stroked them, he bucked forward, thrusting his cock deeper into her throat.

Cobra pulled her hair hard and her eyes watered. "I fuckin' love seeing your tits sway as you suck me. It's so damn hot." Another hard pull, and she thought for sure he'd tear out a handful of her blonde locks.

Dakota's strokes became quicker, harder, and with a small suck at the end of every pass.

"Fuck, you're gonna make me blow, but I wanna be inside you." Cobra pushed her backward off his dick, and Dakota made a small whimper.

She leaned back on her knees, her eyes fixed on his hardness while she wiped her mouth with the back of her hand.

"Get up, sweetheart," he said gruffly, holding out his hand to help her up from the floor. "Turn around with your hands on the wall."

The scrape of his calloused fingers down her back sent a flurry of quivers through her body. When Cobra ran them around the back waistband of her panties, she clenched her thighs together and wiggled.

"Keep your legs wide open," he ordered, and she quickly complied. "Perfect," he murmured as he trailed a single digit over the lacy fabric, down the crevice of her ass.

"Oh, Cobra."

He ran his finger back and forth between her inner thighs, pressing the peach fabric of her panties between her aching, swollen lips.

"Cobra," she croaked.

"Does that feel good?" he whispered.

"Yeah..."

"You're so damn wet."

"I was in the pool," she said between breaths.

Cobra hooked his fingers into the dainty fabric and yanked them down to her ankles and she stepped out of them. He moved her hair from the back of her neck, gently biting and then blowing away the wetness. Dakota jerked and gasped, her hips swiveling against the air. A small patch of goosebumps raised up along her skin.

"You like that," he said matter-of-factly as he slid his fingers between her legs and teased along her glossy lips. "Yeah... you're fuckin' soaked."

"The pool," she whispered.

"Uh-huh."

Two digits delved into her, and Dakota's whole body went rigid at the contact. Her muscles pulsed against his fingers and she cried out when his free palm came down on her ass cheek.

"Yeah, you're fuckin' dripping. You still saying it's the pool?"

"No," she moaned.

"Didn't think so."

Another smack on her behind was followed by a gentle massage of her stinging cheek as he thrust his fingers in and out of her. Dakota looked over her shoulder at him, heat spreading through her as she tracked his every movement. Cobra's lips twitched in a cocky half-smile as he drew his T-shirt over his head and tossed it on the floor, followed by his boots, socks, boxers, and finally, his jeans.

Dakota's breath hitched, and she pushed away from the wall in desperate need to touch him, to feel him.

"Hands back where they belong," he commanded, his palm in the middle of Dakota's back, pressing her upper body lower. "Ass back in the air and legs spread wide."

"But I want to feel you," she whispered as she complied with his orders.

Cobra didn't answer, and from the corner of her eye, Dakota saw him pick up a packet and tear it open. Excited tingles streaked through her, and she closed her eyes in anticipation.

His cock slid over the crack of her ass then pressed against her aching sex. "Do you want it?" he rasped, slipping two fingers into her.

"Yes," she moaned, arching back and forth trying to get the friction she craved, yet utterly helpless with her palms planted on either side of her head. "Cobra…"

He let out a low chuckle, then yanked her ass out further. "Beautiful," he growled as his free hand inched toward her pulsing pussy.

The first stroke on her clit rocked through her, and her whole body jolted in place as she cried out.

"Cobra, please. I need you," she panted.

He pulled his hands away from her pussy and leaned over her, covering her body with his own. "Have you been a good girl, Dakota?"

"Yes," she answered, her body aching for him to enter her.

Cobra entwined his fingers in her hair and gave it a hard tug, and Dakota sighed with pleasure and spread her legs even further.

Then, in one savage movement, his cock plunged into her.

"Oh!" She pushed her ass back toward him.

"Fuck, Dakota." He thrust into her hard and rough. "You feel so fuckin' good." He panted while hammering into her over and over.

"It feels amazing," she said, her body pushing toward the wall.

"It's gonna get better, sweetheart. Fuck, you look hot as hell, you know that?" His lips and tongue slid down her spine, and she cried out in pleasure when one of his hands tugged her nipple as he kept slamming his dick into her heat.

Then his finger slid down her belly to her throbbing clit and tapped it—hard.

"Shit!" she cried.

Another tap. A slap. Then another.

The most intense currents of pleasure sizzled through her, and she writhed and wiggled while shoving her ass back at him.

"Fuck, darlin'," Cobra said as he kept up the relentless pounding.

"Faster!" she cried.

The slap of naked skin against naked skin, the scent of sweat and passion, and guttural moans filled the room.

When he gently stroked the side of her hardened nub then pinched it, pleasure splashed over her, blocking out all sound, until there was nothing but the explosion of sensations—deep and primal, as her screams echoed in the room.

Dakota was barely aware of the feather-light kisses caressing her back, or the steely arms nestling her then lying her down on the bed. Her limbs were rubber, her body hummed in satisfaction, and a delicious purr of delight still tickled deep in her pussy. It was only when the mattress sagged next to her that the wispy haze of ecstasy slowly dissipated. She rolled over on her side and met the tranquil gaze of Cobra.

"How are you?" she asked tentatively. Her orgasm had been so intense, so unlike anything she had ever experienced, that she'd been transported away, forgetting about him. Dakota didn't even know if he'd climaxed, but assumed that he had.

"Real good, darlin'." He bent down and brushed his lips across hers. "You?"

"Oh, yeah. It was incredible."

He squeezed her lightly, then drew her closer to him. "I mean with us doing it."

"Of course ... yeah." She pillowed her head on his chest, listening to his heartbeat.

"That's good." He kissed the top of her head.

For a long while they lay there, legs tangled, arms entwined, bodies fused. The only sound in the room was the hum of the air conditioner until Cobra's light snores competed with it. Dakota carefully moved his arm from hers then slid off the bed and padded to the bathroom.

The fluorescent light hummed above, creating shadows to Dakota's eyes, nose, and chin. She wondered whoever thought this type of lighting was a good idea for a bathroom. Turning away, she reached over and grabbed one of the bath towels, then drew the shower curtains open, and turned on the water. The mildly hot water beat down on her skin and she tilted her head back and let the water wet her hair.

Dakota had never imagined having sex could be so intense and emotional. She peeled the paper wrapping around the soap. It wasn't Cobra's sexual expertise that surprised her, it was the way she reacted to it. It was like she was looking down from above at another person as the passion and lust exploded inside her. And she'd actually cuddled next to him afterward, and ... she didn't feel dirty or cheap.

The scent of jasmine and citrus curled around her as she scrubbed the lather over her skin. *How did he do it?* Each time she'd had sex with a man, she was detached, and afterward she'd feel used and soiled, even if she had an orgasm. But with Cobra, it had been what Dakota had always thought sex should be, but all that was destroyed by one single night.

Don't go there. Don't think of it and ruin tonight.

But it was too late. The room grew smaller and the steam cleared, and instead of seeing the white tiles in the shower, she saw the colored lights strewn around colorful tents, and children laughing and pushing each other as they raced off to the rides. The smell of buttery popcorn and fried onions replaced the soap's scent, and Dakota was back at the carnival in Pocatello on a crisp early September night. How excited she'd been to go that night. Silly, romantic notions filled her head as she waited for her date to pick her up, three blocks from her house.

"I thought we were going to have such fun," she muttered.

The images sharpened as the memory of that night filled her mind.

The roar of the roller coaster tore into her brain, taking away all her instincts to protect and guard herself, throwing her life into a loop. There was nothing but shifting tracks. Screams. Her small whimpers while he grunted on top of her; his weight driving her into the dirt underneath. Each shift forward dug her deeper into the ground until she imagined she would be engulfed by it. Maybe become one of the worms.

His breath was hot and stank of soda, and his sticky fingers pinned her wrists to the ground. The rough scrape of his jeans against her inner thighs: that little detail made hot tears trickle down her face. He hadn't even taken his pants off. She was that unimportant while he drove into her over and over again.

Before, the pain had been sharp, immediate, eating her alive from the inside out.

Now there was nothing, only echoes of emotions, sound, and who she was before this moment—who she would never be again.

When Dakota came back to herself, she was sitting on the edge of the bed with a towel wrapped around her and Cobra's cut in her lap, slowly stroking the leather over and over again. An odd sensory comfort as tears poured out of her eyes, but she didn't feel them inside, only knew they were coming because of the constant splash against her skin.

"Dakota?"

Cobra's deep voice cut through the mess of her past and she jerked her head up and darted her eyes around the room. The mattress moved, and then he was kneeling down in front of her.

"Sweetheart, are you okay?" Concern laced his voice. "What's wrong?"

Dakota sniffled and wiped her nose with the corner of the towel. "I'm okay. Sorry, if I woke you up."

"No problem." He grasped her hands in his. "Tell me what's going on."

She shrugged, then stared down at the carpet. The sound of water filtered into the room from the bathroom.

"Did you leave the water on?" he asked gently.

"I must've. I was taking a shower and then …" Her voice trailed away.

Cobra stood up and stroked her cheek with the back of his hand. He took his cut away from her, placed it on the chair, and then walked away to turn off the shower. The sudden silence startled her, and Dakota lifted her head just as he came toward her with a towel in his hand.

"Come over here," he said as he leaned back against the headboard.

Dakota let him tug her to him then settled between his legs. The numbness began to lift as Cobra carefully towel-dried her hair, gently untangling the knots with his hands before drawing her back against him. He brought the covers up over her, and then wrapped his arms around her.

"Please," she whispered, "keep holding me."

"Let's lie down," he said as he shifted.

Dakota moved over a bit and Cobra lay down on his side.

"Come here, darlin'."

She grasped his hand and lay down beside him. Cobra curved the front of his body around her back and wrapped his arms around her waist. It was like he was shielding her with every part of himself. Dakota's head lulled back against his chest, and she snuggled deeper into the covers.

"I'm here, sweetheart. I'm here and I'm not going anywhere." His lips pressed against her right temple.

She held his hand and tucked it close against her neck, just under her chin. The heat from Cobra's body warmed her, his scent comforted her, and the way he cradled her made Dakota feel safe.

Her eyelids grew heavy and drooped, and all at once, she dropped off to sleep.

CHAPTER FIFTEEN

COBRA

COBRA WOKE UP with his arms around Dakota, and pins and needles tingled through the numbed left one. He blinked through blurry eyes and looked at the slim girl spooned into him, her ass pushed into his crotch. Trying to get the feeling back in his hands, he wiggled his fingers, careful not to wake her.

The night before, Cobra had been hell bent on making sure that *he* would be a lasting memory in Dakota's mind, one that she'd whip out when her next boyfriend wasn't satisfying her right. But now, in the weak sunlight filtering in through the curtained window, the thought of her with any other man was a burn in Cobra's gut and a sour taste in his mouth. Dakota wasn't just another chick, another fuck, and the previous night wasn't just another night of fun.

Cobra's gaze roamed over her again. She had the sheets pulled just above her breasts, and her golden hair spilled over the pillow, catching the sunlight that trickled in through the small gap in the curtains. *She looks so fuckin' beautiful.* Gently, he bent and kissed the top of her head. She stirred, nuzzling tighter against him.

Dakota was different than anyone he'd ever been with before. This had never happened to him. One pretty woman had never been any more important than the next. He couldn't explain it, but she'd touched him in a way that he wasn't used to, and he didn't know what the hell to do about it.

Dakota moaned in her sleep and slightly rolled away from him, so he tugged his arm out from under her and massaged it back to life. During the night, Cobra had awoken a couple of times to Dakota tossing about in a troubled sleep, and he'd debated about whether he should wake her up or not, but then she'd calmed down and settled back next to him. As he looked at her sleeping now, peacefulness was spread across her face, and whatever nightmare had haunted her hours earlier had crawled back to the shuttered recesses of her mind.

Cobra wasn't sure what shadows lurked in the corners of her subconscious, but he aimed to find out in time. He hated that something dark and disturbing was buried inside her, digging its way out to torment her. Cobra wanted to take care of her. The thought that he was planning on her being around long enough for him to figure her out startled the hell out of him. He rubbed a hand down his face, closing his eyes. Shit wasn't supposed to go down like this between them. But something had shifted in him—in *them* the night before that sure as fuck shouldn't have, and what the hell was he supposed to do now?

Dakota was amazing: fiery, sweet, and sexy. She was a breath of fresh air in his stale life. She didn't deserve whatever shit from her past was tormenting her present, and there was no fucking way she should deal with it alone.

Cobra blew out a silent breath into his hand and blinked, staring at the shitty, rundown motel room where they'd been spending the majority of their time. He should be doing better than this for her; Dakota didn't deserve leaky taps and rug stains. Cobra looked back at her, gently tracing his thumb across her cheek and sweeping several strands of hair from her face. When she made a small noise, he almost jerked backward, worried he woke her up, but she didn't move at all. Her breathing deepened and he pulled his hand away while shifting off the bed.

After showering, Cobra walked into the main room and glanced over at Dakota. She was still asleep. He bent down and picked up his boots then pulled them on before riffling through his bag until he nabbed a piece of scrap paper and a pen. Scrawling a quick note about grabbing breakfast and that he would be back soon, he placed it on top of his pillow and scooped up his keys.

When Cobra hovered by the door, he waited, for what he had no fucking clue. There was something magnetic about her … something haunting and right. His gut pinched tight when he thought of anything happening to her. A sigh hissed through his lips as he put his hand on the doorknob. It was stupid as hell to think he'd have anything to do with her life in the future. *Only dumbasses plan their lives. I'm a fuckin' nomad. I go where I want, when I want. I'm a damn moron thinking 'bout all this feely shit. Dammit.*

The truth was Dakota and he were on two very different paths in their lives. Cobra had enough on his plate with the MC and just making his own way through life. He couldn't fix the whole goddamn world, so he should stop trying and just take care of himself.

How did this shit become so complicated? Cobra groaned and leaned against the door while he watched her roll over and face his pillow. He sucked in a breath and held it, but Dakota didn't stir. A burst of warm light poured into the room as he opened the door then quickly closed it behind him. The sticky heat bored down on him as he ambled to his bike then hopped on it.

A little mind declutter was what Cobra needed right at that moment. A long ride could put a stop to all the conflicting feelings that kept bubbling up inside him. None of the back and forth thoughts about Dakota and what he should do would stand a chance once he hit the open road. Between the wind whipping through him and the roar of the engine, there'd be too much damn noise for him to listen to any of it. Turning left out of the parking lot, the scream of the engine shattered the silence, and Cobra sped away.

After two hours of hard riding, Cobra felt more grounded than he had earlier in the morning. He'd swung by the Pirate Donut House and picked up donuts, bagels, cream cheese packets, and hot coffee.

Opening the motel room door a bit, Cobra peeked into the room and glanced at the empty, messed up bed. He stepped inside and put the bag of goodies, the thermos of coffee, and his keys on the table, smiling when he heard the rush of water coming from the bathroom.

"Hey," he knocked on the door. "I'm back with breakfast and coffee. Do you need anything else or can I dig in without you?"

"Help yourself," she said above the water. "I won't be much longer."

"Sure." Cobra hesitated and scrubbed his hands over his face, barely feeling the prickle of his unshaven cheeks. "You up for going on a little trip with me today?"

No sound behind the door.

Shit. She's probably feeling as confused as I am about last night. Or maybe she has regrets about it. I shoulda held back. Way to go, asshole. He punched his thigh and gritted his teeth. Before he could ask her if she was doing all right, his phone went off with a loud ping and he took a step away from the door.

Iron: *Got a lead on Big Pat. We need u to stand with us on this one, bro.*

Cobra flicked the text away with his finger. *Fuck!* He rubbed the back of his neck, already feeling the tension slip back into him. Grinder needed him, and Cobra knew he wouldn't turn away. No matter if he was an active member or a nomad, the MC was in his blood. His brothers were his family, and when they needed help, he was there. Cobra knew if he ever called on any one of them, they'd help him out in a second. That was what the brotherhood meant, and no citizen could ever in a million fucking years understand that.

Cobra: *I'm in. Lemme know what u need me to do.*

He stared down at his phone for a couple of minutes. With an exasperated sigh, he raked his fingers through his hair, his gaze drifting back toward the closed bathroom door. Another ping.

Iron: *Sure thing, bro. We'll be in touch.*

Cobra wiped his palms on his denim-clad thighs. Damn … he just wanted to spend the fucking day with Dakota.

Cobra: *Later, dude.*

He slipped the phone into his jeans pocket. Cobra would wait until his club called him then he'd be there all the way with them in solidarity.

"What were you saying?" Dakota peeked her head out the bathroom door with a towel wrapped around her; her hair was in a loose knot, damp strands curling by her ears.

The corner of his lips twitched while he gazed at her rosy pink cheeks and her shining eyes. His gaze dropped down to the small swell at the tops of her tits, and his dick stirred. Snapping his attention back to her face, he crossed his arms over his chest.

"I was wondering if you wanted to get the hell outta here for the day. Go on a little adventure before work tonight."

"Sounds nice. What did you have in mind?"

"It's a surprise, sweetheart."

Dakota's eyes widened, and she licked her lips. He watched her try to hold back a grin, but she lost the battle when a small laugh came out of her mouth.

She's so damn cute. Cobra cleared his throat. "We'll leave after breakfast. Do you need your clothes?"

"I got 'em in here. Thanks."

Why was he constantly trying to look after her? The problem was, Cobra had a bit of a white fucking knight complex, which he acknowledged, and it had gotten him in trouble in the past. The whole reason he ended up doing a stint at High Desert State Prison was because he was protecting a woman he'd hooked up with in Las Vegas. He and Iron, Hulk, Brute, Viper, and Breaker had gone to Vegas on club business to take care of a couple of dudes who'd skipped out on paying back a loan they'd owed the MC. Cobra had met Sharie at a strip club the night before, and he'd brought her back to his hotel room. They'd spent the following day fucking, then he took her out for a steak dinner before they went to a bar on the Strip.

When Cobra had come back from the bar's restroom, two guys were disrespecting Sharie, and he warned them to back off. They laughed and told him to fuck off and that his biker patches didn't scare them. Cobra turned away in an effort to calm down the rage that was building inside him, but one of the fuckers pulled at Cobra's cut and the fury exploded inside him like a volcano. Soon the three of them were throwing punches, and at the end of it, the two guys were down on their asses, and Cobra was stomping them with his steel-toed boots. The law said the boots were a deadly weapon, and since the jerks required some stitching to patch up their injuries, Cobra ended up doing time for felonious assault with a deadly weapon—a Class 5 Felony.

And now he was back and wanted to protect Dakota, to make her life okay and be there for her whenever she needed anything. Hell, he was in over his head and there was no stopping it. Cobra pushed that thought into the back of his mind and concentrated on the soaking wet woman in front of him who was modestly hiding herself behind a door after everything they had done together the previous night.

He suppressed a chuckle. *As if I didn't see everything.* Like flashbacks weren't playing through his mind on warp speed. His shoulders tightened, remembering the warm heat of her mouth closing over his cock. He bit his lip until the pain jolted him back into the present, and Dakota looked at him strangely.

"I've got everything covered if you want to start without me." Her gaze ran over him from head to toe. "Are you zoning out on me?"

"Nah." Cobra unfolded his hands then shoved them in his pockets and rocked back on his heels. "I'll save you a chocolate glazed."

"Okay."

Cobra made it a point to not look back down at her cleavage even though it stared him in the face from above the towel line. They both stood there as she opened the door a little bit more, an almost anticipatory look in her wide eyes as they locked with his, and his hands went to fists in his pockets.

One slip and that small fucking scrap of a towel would be on the floor.

A low growl leaked out from his lips, and he took a deliberate step backward toward the donuts. Nope, he wasn't going down that road. He needed to keep his cock in his pants and his head on straight.

Yeah ... easier said than done.

Dakota closed the door and Cobra walked over to the table, unscrewed the thermos, poured the hot coffee into a mug, and brought it to his lips as he stared out the window at the distant mountains.

CHAPTER SIXTEEN

DAKOTA

As they rode around the sparse dirt trail, Dakota wondered how she'd gotten to this place with a man who, on the outside, was everything she should've run away from—far and fast. But Cobra was different than the façade he put up. She adjusted her hands on his chest and shivered as the subtle touch worked its way through every inch of her body. The night before had been incredible and mind numbingly horrible at the same time. Her mouth went dry at the thought of it, and she took a few deep breaths. She needed to get a hold of the feelings before they drove her into the ground.

Despite her freak-out, Cobra had been sweet, patient, understanding, and so respectful. It was as if his tough exterior was a barrier to keep other people from seeing the goodness that was inside him. As Dakota's hands clutched his black T-shirt tighter and she nuzzled her face into the back of his leather-scented cut, she could feel him chuckle by the vibrations in his chest. Things were surprisingly easy with him in a way she'd never expected or anticipated. It was the first time after a flashback that Dakota could stand to touch someone before her forty-eight-hour time limit was up.

For so many years she'd have to cordon herself off from men after a flashback because she couldn't bear any physical contact. It made it impossible to have normal relationships, but with Cobra she hadn't felt the need to detach from him after they had sex. There was something about him that made her feel cared for, secure, and cherished. The mixture of feelings swirling around inside her made it feel like her head was about to explode.

"We're almost there," Cobra shouted above the rumble of the engine. "Hold on, it's gonna get bumpy."

Dakota clutched on to him even tighter as they bounced over the rough terrain. During that moment, realization that she *really* trusted Cobra hit her, and it was a very scary and sobering thought.

Dakota took a deep breath of the thick, fragrant air and finally focused on their exquisite surroundings as they rode up a small, narrow dirt trail. The midday sun was high in the expansive blue sky, the fresh smell of pine, of woody plants, and of sweet wildflowers pervaded the air; and high above, hidden among the pinecones of the fir trees, finches sang their melodious strains rising above the other sounds of the forest.

The bike came to a stop, and Cobra lowered his feet and turned off the engine. Dakota's arms dropped away from him as she leaned back. He grasped her hand and helped her off the motorcycle before he swung his leg over the leather seat. He pulled her close and brushed his lips across hers.

"You good?" he asked, breaking away.

"Yeah. The ride was rough but all this"—she waved her arm around in a gesture that encompassed the landscape—"made every bump totally worth it."

Cobra snagged her hand and tucked it in his as they walked through a cluster of trees that soon revealed a shimmering expanse of water in front of them.

Dakota stopped in her tracks, frozen by the beautiful scenery before her. The lake lay blue in the bright light of the sun, the rippled water running right to the edge, washing over rocks that etched some of the shoreline. Tall pines and evergreens bordered the lake, chaotic in their spacing. The soft whispering of the trees caressed her, and she squeezed Cobra's hand.

"This is magical," she murmured.

"I know how much you like water, so I wanted to share this with you. How does this compare with the watering hole you told me about?"

A cozy, warm sensation spread through her, and she blinked rapidly to prevent any tears from rising.

"I can't believe you actually remembered that."

Cobra's chuckle was low and deep. "I do listen when you talk, darlin'."

Dakota pulled her hand out of his and flung her arms around him. She hugged him fiercely, relishing the closeness. "Thank you for remembering—for caring."

He wrapped his arms around her waist and pressed her tighter against him. She loved the hardness of his body, the softness of his touch. Dakota had never known anyone like him; so kind, so passionate, so wonderful to be with. At times, her suspicious mind wondered if he was for real, but when he'd do something so selfless, her misgivings evaporated.

The desire between them sparked stronger than ever. She wanted to get closer to him, fuse them together, crawl inside his skin. Everything at that moment was perfect, and ever since that night when she was fourteen and her whole damn life as she'd known it stopped, nothing had ever been right until now ... with *him* ... standing by the lake.

Smiling, Cobra rubbed his chin against her temple, the hint of scruff on his jawline lightly scratching her. He cupped her jaw, tilting her chin back. The naked heat in his eyes seared her. Her heart slammed into her throat.

"Dakota ... fuck ... darlin'. *Fuck*." His lips crushed hers with a fierce demand that took her breath away. He kissed her again and again, his pants as rapid and labored as hers.

Excitement rippled through her. Cobra squeezed her tighter to him, and her breasts squashed against his firm chest. Dakota felt the bulge between them grow long and thick against her. A wash of goosebumps spread along her body as she dug her fingernails into the back of his neck.

Then the shrill ring of a phone shattered the moment. It sounded so damn out of place in the natural setting, but it kept ringing until Cobra pulled away.

"Fuck!" Shoving his hand into his pocket, he pulled out his phone and glanced at it. A frown burrowed between his brows. "I gotta take this. Sorry, darlin'." He walked away and stood by a tree, his back to her.

Dakota inhaled and exhaled in rapid succession as she tried to calm her body down. The phone ringing was probably for the best. The fear of falling hard for him niggled at the back of her mind. Cobra was a nomad who'd be pulling up stakes anytime, leaving her far behind. She'd miss him for sure, but she'd deal with it *if* she didn't do something stupid like fall in love with him. If that happened, his departure would shatter her heart. She just couldn't let her feelings tear her apart, especially since she'd managed—for the most part, to keep her life somewhat together.

Dakota walked over to the lake, bent down, and let the cool water run through her fingers, reveling in the beautiful surroundings and the peacefulness. Behind her, she heard the low murmur of Cobra's voice, and she wondered if the call was about club business. Not wanting to mar the rapture of the moment, she stared at the hypnotic movement of the hydrilla fronds just below the water's surface.

The heavy crunch of footsteps from behind made Dakota smile and she looked over her shoulder. "Finished with your call?"

"Yeah," Cobra replied gruffly. He pointed to a large rock outcropping off to the side of the lake. "Let's go over there." He walked beside her without taking her hand in his, and she wondered if the phone call had upset him.

They ambled toward the rock in silence, the only sounds coming from the gentle lapping of water on the shore, the slight rustle of leaves, and the twitter of birds. Cobra climbed up and reached out his hand to her. Dakota grabbed it, and he hoisted her up on top of the boulder. It gave them a perfect, unobstructed view of everything, including the vast mountain range that seemed to stretch toward the sky in the background.

Cobra moved to the center of the rock and sat down.

"Come here," he said, extending his arm.

Dakota gripped his wrist, and he tugged her forward and arranged her in front of him so that she sat between his legs with his arms wrapped around her waist and her back curled to his front. "That's perfect," he muttered.

Comfort soaked through her body, and Dakota tipped her head back and looked up at the clouds. If she squinted hard enough, maybe she could find some shapes. It was a silly game she used to play when she was young and carefree … and before everything in her life flipped upside down.

The wind murmured through the space, making small shushed and hollowed noises through the foliage. It was as if everything in their world was magnified, waiting to be captured with every breath.

"I can feel your heartbeat," Dakota said, looking at the ripples in the lake as she sagged back into his tight embrace. "Ba-boom, Ba-boom, Ba-boom."

Cobra laughed at her silly mimicry and squeezed her around the waist, nuzzling his nose into her hair.

"You smell fuckin' awesome," he whispered next to her ear.

All the small hairs on her body stood on end as her skin became charged from the sweet and caring gesture. Rather than overthinking what it meant, she gave in to the feelings, the inner peace that seemed to be weaving through both of them in that moment.

"This is nice," she said.

"Yeah." He placed his chin lightly on the top of her head.

For several minutes they sat entwined together, listening to the sounds of nature, relishing the quiet time with each other. Then Dakota ran her fingers over his forearm and felt the light ridge of raised skin beneath them. Her hand froze in place, and she remembered the same imperfections on his otherwise perfect body across the width of his back. Scars. Had he been in an accident?

"Whatcha thinkin'?" Cobra grasped her hand and moved it away from his forearm.

"How wonderful it is to be with you right now."

He kissed the top of her head. "Ditto, sweetheart."

Dakota bit the inside of her cheek, inhaled, then slowly exhaled. "Have you ever been in a motorcycle accident?"

"Yeah. Shit … every biker I know has been in one. Usually it's because a cager isn't paying any fuckin' attention to the road, or the biker's speeding, drunk, or just not watching out."

"What's a 'cager'?"

"People who drive cages—vehicles."

"What happened with you?"

Cobra shrugged. "I didn't see an oil slick and wiped out. I got scratched up pretty bad, but I wasn't going that fast because the weather conditions weren't that great. It wasn't anything major like some of my friends have had."

"Did you scratch up your back?" she asked.

"No, just my left side. Why?"

Dakota swallowed hard. "I thought maybe that's where you got the scars on your back." She felt Cobra stiffen behind her.

Several minutes passed without him saying a word, and she was just ready to fill in the silence when he cleared his throat.

"I got those from my old man."

A simple enough statement that carried so much behind-the-scenes sadness.

"Your father did that?" she whispered.

"Yeah. He was a strict disciplinarian—a Marine. He ran the fuckin' household like a goddamn bootcamp."

"Oh." Her hushed response fell into the air between them.

"Yeah … growing up with my old man wasn't fuckin' great." Cobra let go of her waist and rested his hands on her shoulders. "Short version, I had an asshole bastard for a father and a traitor for a mother who bolted after the old man was sent to Chino for doing shit to my sister. My brother, my sister, and I all ended up in different foster homes, and I got the fuck outta there as fast as I could. I ran away when I was sixteen and never looked back. There you go—childhood in a nutshell."

Dakota winced and licked her lips. "How old were you when you went into foster care?"

"Twelve."

Her heart ached for him. "I'm sorry," she said.

"What for? You didn't do anything. Life can be a piece of shit sometimes, but it's what you do with it that counts."

"I suppose. Is your dad still in … prison?"

"Nah, the bastard got out after only a few years. I don't know where the fuck he is, and that suits me just fine. The only thing I liked about growing up with good ol' Mom and Dad was living in Oceanside." Cobra twirled a strand of her hair around his finger. "That's in Southern California. Big Marine base there. I loved sitting on the sand and watching the waves crash on the beach then pull back." He chuckled. "I can't tell you how many times I wished I was one of those damn grains of sand the ocean took from the shore, floating away, going to new places … getting the fuck away from the chaos of our house."

"Is that why you joined the motorcycle club—to get away?"

"Not really. I joined because it was the first time in my life I felt like I was a part of something. The club was the family I never had … the loyalty and trust not one of my goddamn parents ever gave me or my siblings. The club was my lifeline, and it still is. It's just that after going to prison, I decided to go nomad. I had to sort out a bunch of shit inside me, and I didn't want to end up back in the pen."

"Why did you go to prison?" Dakota held her breath.

"Some fuckers messed with me and I fought back. Turns out I was a better fighter."

"Did any of them ... die?"

He nuzzled the side of her neck then kissed it softly. "No, sweetheart. It was just a bar fight. The assholes were clean cut, and I was a member of an outlaw club. Not hard to imagine why I ended up in the joint and they didn't."

"That's so unfair." Dakota tilted her head back and locked her gaze on his.

A half-smile tugged up the corner of his mouth, and he ran his thumb lightly over her bottom lip. "That's the way life plays out, darlin'."

She settled back against him. "Yeah, it seems that way."

"I'm guessing you didn't have an ideal home life either." Cobra gently kneaded her shoulders with his fingers.

"No, everything was fine. It was all good ..." she trailed off and glanced into the distance, her vision of what she was seeing fading into old memories that had a tendency to taint everything. "My parents loved us. They worked hard and had decent jobs. My dad was a long-distance trucker so he wasn't home a lot, but when he was, he always spent time with us. My mom worked hard at the grocery store, and we had enough to afford a decent house and food on the table. I have four siblings—I'm the third kid in a family of five." Dakota swallowed past the sudden tightness in her throat and felt herself pulling away from him, curling into herself as if she was powerless to stop the motion. "Typical childhood. For the most part."

"Uh-huh." Cobra's tone sounded like he didn't believe her, and she laced her fingers together, unconsciously squeezing as she tried to focus on everything that was happening outside herself while her body reprocessed old wounds. "You're tense as fuck, sweetheart. Every time I touch you, you flinch backward. Do you think you might want to talk about that?"

Dakota breathed out through her compressed and tightened lungs, her whole body a mess of jitters. She'd never talked about *it* to anyone before. There was so much piled inside her that she'd never addressed, acknowledged, or even understood, and now it was raw and ripping through her whole life. *Fuck.* Dakota squeezed her eyes shut and tried to ignore the sudden shaking rippling through her body.

"It'll make you feel better." His low, calm voice enticed her.

Maybe it's time. A huge part of her *needed* to talk about the incident, and Cobra was someone she could count on to take care of her and listen to everything she had to say without condemnation. He was a safe space.

A small whimper escaped her lips and she heard him making small, shushing noises trying to soothe her as she geared herself up to speak about her past.

"Take your time, Dakota," he whispered, his body heat comforting her. Cobra circled his arms around her waist and gently squeezed.

"When I was fourteen, my older brother's friend used to come over a lot. We'd known each other since I was little, and he watched me grow up. His name was Taylor." Dakota choked on her words and took a few minutes to breathe, compose herself, and get back into it. "The summer before high school, things started changing between us. It was so damn hot. It was one of those summers where you could barely breathe because the air was thick with humidity. All us kids lived at the swimming hole that season." She shuddered.

"It's okay. I'm here," Cobra said in a low voice.

After breathing in and out a few times, she rested her head against his chest. "My brother Luke—he's two years older than me, and his friends would hang out with me and my friends. Taylor always came because he was Luke's best friend. He was practically a member of our family. Anyway, one time when we were at Monkey Rock, Taylor told me there was something he wanted to show me, and he took me away from everyone to an area surrounded by trees and bushes. He backed me up against a large tree and kissed me. A bunch of butterflies swarmed in my stomach, and I felt weird and good and scared all at the same time.

Taylor always told me how pretty I was and how much he liked me. I didn't know what any of it meant, only that I loved the way he looked at me and how he made me feel special."

"And your brother didn't know Taylor was doing this to you?"

Dakota shook her head. "Luke would've beaten the shit outta him if he knew. But I *did* like the way it felt when we kissed."

"That's normal," Cobra said as he smoothed his hand over her hair.

"So, for the rest of that summer, Taylor would catch me alone or try to engineer our time together. We spent endless minutes glued to each other … kissing, and sometimes he tried to take it further, but I never let him. It didn't feel right. I didn't want to do it. Taylor seemed to have full possession of my body when we made out, like he wanted to own me, and it sent my brain spinning away for a little while until his hands went somewhere I didn't like and I had to stop him."

Dakota took a deep, shaky breath and squeezed her eyelids closed trying to block out the sunshine. There wasn't room for any sunlight to enter her world while she relived the memories; she had to submerge herself in darkness and let everything else fall away.

"When the carnival came to town, Taylor asked me to go with him as a secret date. He said we couldn't tell anyone because we'd both get in trouble if anyone knew. I was fine with that because I knew my brother would be pissed if he found out his friend was dating me. I also knew that my parents had a standing rule that no one dated until they were sixteen, which was two years down the road for me, but I was crazy about Taylor so I snuck behind their backs. Taylor kept telling me how much he liked me—he was consistent with his affection. I didn't want that to go away. So I agreed to play by his rules and meet up with him without anyone else knowing. Looking back on it now, I'm fully aware it was a recipe for disaster. I was a stupid kid—"

"Whatever happened, it wasn't your fault, sweetheart. You have to know that now. None of it was ever your fault, no matter the fuckin' situation," Cobra said.

Dakota nodded, though she wasn't sure the words even penetrated all the way. But a small bit of weight lifted off her shoulders. She hung her head and opened her eyes, looking at a patch of moss on the rock's surface. Cobra's breath pressed against her neck, warm and comforting.

"The night started off totally fun and magical, and Taylor kissed me at the top of the Ferris wheel. We went on so many rides, and he won a big-ass stuffed bear for me at one of the games. My folks thought I was with my girlfriends, so I remember being a bit on edge that I'd be caught. Then he told me he wanted to show me something and he took me under the roller coaster …" Dakota stopped with a small noise as her insides turned to stone and then liquified. "He said it was the coolest spot in the park. It was loud, kind of scary, and I had a perfect view of the cars as they sped by on the tracks from above me." She ran her hands over her arms. "That's the majority of what I remember from that night when it's not coming back in flashbacks."

Dakota strained beneath her skin, the sensation of ants crawling across her flesh made her nerves a mass of tingles.

"What happened?" Cobra whispered.

"He raped me."

CHAPTER SEVENTEEN

COBRA

"THE FUCKIN' SONOFABITCH," Cobra muttered, unable to ignore the white-hot anger that had both his hands clenched into tight fists at his sides.

Every protective bone in his body tensed from thoughts of killing the bastard with his bare hands—to retroactively taking out payment on Taylor's flesh over a month to two-month span, solely keeping him alive to endure more torture, pain, and Cobra's wrath. The well-planned fantasy flashed through his mind in less than a nanosecond.

"What's his last name, Dakota?" he gritted out through clenched teeth.

"It's not important. Don't worry about it."

"Are you fuckin' kidding me, sweetheart? There's nothing more important than what you just told me. No wonder ..."

Cobra trailed off remembering how troubled her sleep had been the night before. The nightmares were flashbacks and that fucking-excuse-for-a-man created them. What kind of fucking piece of trash raped a fourteen-year-old girl? Cobra had done some fucked up things in his life, but never anything that violated a woman. It took every ounce of willpower for him to curb the urge to crush her to his chest and never let her go, to always keep her safe. But now wasn't a good time to go all possessive on her, he could pick up on it by the tense, frail lines of her body.

"Is there anything else you want to tell me, darlin'?"

"This is, uh, this is the first time I've talked about it—with anyone."

"I'm honored you shared it with me."

His words didn't even fucking cover the emotions bubbling up inside his chest. Cobra's insides seethed, and he was so sad for her and what she must've gone through that night. *And to hold all that shit in for all these years? Fuck!* On the outside, Cobra tried to be her rock.

"Afterward, he smiled at me and acted like nothing had happened and dropped me off about a block from my house. He tried to kiss me again, but I pulled back and somehow jumped out of the car and ran toward my house. Everything was such a hazy blur. I know when I came to again, I was in the shower washing myself over and over again. I wrapped my underwear in a plastic bag and threw it out … so my parents wouldn't see … the evidence."

"He didn't try—" Cobra let the words hang between them. She would pick up on what he was putting down and he sure as shit didn't want to retraumatize her by saying them out loud.

She shook her head. "No, Taylor didn't touch me again. But it was awful. I still saw him all the time. He and my brother were still best friends, and Luke had no idea what had happened—I just couldn't tell him, or anyone. The worst part was that we went to the same high school. Whenever I'd see Taylor, I'd try to ignore him, but he'd leer at me whenever we crossed paths."

"Is that why you moved away?"

"Not exactly." She seemed to fold into herself even tighter. "The reason I left home was because he tried to do it again. After he got out of high school, he went away to college and I was so damn relieved. I tried to move on, got a job at a tattoo parlor, and was feeling better than I had in a long time, but … Taylor," Dakota's voice seemed to scrape out the motherfucker's name, and Cobra could barely stop himself from punching the nearest rock, "came back to town and found me one night at the tattoo shop and booked an appointment. I had no idea *he* was the client, and when I saw him I freaked-out and started having a panic attack, so he left. Later that night … he tried to attack me again—in the alley behind the shop where I worked. He was waiting." Her voice hitched.

Cobra held her tight. "It's okay—I'm here. Get it out."

For several seconds Dakota just stared out into the distance, then she sighed and her shoulders slumped. "He grabbed me and called me so many horrible names, but this time I reacted. I sprayed mace in his eyes and ran like hell. When I got home, I didn't tell anyone. But I couldn't stay in Pocatello anymore. I didn't feel safe. He'd made every second of my life a waking nightmare. I had no doubt that it would happen again if I didn't leave, so I bolted. Since I left, my family and my whole life was ripped off its axis."

"So you ended up in Idaho Falls?"

She nodded.

"Then what got you running again?"

"The bastard … *again*." Cobra growled and she patted his hand. "I'd been living in the city for about a year, and one night while I was at a bar with some friends, I saw *him*. He didn't see me because he was too busy groping a girl he was with. Of course, I started to panic, so I made up some BS to my friends and left. For the next few months, I was living like a hermit: I'd go to work then head straight home. I was scared to death to do anything else. Then, he called me one day and left a message saying that he'd just found out I lived in the city too. The SOB wanted to 'get together' for a drink. After I heard the message, I took out a map, closed my eyes, and let my finger fall down. It landed on Philipsburg. Since the town's so small, I was pretty sure he'd never heard of it or would ever move there. I packed up my stuff, loaded up my now-busted car, and met you."

"I'm glad we were on the road at the same time," Cobra said in a low voice.

Dakota took a deep and shaky breath in front of him. It wasn't until then that Cobra realized she was quietly sobbing, curled into herself as she used her forearms to wipe under her nose. He'd been so consumed with vengeance that he hadn't noticed her obvious pain.

"Oh, sweetheart." He tugged her up and peppered the side of her face with feathery kisses. "Normally when there's a problem, I fight my way through that shit. I tear apart whatever caused me pain until it's no longer a threat, but fuckin' hell, I don't know how to do that for you, sweetheart. I'm so damn sorry."

"It is what it is. I shouldn't have told you … you must think—"

"Don't even fuckin' say it. I don't think anything bad about you, little one. So don't even think for one fuckin' second I would judge you for what some scumbag did to you."

Cobra watched as Dakota snuggled closer to him. He wrapped his arms tighter around her; more than ever, he wanted to be her safe haven, protect her from everyone and everything.

"How can I comfort you, sweetheart? Tell me. Anything."

"Distract me. Please. Everything's coming back again and I'm not…" her soft voice cracked, "I'm not ready yet."

"Okay … okay." Cobra pushed away the anger and focused on taking her mind off of it. "When I ran away from one of many shitty foster homes, I hitchhiked to a relative's house in Billings—that's how I ended up in Montana. The relative was a distant cousin of my mom's, and I remember a couple of times we went to visit her when my old man was deployed. So, as much as I settled in, I couldn't keep my nose out of shit; as a result, she 'asked me to leave' after I graduated high school. While I was living with her, I met a neighbor who had the baddest-looking Harley-Davidson I'd ever seen. Turned out he was a member of the Steel Devils MC. He was in the charter chapter, so when my cousin kicked me out, I made my way to the national chapter in Missoula, where I ended up prospecting. It took me two years and a laundry list of bullshit tasks, but I got my full patch in the club and that was the best fuckin' day in my life."

Cobra hesitated and cracked his knuckles, unable to rip his attention from the back of her head as she sat in front of him. While the rest of the shitty world turned on its axis, he was grounded with only his worry for Dakota.

"Anyway, I got a reputation for being untouchable—a ruthless, calculating motherfucker, and they promoted me to their enforcer as a celebration of those *gifts*." He snorted as he remembered Grinder's awe at the depth of Cobra's rage. "I took my job seriously. If anything, my father had engrained in me a sense of not giving a fuck when you fought, you laid it all out on the table—much like he did when he was beating us or my mom. That fun little tidbit played into my life as an adult, and I would take on any fucker who stood in my way. My rage had an outlet—boozing, partying, kicking ass, and fucking. Pretty simple.

"After those two whining pussies in the bar touched my cut, I saw red, and the whole world rained down in blood. When I came back to myself, the fuckin' badges were slapping handcuffs on me, and I was thrown into the back of a cop car. Those fuckers landed me in prison. And when I got out, after doing three years, I wasn't too fuckin' keen on doing more time, so I shut down and tried to get away from the violence. Too bad no one else got the damn memo because my reputation follows me like a brand on my skin."

Cobra coughed and rubbed his forehead, as if digging up all this old shit was wearing him down just thinking about it. There was truth to it. Nomad had been a way for him to sort out his shit, removed from all the violence that he saw on the daily. It was a way to get clean and take a hard look at his life as a loner and see what really existed for him outside of his previous ways of coping with stupid shit and a fucked-up life. Everyone had a fucked-up life, but it was the choices you made afterward that sealed it.

"Prison must have been horrible," Dakota said so softly that he almost didn't hear her.

"It wasn't a fuckin' good time, that's for sure. I learned the value of freedom and how much I was taking it for granted every day."

"Did you exorcize your aggression?"

"Not exactly an environment where you can stop fighting, you know?" Cobra scoffed and cracked his neck, looking off into the horizon, his mind only seeing the violence in the prison yard. While he was in the joint, it seemed like the noose of living or dying tightened around his neck every single day. He shook his head, scattering the memories. "But I got out, and that's all that fuckin' matters."

"Were you seeing anyone special during that time? I mean, it must have been lonely and you probably had a woman on the outside or, at least, after you got out."

Cobra almost smiled as her voice grew a little bit stronger and surer, but the idea of having anyone in his life during that time was insane. After he'd been released, he needed to make up for lost time, so, for about a year, he'd fucked his way through a lot of the cities and towns he'd passed by.

"No one serious."

He kept the details to a bare minimum, not wanting to scare her away. Cobra didn't want her to think that she was just one of many who wet his dick. Dakota wasn't—she was different and becoming very special to him.

"Have you ever had a serious girlfriend?"

"Nope."

Dakota's shoulders slumped a bit. "Oh," she muttered.

"Sweetheart, you have to fuckin' understand something here..." Cobra brushed her cheek with the tips of his fingers. "I don't do this shit. You and me? Talking? No way. When I'd hook up for a bit with a chick, we'd eat dinner together and co-exist." He bent down and kissed her lightly on the lips. "I'm different with you. Don't think this is my damn MO or something with a woman."

He cradled her in his arms, clutching tighter each time she trembled.

CHAPTER EIGHTEEN

DAKOTA

Dakota wiped at her face with both hands. "Thanks for listening to me."

"No problem, sweetheart. Don't even think anything of it. You talk when you need to—I'm here."

A small smile flew across her face. It was gone as soon as it appeared, but the feelings that came with it only shifted to the surface and wouldn't be pushed down—even if she'd tried. A soothing sense of giddiness made her head light and fluffy with all of her thoughts spinning around, and Dakota couldn't grab them. Calm flooded through her muscles like thick syrup as she dissolved back into his arms.

"Is this what trust feels like?" she asked as Cobra rubbed her shoulders with a sigh, neither of them looking at each other, their gazes fixed off into the distance.

"How the hell do I know?" Cobra laughed, raw and loud. "What I do know is that you aren't like anyone I've ever met in my life. You keep me on my damn toes, and you scare the fuckin' shit outta me, kid."

"Same," Dakota breathed out the word and licked her lips.

"You're the first person I've talked to about this shit, you know."

For some reason that shocked the hell out of her, and she physically jerked at the knowledge. Dakota knew he was quiet and withdrawn most of the time, but she also knew he had brothers in the MC and figured they must've heard some of his history over the years.

"I can't believe your MC friends don't know about your past," she said.

Cobra shook his head back and forth. "When you're an enforcer, people expect you to be untouchable, sweetheart. No room for a sob story background or drama bullshit. I used my demons to fuel my job."

"That's not fair to you. I'm sorry." Dakota felt for him, knowing what it was like to keep deep, dark secrets and the need to continually run from them until the running had become her whole life. "Thank you for telling me."

"Yeah."

They sat together, wrapped in each other's arms, ignoring the ticking clock that had followed them both through their lives. A push and pull with time that had marked every choice and defined every decision.

"This may seem like a weird question considering that we've been staying together for almost two weeks, but what exactly do you do for a living?" she asked, changing the subject from their tortured pasts to the present.

"Landscaping—a fancy word for mowing grass and trimming hedges. It pays for what I need. I've been a 'Jack of all trades' for a long time now."

"But you've been visiting the MC too."

"Are you asking if I do anything for them?"

Dakota nodded, her stomach churning and not entirely sure she wanted the real answer. Would it change her opinion of him, knowing he was back crushing skulls or other questionable activities?

"It's complicated, but it's also club business."

"Which means?"

"It stays in the club with the brothers."

She wrinkled her forehead and her mouth turned downward.

Cobra laughed. "That's the way it rolls in the outlaw world, darlin'."

He pulled back and rose to his feet then offered her his hand. Dakota stared at it, suddenly unsure if she was willing to join the real world again after everything they'd been through together in this place. Cobra must've picked up on her hesitation, because his brows rose slightly, and he cocked his head at her in a silent question.

"We can't stay here forever. It'll be time for me to take you to work soon."

"Ugh, you're right." She rolled her eyes and grabbed his hand as he pulled her up and led them both back to the bike. "They probably won't be too understanding if I called in sick so soon on the job."

He chuckled. "Probably not." He swung his leg over the seat and straddled the bike. "We'll grab barbeque for an early dinner, then I'll take you to the ink shop."

"Sounds like a plan," she answered, sliding in behind him.

Dakota wished she could hang out with Cobra for the rest of the day, then spend the night buried under the sheets with him. The night before, she had an aggressive SOB who had wanted a swastika on his forearm and then an idiot who'd wanted a tat on his dick. She hoped her shift that night would bring in a saner group of clients.

After some really good ribs and potato salad, Dakota waved goodbye to Cobra then entered the tattoo parlor. She was still worried that her slip up in telling Cobra about the rape would color his entire opinion of her, regardless of his repeated assurances to the contrary. Men didn't get over the whole tainted, sullied-goods thing so easily.

Dakota sighed and wiggled the mouse to activate the shop's computer screen. She had at least another five appointments to navigate through, mostly consultations, just talking and walking them through the process. After that, as long as she didn't get any surprise walk-ins, she could be home in a little over three hours.

A whole three damn hours to imagine all the ways Cobra could bend, lick, suck, and thrust his way into her sex hall of fame. Not that the list was that long or anything: quite the opposite.

She grimaced and made a couple of notes in the computer next to a client who was showing up to consult about a cover-up tattoo. Those were tricky and, most often, some of her least favorite work. While some artists loved the puzzle of it all, Dakota found that covering up a person's ink so no one saw the original as a frustrating labyrinth of possible things that could go wrong. Much like her rusty sex life, it was a lot easier to jump into the act when she had a clean slate—unfortunately, that wasn't their reality. It never would be, either.

"You look like you're thinking awfully hard there, honey. You might want to lighten up before you get wrinkles."

Dakota glanced up as a shock of surprise whipped up her spine. An older woman was standing in front of the counter, adult braces gleaming in the shop lights, her blonde bob cut severally to her chin.

"Oh, hello. I'm sorry, ma'am, I didn't see you there. How can I help you?" Dakota blinked a few times and tried to get her heart rate back in line. Her thoughts slowly started to re-register to what was happening in the real world versus what had been going down in her head.

"I'm here for my appointment, if you can manage that with everything else you have going on up there?" The woman reached across the counter and tapped a bright-red fake nail on the side of Dakota's temple. "Please, tell me it's a man. If it's not a man, you shouldn't be paying it any mind."

Unable to wrap her mind around what was happening while she scrambled for another answer—any other answer than the truth—Dakota found herself babbling helplessly about what was actually going on in her life. It was as if she were living outside her body, watching herself stumble over her words to this older woman.

"Ah, so it'd been awhile since your flower had been plucked, and now that it has, you want it all the time, right?" The woman grinned again and leaned one elbow on the counter, giving Dakota a knowing glance. "Jump him, don't think about it, and don't take no for an answer. He'll appreciate you telling him what you want."

She winked and Dakota's eyes widened. This was … utterly insane. There was no other word for it.

"Sure," she replied, mindlessly tapping into the keyboard a bunch of useless symbols so it looked as if she were busy doing her job. "What exactly can I help you with, Mrs.—?"

"Tawny Delanie."

Before she could absorb that gem of a name, the woman launched into a detailed depiction of her ideal tattoo, which included the baby Jesus holding a box of Cheez-its, surrounded by a field of wildflowers with two banners on the top and bottom with important dates. After that consultation, the rest of the night flew by with nothing quite so colorful, but anything else seemed easy after Tawny.

Dakota racked up a list of drawings she would have to complete and kept a running tally of how much time she estimated they would take outside of the shop. By the time her replacement, Jackson, stumbled in to close up and handle all the machines, she was itching to fling herself out the door and onto the back of Cobra's Harley.

"Dude's out there," Jackson snorted and pointed with his thumb to the purple bike she saw waiting across the street, painted by the shop signs down the block.

"Thanks."

Dakota cleaned up her work station with trembling fingers and threw everything in her bag; she typed in her "logged-out" time and was out the door before she could process what had made her quicker than normal. What she *should do* was stay back and pick Jackson's brain. Figure out the shop's inner workings, ask about their clients' intricacies so she could play off them later as she developed her own clientele.

Instead, she was moving straight into Cobra's arms as if nothing in the world could stop her single-minded trajectory.

"You look … intense," he remarked lightly, looking her up and down before handing her a helmet.

"Long shift," Dakota muttered and swung herself over the back of the bike.

Her attention zeroed in on the nape of his neck. It took everything inside her not to place a kiss on his flesh before licking up his neck and letting the lightly chilled night breeze tickle his skin. Instead, she bit her lip and told herself to cool her damn jets and wait a little bit, read the situation rather than pounce on him like a cat in heat.

"Work rough tonight?"

Dakota nodded as he opened the motel door for them both and lifted his T-shirt over his head then flung it across the nearest chair.

"Wanna talk about it?"

"Not really—just some pain in the ass clients and some strange ones too. I guess an ordinary day in an ink shop. How was work for you?"

"Hot as hell and it felt longer than usual. I've gotta take a quick shower." Cobra walked to the bathroom and closed the door behind him. A few minutes later, she heard the sound of running water. She sat at the edge of the bed and reached for the room's telephone on the nightstand and, cradling the receiver in the crook of her neck, she dialed Pizza Madness. On the fourth ring, the employee picked up and she ordered their usual two medium deep-dish pies, one with pepperoni, one with extra cheese. Dakota hung up the phone, stood up, walked over to the wall nearest to the window, and parted the curtains a little and looked out. *Have things changed between me and Cobra?*

"You clearly got something on your mind, sweetheart." Cobra's voice startled her out of her musings, and she spun around.

Dakota dipped her gaze to the short white towel snug around his waist then slowly drew her eyes up over his chiseled abs and chest.

"Am I gonna have to get it out of you, or are you gonna tell me?"

Her skin pebbled at his low voice, and she bit her lip, trying to push away the immediate effect that was whipping through her body. No, it wasn't the time yet. Hell if she knew exactly when the time would be good enough, but it wasn't now, regardless of the fact that every fiber of Dakota's being was urging her to dig her nails into his finely muscled back and yank him forward until their lips crashed together. She could feed on his mouth to the point where she couldn't hear any more doubts against the onslaught of her excited pulse against her temples.

As he slipped on a clean pair of jeans and T-shirt, she watched his every movement. He glanced up and caught her gaze.

"You look like you want to devour me, sweetheart."

"Funny, you're not that far off…"

"Oh?" Cobra took another step forward into her personal space, all teasing suddenly was dampened to a seriousness that ratcheted the tension between them up a few notches.

"Come here," she whispered, wrapping her palm around the back of his neck.

CHAPTER NINETEEN

COBRA

WHILE DAKOTA'S TONGUE lightly traced his lips, Cobra angled his hips forward to press her against the wall as she made a muffled noise of pleasure. Clearly, she wanted to take the reins for the night. He wasn't used to a woman in charge, but it was an interesting change of pace. Cobra wondered how long he could roll with it before the beast inside him took over and ate her up in a single bite.

Her hand on the back of his neck lightly tugged downward, and he laughed, struggling against her pushes to get him on his knees. Clever little fucking minx wanted worship? All right, he would make her knees so damn weak and have her beg him for more before she screamed out his name.

The air from the AC blasted cold as Cobra slid down to his knees in front of Dakota and traced his hands down her curves while her head arched backward against the wall. Her hand still rested on the top of his head and he squeezed either side of her hips before slowly riding her skirt up to reveal a tiny sheer thong.

He licked his lips as a jolt of lust landed right on his stiff cock. "Fuck." His rough voice caught in his throat as he looked up into her wide, startled gaze. "You've been wanting this."

"The. Whole. Time. I. Was. At. Work."

Each word was whispered, though that didn't make them less powerful.

Cobra rumbled appreciatively, loving the idea of this sweet little woman keeping her thoughts free of anything else but him. The image of Dakota almost naked under that skirt of hers, dreaming up all kinds of scenarios of them fucking was enough to make him blow right then and there.

He bunched the flimsy material of her thong between his fingers and ripped the sheer fabric apart.

"Oh God," she whimpered, her hips gyrating forward as her eyes fluttered closed. Dakota's hand clasped into the hair at the top of his head.

"I haven't even fuckin' touched you, sweetheart," he growled, burying his face between her legs as he used his hands to pry apart her thighs so that one leg was on either side of his head. "I know you're gonna taste fuckin' delicious."

"Please, Cobra," she moaned, already primed for him.

Her scent of arousal was thick in the air. He slipped his tongue out to lightly trace the outer lips of her pussy at the same time he reached behind her to palm each ass cheek. Dakota gasped as he yanked her forward and dove into her heat. One light tease had outdone all his patience and Cobra sucked on her tight little clit as she scrambled and made small noises above him while her hands pawed at the top of his head.

"That feels so good!" Her thighs shook on either side of him as she cried out and tried her best to thrust into his mouth to get more friction.

"That's it, darlin', ride my face with your wet little pussy. I want your juices all over it," he smothered against her. "You taste so damn sweet. Keep it up. That's it."

Cobra talked her through it. Flicking her clit with his tongue, sucking like a two-thousand-dollar vacuum, and gently tonguing her opening, and Dakota went wild, like a hellcat on steroids.

Meanwhile, his cock was fast approaching blue ball status. Cobra was so hard, every small adjustment made him wince from the pressure of his jeans against his dick. He hadn't been this horny since freshman year when he'd been getting off twelve to fourteen times a day and was afraid he was going to wear a hole through his flesh. But something about Dakota made everything feel brand fucking new. He didn't give a shit if his dick fell off in the process of pleasing her, so long as she got exactly what she'd been dreaming about all damn day.

"I'm … I'm …" she panted, unable to get out the words.

"You're sure about this, sweetheart?"

She was dripping down her thighs. Her body was more than sure—but he wanted to make certain her mind was in for the ride.

"Yes." She breathed out with a whimper. "Yes. Please."

"Tell me, sweetheart."

Her lower lip trembled and he lapped up a bead of her liquid heat as it slid down her inner thigh. When Cobra looked back up at her again, her jaw was clenched and her expression looked like the feral intensity of a leopard just before it pounced on its prey. Primal. Raw. Fucking gorgeous.

"I want this, Cobra. I want you. Do it. Now."

Well, fuck, that was good enough for him. He pulled himself up and scooped her into his arms then threw her on the bed. Dakota barely had enough time to make a sound before Cobra was on her, over her, yanking at her clothes like a madman. All he wanted was to see her soft, silky skin. With every article of clothing he discarded, his mouth followed his hands, licking, kissing, and teasing the fuck out of every inch of her flesh until she was a moaning, helpless mess.

Dakota fluctuated between grabbing him by the hair or shirt to kissing and groping his ass. At one point, she tried to drag his hands, his mouth to where she wanted him to be on her body, but he ignored her efforts. Cobra kept teasing her, making her body quiver and pebble as she moaned and pleaded to no avail. He was unmovable.

"You want some more, darlin'?"

Dakota huffed and dragged her nails over his chest across his T-shirt as if she were trying to rip it off him. With a huge fucking grin plastered across his face, Cobra yanked his shirt over his head. Next came the boots and socks. Then the jeans. Finally the boxers. He didn't make any kind of show out of it or entice her to open up her eyes as she whimpered and writhed beneath him. Nope, he wanted it over with, so they could move on to more fun things.

Cobra had promised her a fuck ton through his body language, and as he nabbed the condom he kept in his pants pocket for emergencies, he knew there was only one other thing he had to say before he dove straight into her.

"Sweetheart, do you have a favorite position?"

Cobra was acutely aware of memories that had leveled Dakota the last time they fucked. He still wasn't sure if it was something he'd done that reminded her of that asshole, but he didn't want to take his chances in triggering any shit from her past. But Dakota simply shook her head. Her brows furrowed, her breasts trembled, and her little rosy nipples begged for his mouth.

He grabbed her ankles and maneuvered so they were both sitting on his left shoulder, moving her so that one ankle crossed over the other one. He kept them pinned to him with one hand and guided his condom covered dick to her slick entrance with the other one.

"I need you," she spoke softly, low enough he almost didn't catch the words.

Cobra didn't hesitate again. The first inch inside her tightness was like finding heaven and coming back on the other side again. So fucking magical. Dakota was perfect in every way, and he groaned, locking his eyes on hers.

"That's right, sweetheart. Look at me. I wanna see the lust in those pretty eyes when I fuck you senseless." A sheen of sweat glistened over her face as pure bliss played across it. He pushed in more. She groaned then bucked and arched her back toward him.

"Fuck, you're greedy for me," he said. Damn, Dakota was a hot cutie who was driving him fucking crazy at the moment by the way she used her hands and pushed up her hips to coax him to move deeper inside her. Cobra wanted nothing more than to pummel in and out of her, to bite and suck her tits, and touch the one spot he knew would set her off like a geyser, but he held back and kept teasing her.

"Cobra, please," she begged.

He dipped his head and sucked one of her rigid nipples into his mouth, teasing it with his tongue and teeth. A throaty moan fell from her lips.

"The sounds you make get to me," he whispered in her ear, flicking the pebbled bud with the tip of his index as he slid his other hand under her and held the soft curves of her ass.

"It feels good," she panted, bucking against him. "I'm ready for you."

"I know that," he said then resumed ravaging her tits as he slowly moved in and out of her. It was the hardest damn thing he'd ever done, because all he wanted to do was fuck the hell out of her, but Cobra knew it would be so much more intense for Dakota if he went slow.

"I ordered pizza," she whispered.

His hands tightened around her body.

"Your concern is the *food*, sweetheart? Or are you using it as an excuse for me to pound into you, so you get what you want outta me?" he rasped and withdrew himself until his cock was barely in her opening, resting there while she fought and cried out frustrated protests.

"That's not how this shit works, darlin'. Bad girls don't get what they want. Besides, fuck food—I got all I need right here." He buried his finger between her wet pussy lips then brought it to his mouth and licked off her sweet juices.

Dakota's gaze fixed on his movements as if fascinated and drawn to them.

"Want a taste?" he asked, bending his head down so his face was mere inches from hers.

She nodded, and he crushed his mouth on hers and shoved his

tongue through her parted lips. After a long, deep kiss, he pulled back and before Dakota could say anything, he plunged all the way inside her tightness, and she arched into him with a small, shocked moan. A shudder flung down his back. Fuck, Cobra would be happy to hear that noise for eternity. Such a small sound, yet so damn gratifying, and he sure as fuck was going to make her do it again for him.

Another long, slow-gliding withdraw then he slammed back inside again.

"Oh, shit," she gasped. This time she practically jackknifed off the bed, whimpering and clawing at the sheets.

"Damn, sweetheart." He chuckled, lightly biting her calves. "And this isn't anything yet."

CHAPTER TWENTY

DAKOTA

Dakota clung to the sheets as Cobra tore through a teasing tempo above her with just enough action to drive her crazy, but not enough to send her spinning over the edge into orgasm oblivion. He was careful, calculated, and downright masterful, and she held on to every pleasant sensation that wrung out her nerve endings. Dakota knew deep down, in some small space, that this was what sex was supposed to be like between two people. A connection so raw and bone deep, she felt shattered and built up all at the same time.

The fact that she had found it with Cobra was insane. But also oddly … right. While he filled her in every possible way, she struggled against the back and forth tease that he was tightening through her flesh. Every time she thought she was onto him, he would change it up by lighting up another bulb on her physical switch board that would send her sky high all over again in a new way.

What Cobra was doing to her erased everything; it made her shiny and new, as if this was her one and only experience, because in a way, that was true. A subtle ache started in her chest and flushed across her skin, a weird rawness that stemmed from some kind of physical relief Dakota hadn't known she'd needed after all these years. Her inner walls pulsed around his cock, and he caught his breath, nearly halting a long thrust, before he grabbed her ankles and pulled upward, deepening the angle yet again.

"Oh, fuck," she breathed out on a long groan, breathless as he rammed inside her even deeper than she'd ever thought possible. It was as if every part of him was touching every part of her—everywhere. "Don't stop. Don't you dare stop."

A rumble and a grunt were her only answers.

Dakota felt his free hand explore between her legs, and she was afraid she'd fall to pieces before Cobra located her tender button. Her mouth opened—wordless, as ecstasy jerked her limbs tighter and tighter.

"Oh fuck, that's it, sweetheart. Let it come," Cobra coaxed her gently. "Give into it. Give in, let it take you."

"Oh … oh … oh …" she kept saying over and over like a chant. Dakota was on a high as Cobra shoved into her hard and rough while flicking her hot button at the same time.

"Dakota," he said through gritted teeth, his balls slapping against her ass as she bucked against him. "You're so fuckin' sweet."

A low roar built through the apex of her soul and funneled through her throat and out her mouth. A cry unlike any sound she'd ever made in her life. For a second, everything fell away and she saw stars: small shimmers bursting to life across her closed eyelids. Her fingers went numb and limp against the damp sheets; her body wrung out from the shivers that were curling her spine with pleasure.

"Fucking hell. Oh fuck—" Cobra stole her words away with a kiss that nearly took her breath with it. His green eyes smoldered with lust and something darker and deeper.

Dakota strained against him, yearning to make another orgasm come faster and harder than the one before, knowing it would bring him just as much joy. This next one could be the two of them coming together.

Her arms went around his neck and he hissed. His skin was flushed and slightly sweaty, but his movements never wavered in their intensity. Cobra was definitely a marathon and not a sprint, which made her feel luckier than she could fathom. Dakota squeezed her legs together, pressing her thighs as hard as they would go as she strained beneath the heavy blanket of orgasm that hovered over her. It was so damn close, nearly smothering her again in a soft yet shattering peace.

Still, he hadn't let up on her clit, and she held her breath as his finger played with her hardened nub in small, short circles and tiny flicks at the same time alternating with deep, hard presses while he pounded into her. Nothing gentle about it, nothing sugary sweet or any version close to lovemaking that she'd seen on TV. But it was more attentive and tender than anything she could ever imagine. For her, it blew all the love scenes she'd read in her mother's romance novels out of the fucking water.

"Damn, darlin'. The way you grip my cock so tight is fuckin' good," Cobra rasped, still anchoring her to him with one hand on her hip, where she imagined she would wear his bruise in the morning.

"Close … so close," she gasped.

"Yeah. Fuck," he grunted.

Cobra dove forward and sucked her nipple into his mouth, then pinched her sweet spot and the second orgasm tore beneath her skin in an unstoppable wave of ecstasy causing Dakota to writhe from the power of it.

His breathing ripped out of him in short huffs then he stilled, tensed, and stared deeply into her eyes then thrust so far forward that she thought he was trying to claim every inch of her—all the way to her soul.

"Dakota. Fuck!" he cried. His eyes glowed in the moonlight through the large crack in the curtains, and then he collapsed on top of her, moving her thighs to either side of his hips as he burrowed his head into her neck. His heart thundered against her chest.

After a long pause, he cleared his throat with a small cough. "That was fuckin' intense."

"Yeah, it really was." She laughed softly.

There was a sharp knock on the door and both of them jerked up like puppets on a string.

"Who the fuck is it?" Cobra said.

"Uh … you ordered a pizza?" a muffled voice said behind the door.

They both busted out laughing, then Cobra brushed his lips across hers and struggled to untangle himself from her body and the sheets. He bent down and scooped up his jeans from the floor and shrugged them on, then stumbled toward the door.

A guy in his late teens pushed up the glasses on the bridge of his nose. The aroma of pepperoni wafted into the room, and Dakota's stomach growled.

"We forgot you were coming, but I'm fuckin' starved," Cobra said as pulled out a wad of bills from his pocket.

The pizza guy looked over Cobra's shoulder and his face reddened when he saw Dakota sitting up in the bed with her hand clutching the sheet over her breasts. She smiled and the young man averted his gaze and handed the boxes to Cobra.

"Smells good." He glanced over at Dakota and winked then turned back to the guy in the doorway. "How much do I owe you?"

She giggled under her breath, certain that a generous tip was on the guy's horizon.

CHAPTER TWENTY-ONE

DAKOTA

"Isn't today your day off, sweetheart?" Cobra kissed her temple and slid out of bed as the afternoon sunlight slipped through the worn curtains.

"Yeah, and I'm going to spend it doing laundry. Real fun, huh?" Dakota replied.

"I wish I could call off, but Ryan and Sergio weren't at work yesterday, and the boss was fuckin' pissed. We need the dough, so I'm dragging my ass there today."

"That's okay—we have a lot of laundry. I'm going to wash the sheets too. We can do something fun tonight."

Cobra shook his head, the fine lines deepening on his forehead. "Sorry—no can do. I've got some shit I gotta do tonight, but I'm a call away if you need anything."

Dakota watched as the sweet man slung himself into his tight-fitting jeans, a flush of desire spread through her as she enjoyed the view. The past few weeks had fallen away into a blur of bliss. When she wasn't at the tattoo shop and Cobra wasn't working, they were either having fun in bed or on his bike, exploring the backroads around the area. Each day, each moment, they seemed to grow closer, sharing stories from their pasts, and trusting one another implicitly. Dakota found it almost impossible to believe that she had found such trust and intimacy in a man. Cobra made her feel safe and protected, cherished and respected, and she never thought that would ever be possible.

"Whaddaya got going tonight?"

Cobra shrugged then sat on the chair and pulled on his boots. "Club business."

Dakota knew that meant *that* conversation thread was over. Whenever he'd tell her something was club business, a slice of fear crept down her spine, and worry set in until he was back home safe and in her arms. She'd never felt the depth of emotion for any man the way she did for Cobra.

The only guy Dakota thought she'd loved was Justin, her old high school boyfriend. They'd dated for a year and a half, and when she'd been ready to finally make love, it was disastrous. The flashbacks had gotten in the way, and she couldn't tell Justin about the rape. After time, she'd learned how to block them out while they were together, but the sex with Justin had seemed more like a chore than a pleasure.

Dakota had given up her dreams of going to college because Justin had told her he wanted her to stay in Pocatello with him and professed his undying love for her. He'd decided to forgo college in lieu of a job at his uncle's mechanic shop. Dakota needed Justin in her life to feel worthy and important, and to keep Taylor away, so against her mother's advice, she agreed to stay in Pocatello and work.

A week before her senior prom, Justin dropped her and took another girl, Larissa, instead. Dakota was devastated, embarrassed, and mortified. Right after graduation, Justin had married Larissa, who was four months pregnant. Dakota's heart had grown colder, and she swore off guys and concentrated on learning a skill. She'd always been artistic and loved tattoos, so she studied hard and did an apprenticeship at Inkworks. She'd avoided Justin and when he'd called her in an attempt to rekindle their relationship, she hung up on him. *So many men are such fucking idiots.*

"Are you okay? You look like you're thinking too much."

Cobra's deep voice pulled her back to the present.

"Yeah, I'm good."

He narrowed his eyes. "You sure?"

She nodded.

"Okay then," he said as he walked into the bathroom.

Dakota pulled her knees up and wrapped her arms around them. Cobra was so attentive, kind, and caring, and he gave her space when she needed it. The relationship she had with him was healthier than anything she'd experienced in her past, but that didn't mean the demons had flown out the window. Dakota still had moments when she needed to stop them. Times when flashbacks seized her hard enough that she needed to be away from everything and everyone. Cobra understood that and never criticized her or got insecure about it. She considered herself lucky to have found such an amazing guy.

When Cobra came back into the room, she looked up at him. "How long are you working today?"

"Landscaping until five and then I gotta go to the clubhouse." Cobra turned around as he threw on a sleeveless white muscles shirt. He packed a black T-shirt in a small bag.

"So it'll be a late night for you," she said, throwing her hair up into a tie she kept around her wrist.

"Probably. I'll text you when I'm on the way back from Missoula."

"Sounds good." Dakota smiled as he came over to her side of the bed and kissed her with a series of slow, lingering moves that left her breathless and weak.

"Try to enjoy your day off after you get done with the washing." Cobra cocked his head, studying her for a beat before he opened the door and walked out.

Dakota missed him the minute he was gone. She leaned her head back against the headboard and closed her eyes, swallowing the lump in her throat. The vibration of her cell phone startled her. She shook her head at the way she jumped at the familiar sound. Dakota watched the yellow device rattle along the top of the nightstand, and when it reached the edge, she grabbed it and looked down at the screen. *Luke.*

"Hey," she said.

"Where the hell are you?" her brother replied.

"I'm fine. How're you?" She straightened out her legs on the mattress.

"Mom's worried sick about you. She's been trying to call you for over three fucking weeks, Dakota. Why in the hell haven't you answered your phone?"

The truth was she didn't want to deal with any of it. When she took off from Idaho Falls, Taylor had called and texted several times asking to see her. He'd found out she lived there from Luke. Dakota had decided to turn off her phone and forget about it for a while. When Cobra had given her the burner phone, she'd left a message for her mom telling her she was okay and she'd be in touch soon. Now that Cobra was in her life, Dakota had taken out her phone just that morning and turned it on.

"I had problems with it. I left a message for Mom saying I was all right."

"That was a while back. Get real. You're such a fuck up."

Dakota winced at his words. "Nothing's changed—I'm still all right."

"Mom has been going crazy wondering why you left Idaho Falls. You owe her more than one damn message."

"I know," she whispered. "I'll call her after we hang up. How are Mom and Dad?"

"Besides being worried about you, they're okay. Where are you?"

"Montana. I just needed a change."

"Where in Montana?"

Dakota bit the inside of her cheek then sucked in a sharp breath. "Billings." She hated lying to her brother but she couldn't take the chance that Luke would tell Taylor where she was if she told him the truth.

"Why are you there?"

"I found a better paying job and, like I said, I needed a change. What've you been up to?"

"The same—working. Taylor said he tried to get a hold of you in Idaho Falls but you never returned his calls."

The room grew smaller and stuffier, and even with the AC at full blast, Dakota felt hot as hell. "Yeah, well, I was real busy."

She wished she could tell him the truth, but Dakota knew Luke would never believe her. They used to be so close when they were kids, but after what Taylor did to her, they'd grown apart. Luke had often accused her of becoming sullen and withdrawn, and he'd been right, but he never asked her if anything was wrong, or why she'd changed.

"I think he was offended that you dissed him."

"I've got to get to work. I'll give Mom a call—promise."

"When are you coming home for a visit?"

"I'm not sure. It's a new job so I won't get any time off for a while. I really have to go. Thanks for calling."

"Just make sure you call Mom ASAP, got it?"

"I said I would."

"All right then. Take care of yourself."

"I will. Bye."

Dakota stared at the black screen for several minutes. *I should've told him about Taylor. No ... you shouldn't. I need to tell Mom.* But what would that gain? Her mother was worried enough about her, and she still guilted Dakota about being the only one in the family to live away from Pocatello. No, her mother had enough on her plate with her full-time job, Dakota's younger brothers, and trying to make ends meet most months. Nothing would be accomplished by adding Dakota's past baggage onto her mother's shoulders.

After a quick phone call assuring her mother that she was more than all right, Dakota turned off her phone then put her feet on the cheap carpet and stood up. She padded over to the two pillow cases stuffed with laundry and picked them up, balancing one of them on her hip.

She slipped on a pair of flip flops, tucked her burner phone into the back pocket of her jean shorts, and headed out the door. When she turned to lock it, one of the pillow cases fell out of her hands and a pair of Cobra's jeans landed on the pavement and something fell out of one of the pockets.

Dakota crouched down; a small business card with Satin Dolls printed at the top in hot pink script took up the majority of it. Not much to go off of, but it was a strip club, given the "Gentlemen's Club" printed below the logo. Dakota flipped the card over and there were words scrawled on the back. "Can't wait to see you, baby. Give me a call soon."

There was a cell number and a name.

"Jenny," Dakota muttered under her breath. She stepped back into the cool room, dropped the laundry on the floor then fished out her cell phone. She hesitated for several seconds. *Whatever I find out, there's no going back. Do I really want that?* Her mind ping-ponged back and forth, wondering if she should put the card on the dresser and go about her business or call the number.

For all she knew, the chick could've been a regular for Cobra before he and Dakota had even gotten together. But there was no way to be sure. And everything had been going so well, too well. It was bordering on too-good-to-be-true between them. At least, aside from all the club secrets and late night rendezvous Cobra had going on with his MC. Should she really take it on faith that he wasn't seeing anyone else on the side while he claimed to be hanging out with his brothers?

With trembling fingers, Dakota tapped in the number for the strip club. She wasn't ready to talk to this Jenny chick yet and didn't want to confront her if it was nothing.

"Satin Dolls, how can I help you?" a sultry voice said.

Dakota took a deep breath and forced some cheerfulness into her voice.

"Hi. I was wondering if you'd seen a guy in there recently, like the past few weeks. He's pretty distinguishable: big guy, biker-type, tats on both arms. His name is Cobra and probably hangs out with Jenny when he's there."

"Oh, uh," the woman hesitated and there was a pause over the line. "I'm not allowed to give out that kind of information—it's club policy."

"Yeah, I understand, it was worth a shot." Dakota's teeth grazed the bottom of her lips, and her hand tightly clenched the phone. "There isn't anything you can do? Anything at all? I promise, I'm not trying to cause trouble for the club. I'm a friend of his sister's and it's family stuff."

There was a sound like the woman had cracked her gum over the line, some murmuring, and then a slight shuffle and static.

"Okay, look, I said I'm not supposed to do this, but since you're his sister's friend, I'll help you. Cobra's a regular and Jenny's his girl when he's in town." The woman sighed, long and drawn out and totally over dramatic. "He comes in to see her. Sometimes they go into one of the back rooms."

"Back rooms?" Dakota asked.

"The ones for private dances, that kind of thing. That's all I can give you, and I shouldn't even have told you that much."

Her heart sank and her knees felt like they would give out.

"Is there anything else? You're tangling up the phone line."

Dakota hung up without saying another word. A sick feeling twisted low in her belly as she tried to clear her head of the information she'd just learned about Cobra—about the man she was seriously falling for more and more every day, and who treated her like gold—the man she'd begun to trust.

While Cobra was taking Dakota out on long bike rides, to dinner, to the lake, and to bed, he'd been watching Jenny strip and do whatever else happened in those rooms. Dakota put her hands against her stomach and bent over, thinking that she might throw up. A small whimper escaped her lips as images of a naked Jenny grinding down on Cobra flashed through her mind like some damn porn flick.

No. Stop. Dakota squeezed her eyes shut and tried to banish the snapshots.

Even though she and Cobra had never said they were exclusive, Dakota thought he would have at least had the decency to tell her he was seeing someone else. Right or wrong, she felt sucker punched by the man she thought cared about her. The realization that Cobra was just another guy who turned out to be an asshole hit her hard.

Tears rushed to her eyes. There was no way Dakota was going to let him know how deeply he'd gotten into her heart. She angrily wiped her wet cheeks. The best way to cope was to put it out of her mind for now, and when Cobra got home that night, she'd ask him about it. If Cobra lied, she'd pack up and leave—it wasn't like she wasn't used to doing *that*. Dakota didn't need to stick around for a man who was nothing but a heartbreaking, self-centered thug who was out to fuck his way across the coast. *He's no different than any other asshole I've met.* She'd be out of there. Simple ... but why did it feel so hard and so sad?

Dakota slung open the motel room door and stomped across the hot tarmac without really seeing anything. The late morning heat slapped her in the face, but she barely noticed it as she hauled the bags filled with some of *his* clothes to the laundry room. Her mind kept spinning around all topsy-turvy with images of her and Cobra mixing with those of him with the stripper. Dakota kept shaking her head as if it would make the snapshots scatter away.

The laundry room was on the premises, but it was in a sketchy basement below the main office. The last time she'd gone there it had given her the creeps, but then Cobra had joined her and all was good. The door creaked open and Dakota flipped on the light switch. Two white washing machines and dryers stood against the wall, and a long table shelf lined the opposite side of the room. As Dakota walked to the machines, she made sure that she didn't look at the cobwebs in the corners of the room; in and out as quick as possible was her goal. She took out a coin purse in her pocket and fished out a bunch of quarters

Cobra had given her.

Dakota stared at the coins, barely able to focus. She took out two quarters and slipped them in the slot, but her attention was like a robot: going through the motions as her heart thundered in her chest. Her temples tingled from the adrenaline that had slipped into her bloodstream the second that woman had answered the phone at Satin Dolls. While Dakota wanted to live in the land of denial and think the best of the situation, it wasn't feasible. Not with the evidence that stared her in the face.

She threw a load carelessly in the washing machine and jerked the settings button, nearly taking off the knob. *This was supposed to be different. I really liked him. I fucking trusted him with my secrets and my feelings.* Dakota swiped her runny nose with the corner of a towel. She rubbed a hand down her face and turned to face the washer, bracing herself against either side of the casing. A swift wave of panic tightened her chest.

"Not now. Shit. Not now," she muttered.

Her whole body shook, the world narrowing and swirling like she was on a fast spinning amusement ride. While her fingers gripped the washer for all she was worth, her throat tightened, unable to catch her breath. Everything was moving too fast. Too much. There wasn't enough time.

"Excuse me."

The male voice floated up through her clogged senses. Dakota knew in the back of her head that she needed to see what he wanted, that she probably had to move out of his way. But her feet didn't move; they were locked in what felt like cement as her knees shook like wet noodles. When she tried to turn, nothing moved and Dakota breathed through her mouth like a spaz.

"You doing okay?"

"I'm … um …" She tried to gulp in air to get out an answer, unsure if she needed medical help or if this thing would pass soon. "I …"

"Never mind. No worries."

A small bit of relief funneled down her system. But not enough to stop the panic in its tracks. She thought she heard footsteps head back up the stairs as she swallowed thickly with a moan, trying to stand up straight, trying to do anything beyond what her brain was telling her, which was to flee.

All of a sudden, the room went quiet—past the soft and quick shush of her blood in her veins and the circular tumble and shift of the washer. Everything came into clear focus. Too clear, too sharp. An overexaggerated sensory overload. She moaned and shifted a little bit to the right.

Then several pairs of footsteps rushed down the stairs. Dakota whirled around and her eyes landed on Jake as he entered the room. The way he stared at her made her flesh crawl.

"I'm almost done," she said, stopping the machine. Her instinct told her to get the hell out of the room. Now.

"You're looking good—a little pale, but pretty as always." His words slid over her like slime.

"Cobra's waiting for me," she said as she stuffed the wet clothes in the pillowcase.

"No, he's not. He's at work." Jake chuckled.

Dakota froze with a pair of dripping sweatpants clutched in her hand.

"It's kinda nice not to have him always around you like a bodyguard." Jake took a step to the side.

Without thinking, she left the rest of the clothes in the machine and slung one of the bags over her shoulder.

"You're not leaving so soon, are you?" Jake asked.

He stared long and intently with an evil glint in his eyes. The hollow sensation in the pit of her stomach coiled into a lump of fear. Dakota shuddered and dashed toward the doorway and Jake stood still, watching her. Then she slammed into someone just as she left the room. A strangled scream tore from her throat as a pair of arms wrapped like steel rods around her waist. She tried to break away, but was powerless in the grip.

"Leave me alone!" she yelled, looking up into the hard features of a man she didn't recognize.

The stranger dragged her back into the room, and Dakota kicked at him and struggled to break free. For a split second, the attacker let go then spun her around, strong arming her backward until she was nearly off her feet. Her arms pinwheeled as she tried to gain traction. From the corner of her eyes, Dakota saw Jake's frosty sneer, and panic overloaded her system even more.

"You got this?" Jake asked.

"I'm good," the guy answered as his hand clamped over her mouth.

Dakota clawed at it, and let out another scream when he removed it.

"Calm the fuck down," he said.

The assailant's hand shoved an acidic rag over her nose and practically down her throat. She squirmed, but the man had her in a vise-like hold. Jake pushed away from the washing machine and walked past without giving her a second glance. Once again, she dug her fingernails in the attacker's forearms, but he just pressed down harder on the rag.

Her mental cries of anguish rose, even as weakness descended on her body. Her legs were like rubber, and she leaned back into him.

"That's it, baby … breathe deeply … just like that," he said in a lulling voice.

Dakota's eyes flickered and closed as her world went black.

CHAPTER TWENTY-TWO

COBRA

"H ERE," GRINDER POURED him a double and slid the shot glass and the bottle across the bar top. "You look like you could use it."

Cobra grunted, picked up the shot, toasted his MC president, and downed the tequila in one long swallow. The liquid caused a fire in his belly. Normally, he wasn't one to drink on the job, especially since he'd gotten out of the joint. Cobra preferred being clearheaded when there was actual shit on the line like lives or a livelihood, but judging by the rest of his brothers, they didn't roll with the same rules.

That night Cobra wanted to be on high alert. Even though this bastard Big Pat was a two-time operator, some unexpected shit could go down if the club was too cocky. He glanced at his phone to see if Dakota had texted him back, but there was nothing. *Probably napping after all that washing.* He chuckled under his breath. The things that woman did to him were off the charts. Each day he found himself growing closer to Dakota, caring more about her, and wanting to spend more time with her. *That* was a first for him.

When he'd left that morning, the forlorn look on her face as he closed the door behind him squeezed his damn heart something fierce. It took everything he had not to blow off work and go back into the room and spend the day with her. It tore him the fuck up to leave her alone, especially at night, but he didn't have a choice. He *had* to be here with his club—they were his family, his bloodline. Besides, club business was club business, and it always came first. Citizens never fucking got that.

Cobra knew that Dakota was dying to know what he was up to with his MC, but even if he could tell her, he wouldn't. There was no reason for her to see how he could deal out damage and revenge with no emotion like he was ordering a pizza or planning out a garden. Dakota saw something different in him. Cobra could see it in her eyes every time she looked at him when she thought he didn't notice. She'd never understand how he could compartmentalize the acts that were required at times in an outlaw world.

"Fuck," he muttered.

"Have another one, bro," Iron said as he set a tumbler in front of Cobra.

He shook his head and pushed it toward his friend. "Nah, I wanna be clearheaded."

"Big Pat's a fuckin' lightweight." Iron picked up the glass and threw it back.

"Even so, we gotta treat each mission like it's war. Trouble comes up when a person lets his defenses down."

"Cobra's got a point," Brute said as he sidled up next to the two bikers.

For the past hour, the club had been planning how to take Big Pat off the dealing circuit. It was bad enough he was dealing date rape drugs, but it was an even bigger thorn in the club's side that the dirtbag was manufacturing meth on Steel Devils' turf.

"Did you confirm the location I told you about?" Cobra asked, sitting back in his barstool and putting his boots up on the one next to him. "The warehouse off of Industry Road?"

"Yeah, we've had a couple of prospects watching it. It's the fucker's meth lab. He's got a bunch of clean-cut pussies working for him, and they keep pretty consistent hours. That dumbass needs to take a fuckin' cue on how to run an illegal business," Viper said as he slapped his palm on the bar top.

"Yeah," Razor agreed. "What the fuck happened to all the *good* bad guys? All we got now is a crop of goddamn posers in their place."

"They just work on greed and no fuckin' brains," Viper replied.

"Ain't that the fuckin' truth." Pee Wee brought the beer bottle to his lips.

"Yeah, well, we're coming for that motherfucker, and he won't know what hit him. We'll show him what happens to pussies who think they can pull something over on the Steel Devils." Hulk punched his fist into the palm of his other hand with a loud snap.

"That's the plan." Cobra tapped his fingers on his knee and looked around the room. "The club gave the fucker a free pass in Lolo, so the way I figure it, Big Pat has used up all his chances."

"Damn straight." Razor took a long drag from his lit cigarette.

"You gonna be up for the fight, dude?" Scarface said as he stood next to Cobra.

"What the fuck does that mean?" Cobra replied as he dropped his feet to the floor and straightened up on the barstool.

"It's just that you've been nomad for quite a while, and the occasional head busting isn't the same as living the life every day."

The two bikers locked eyes, and Cobra clenched his jaw as a surprising burst of anger lit up through his sternum. Along his journey, he'd met nomads who'd lost the passion for the club ways, but not Cobra. The rage that fueled him when he slipped into the white nothingness to handle his job as their enforcer was slithering into his bloodstream now. As simple as flipping a switch, and he was back.

Scarface's gaze sharpened and he grinned, narrowing his eyes. "Fuck, there you are, bro." He punched Cobra on the arm. "Welcome back."

Fury riled him, and Cobra flew off the stool. He reached out as he lunged for Scarface and grabbed him by the neck in a span of a heartbeat.

"Fuck you, asshole!" Scarface yelled as his hand moved toward the inside of his cut for a knife, no doubt.

In a fluid movement of reflex, Cobra swiveled his hips a quarter turn and yanked his arm that was still locked around Scarface's neck, and squeezed harder. All he had to do was flex hard and let his biceps do the work to snap Scarface's neck.

"What the fuck?" the biker choked out as his hands tried to push away Cobra's vise-like hold.

"Break it the fuck up!" Sparky said. He grabbed Cobra by the shoulders and yanked on them.

Reason broke through the fog of rage, and he dropped his arm and stepped back from Scarface.

The biker glared at Cobra as he rubbed his neck.

"We don't have time for this shit—save it for later. We've got a goddamn job to do," the vice president said, his gaze darting from Cobra to Scarface then back to Cobra.

Cobra kicked at the floor then shoved his hands in his pockets.

"I guess going nomad didn't hurt you none." Pee Wee's voice sliced through the tension between the two men.

The corners of Scarface's mouth twitched up before a loud guffaw broke through his lips. Cobra busted out laughing, and soon the cacophony of laughs, whistles, and stomping feet filled the main room.

Cobra extended his hand and Scarface clasped it tightly then pulled him into a bear hug.

"Fuck, dude, your reflexes are spot on," he said as he motioned the prospect for two drinks.

"You better fuckin' believe it," Cobra replied. He took the shot Scarface offered him and let it wash down his throat. *I fuckin' miss this.*

A loud whistle silenced the room and all eyes averted to Grinder, who stood on top of one of the tables.

"You got two fuckin' seconds to finish drinking up. We got some asses to kick and some shit to blow up."

The room filled with the full-throated roar of forty members stomping their feet, fists in air, chanting "Steel Devils forever, forever Steel

Devils" over and over. Cobra's chest swelled with pride as he joined in, feeling a sense of camaraderie with his brothers.

As Cobra walked to his Harley, he pulled Razor to the side. "I gotta ask a favor of you," he said in a low voice.

"What is it?"

Cobra wiped the corners of his mouth with his fingers. "I need some intel done on a sonofabitch."

Razor, Iron, and Brute were the computer brains in the club, and they could find tons of shit on anyone. It blew Cobra away as to how they did it, and Razor was the best of the trio on his clandestine research.

"Sure. Who's pissed you off?" Razor chuckled.

"Fucker's name is Taylor Ruybal. I need to know the asshole's address and where he works."

"Do you have info besides his name? How old is he?"

"He's twenty-two, born in Pocatello, Idaho, and has been living in Idaho Falls as of a few weeks ago."

"Easy as shit, bro. What did the pussy do?"

Cobra stopped in his tracks as anger smoldered inside him. "He messed with my woman."

Razor's eyes widened. "Fucker. And when did you get a woman? Is it that stripper at the Satin Dolls?" He snapped his fingers. "What's her name?"

"Jenny, and no, it's not her. We're friends *without* benefits now."

"Then who's this chick you're ready to kill for?"

Cobra shrugged. "Just someone I met."

Razor clapped his hand on Cobra's back. "I've never heard you call any chick *your* woman. Happy for you."

"Yeah. So I'll text you the shit I just told you about this fucker." He started walking again.

"Do that. If you need any help, I'm down for it. Pretty sure Iron and Brute will be too."

"Thanks, bro. I'll keep that in mind." Cobra shuffled over to his

Harley and swung his leg over the seat.

The thunder of sixteen bikes soon shattered the silence as the outlaws rode side by side on the highway leading to Philipsburg. As they approached the area where Big Pat's warehouse was, they hit the kill switches on their bikes and coasted to a safe location. There was no reason to tip off the prey that the lions were coming for blood.

"The prospects said that they've only seen about five assholes going in and out of here at one time," Brute said as he crouched behind one of the large oak trees across from the property.

"I didn't notice any security cameras when I cruised by the place the other night," Cobra said. "Did the prospects find any?"

"They checked it out and there were none. There are only four big-ass dogs that Sticky and Ringer took care of as we were heading in—the pups should be out for a while. Big Pat's proving once again why he's only a two-bit thug," Iron said.

Cobra and the others chuckled.

"Fuck, this is gonna be too easy," Cobra said.

"Are you gonna be bored kicking their asses?" Scarface's smile widened into a grin.

"Fuck, yeah." Cobra sat back on his haunches and fished his cell phone from his pocket. He checked his messages and calls—nothing from Dakota. He hadn't heard from her since he'd left for work early that morning. Fuck, something felt wrong. Niggling worry bore a hole into the back of his brain. *Maybe she's pissed because I've been gone too long, or maybe—*

"There're only two doors—one in the front and one in the back." Iron's voice broke in on his thoughts. "The prospects broke in through one of the windows last night and unlocked five of the others ones in the basement. None of the moronic SOBs noticed anything off kilter today, so some of us can go in that way and unlock the back door. Four of us can stand watch in the front in case the fuckers try to make a run for it."

The men nodded, and then Sparky made the decision on which

brothers were going to do what. Cobra was one of the brothers who would go in through one of the basement windows.

"Let's move out," the vice president said.

The street was empty, and a thick blanket of clouds blotted out the light from the moon and stars, keeping the bikers shrouded in darkness as they crossed the road. They fanned out, each of them well aware of his position and role in obliterating the occupants and the contents inside the small warehouse.

As they approached the building, Dakota's face flashed in his mind. *Why the fuck aren't you answering me? Are you okay?* Cobra rolled his shoulders and coughed, trying to get his head back in the game. The club was on a mission, and he had to push all thoughts of his woman out of his brain and focus on the here and now. The cold and ruthless reputation he was famous for had to be front and center. Cobra inhaled and exhaled several times until he fell into his detached zone.

Cobra crouched low as he followed Iron, Brute, Pee Wee, and Razor to the side of the warehouse. Brute pointed to a series of windows, and Cobra dropped to his knees and pushed one of them open. "Too fuckin' easy," he muttered under his breath. His hand went to the back of his waistband and felt his 9mm. Cobra never liked it when things were too easy because in his experience it meant shit was about to hit the fan.

"Be on high alert," he said to the others. "This shit is too damn simple for my liking."

The brothers nodded then opened the windows and slipped inside.

Rows of metal tables filled with copious bottles of cold medicine, a plethora of antifreeze containers, drain cleaner canisters, batteries, glass tubes, and Bunsen burners occupied a good portion of the large room. Huge fertilizer bags lined the back wall, and the strong odor of solvents seared Cobra's nostrils.

Brute held up two fingers on his left hand, gesturing everyone forward as they moved as one unit toward the stairs. Like harbingers of death they walked in the darkness, forming shadows that would soon spread wrath on everyone in that fucking building.

When Cobra and Iron reached the top of the stairs, a strong and foul chemical stench hit them in the face, and Cobra pinched his nose with his thumb and index finger. Iron pointed to a steel door, and Cobra quietly walked over and let in four Steel Devils. A flood of antsy excitement dropkicked him in the stomach as he and the others threaded through the darkened building looking for the drug lab. They moved with barely a sound as they secured the different areas. In the distance they heard noise: muffled voices, the whirr of fans, the clang of pots. As they approached the front part of the building, yellow light seeped from under a door. Several of the members flattened against the wall, hiding in the shadows, and Cobra crept over then slowly turned the knob, opening the door ajar. A sliver of light spilled onto the concrete floor, and he peeked in and saw five men cooking meth. Three looked to be in their early twenties and had the same look—clean-cut and preppy—that the fuckers had who'd drugged Dakota. The other two men were older and looked like thugs. Cobra knew they'd have to be taken down first before they took care of the other ass wipes.

One of the douchebags walked over to a table, and within seconds, loud, hard-hitting beats blared through the room. A couple of the guys mouthed the lyrics and swayed with the music as they worked.

Razor motioned to a hallway to the left before he and Hulk disappeared into the shadows. Cobra figured they were going to let in the rest of the brothers, so he waited, poised at the door, watching the assholes mix shit up then pour it into pots on the burners.

A minute passed. The tension crackled. Another minute ticked by. The stress mounted. It seemed like hours, and every muscle in Cobra's body strained to stay rooted to the spot. From the look on the faces of his brothers, he knew they were itching to rush into the room and crack some skulls.

"Yo, what the fuck!" a voice bellowed from behind them. The rush of heavy footsteps made Cobra look over his shoulder. A tall, built man in his thirties held a gun in his hand as he rushed toward the bikers. "Big Pat didn't tell me about you."

Cobra couldn't believe the dude thought he could take on all six of them, and he closed the door to the lab then turned around and watched the guy as he stopped and stared at them wild-eyed.

From the corner of his eyes, Cobra saw that Iron, Pee Wee, and Brute had already taken their guns out.

"Seems like this motherfucker's been smoking too much of the shit they're cooking," Cobra said and the others laughed.

"Who the fuck are youse?" the stooge said.

Iron narrowed his eyes. "The Grim Reaper."

Before the guy could say anything, Pee Wee, Brute, and Scarface were on him, and the man shot in the air. Damned fool, he didn't stand a chance. The three bikers cut him down in a short time. The guy went down in a heap, sputtering and choking on his own blood as it flowed from his cut throat.

"What the fuck?" Sparky asked as he approached Cobra. Several members were behind him.

"The fucker came outta nowhere. Had a gun. I'm pretty sure the assholes inside the lab heard the shot," Cobra said, his eyes fixed on the dude on the floor. The man lay still with a leg twisted awkwardly behind him, a pool of blood spreading around him.

Iron bent down and picked up the gun then wiped the blade of his knife on the dead man's pants. "We ready to get this shit over with?" he asked.

Sparky nodded and motioned to Cobra to open the door.

When Cobra looked inside, it was as if nothing had changed; he couldn't believe the dumbasses didn't hear their colleague's gun go off. The music still blared and he figured it probably had drowned out the shot.

Cobra wrinkled his nose and flexed his fingers around the piece in his hand as he pushed open the door and stepped inside. All of his brothers had their guns drawn as they rushed into the room. The fucking assholes making the shit still had their backs turned as the bikers ambushed them.

"Too fuckin' easy," Cobra muttered under his breath as he put his gun back in his waistband and took out a hunting knife from one of his boots. In battle, he preferred to get up close and personal if he had the choice, and the stupid fucker in white shorts moving his hips to the music just pissed Cobra the hell off.

He covered the distance quickly and in less time than it took for the preppy shitass to figure out what the hell was going on, it was too late. Cobra put his left hand over the guy's mouth, his right knee into the small of his back and his blade against the punk's throat.

One slice and he was down, his small brown eyes glassing over. The fucker bled like a pig, but Cobra stepped away from him and looked around the room. Four other assholes had come into the room with guns drawn, and he had no idea where they'd come from. The scene was like a snippet from some urban fantasy movie where the deafening music played on while fists crunched against jaws, bullets whizzed by, and blood splattered in the air.

By the time it was over, two Steel Devils had been injured—Voodoo taking a bullet in the shoulder and Scarface bleeding from a knife stab in his leg. Big Pat's crew fared much worse—all had moved on to the big meth lab in the fucking sky.

During the melee, someone had turned off the music, or maybe a bullet had busted up the player, but at that moment, only the sound of smashing equipment reverberated through the lab.

"Damn, I thought this would've at least been a fuckin' challenge," Cobra said to Sparky.

"Me too."

"Did Hulk and Razor take Voodoo and Scarface outta here?"

"They're already on their way to Missoula, and Grinder's already called Medicine Man to come over and do his magic," Sparky replied.

"Good thing's Razor's a paramedic," Cobra said.

"Yeah, he knows what the fuck he's doing."

Brute walked over to the duo and nudged Sparky with his elbow. "We ready, brother?"

"Fuck, yeah," Sparky replied.

"We'll use their shit to blow this fuckin' building to hell." Cobra chewed the inside of his cheek and grabbed the bottles of lighter fluid on the counters. "Yo!" he yelled then threw several containers to Pee Wee, Iron, Brute, Viper, and Boulder. The other brothers had gone in the basement and brought up some of the accelerants that were on the metal tables.

"Let's make this baby burn," Cobra said.

Each brother shifted all around the room and poured the fluidt on every available surface, knowing that there was enough flammable, toxic chemicals to light up the place like it was the fucking Fourth of July.

"Crash, boom, bang, motherfuckers," Sparky said as he chucked a bottle of ammonia under one of the tables. "I'm doing the goddamn honors, so get the fuck out." He lit a match.

"I got your back," Cobra said, standing in the doorway. Several of the brothers had left the building and started walking toward their bikes.

A great flash of fire-like lightning immediately ensued, and it sprang up, reaching for the ceiling. Cobra and the others dashed out of the building, running through a black and dismal cloud of acrid, lung-burning smoke. They bolted across the street as they headed to their motorcycles. Cobra's eyes stung and teared, but he didn't stop to wipe them until he was firmly on the seat of his Harley and switching on the engine.

He raised his fist in the air then separated from his brothers, who headed in the opposite direction. Cobra had to get his ass to the motel to find out why Dakota had been giving him the silent treatment that whole day.

Idling at a red light, Cobra double-checked his phone. Nothing from her. *Shit!* She was probably deep in a romantic comedy movie binge or maybe even asleep, making those little snore noises he found so fucking cute. *Yeah, that's it.*

Cobra ignored the bile that rose from his gut and the fear tickling at the base of his brain as he burned rubber and sped to the motel.

CHAPTER TWENTY-THREE

DAKOTA

DAKOTA GROANED AS her eyelids fluttered opened. "Fuck," she whispered under her breath. Nausea roiled in her stomach at the same time that her head pounded like she'd done twelve keg stands.

She blinked, but everything was still blurry. Too bright. Too close to the surface as she struggled to move her aching, noodle-like limbs. Nothing on her body felt right. Everything was slow and Dakota couldn't get her thoughts together as she fought to figure out what the hell had happened.

She was lying on a concrete floor, and she tried to adjust into a more comfortable position. Streaks of bright sunlight pierced her eyes like shards of glass.

Where the hell am I?

Then everything came back in a flash of quick images that left her gasping. *That asshole Jake set me up. But why?* The images kept coming: the stranger who attacked her, a cloth pushed against her face, the light fading to darkness. *I was drugged!* Clammy fear skittered up and down her spine and crept in the roots of her hair. *Maybe he paid that asshole Jake money to take me. Maybe I'm going to be a sex slave. No!* Panic—sheer, terrifying panic—ripped through her. *I have to get out—escape.*

The idea of that man's hands groping her body brought sour bile up into her throat again and Dakota nearly choked. *I can't freak out. Not now. I have to focus.* If she wanted to make it out alive and whole, she had to pay attention to everything.

Dakota's stomach twisted and she bit back her groan. Images of what her kidnapper could do to her whirled through her mind in full technicolor. *No, no, no.* There wasn't time to dwell on the what ifs, and it would only feed her fight-or-flight response. Dakota gritted her teeth as she tried to push up into a sitting position, but she couldn't move.

Above her were bright fluorescent lights that reminded her of the sixth-grade classroom she sat in when she was a kid. *Why the hell am I thinking of* that? Again, she cried out at the relentless pounding in her temples. A bitter taste permeated her mouth, and Dakota wished she had some water to quench the horrible thirst. She was able to turn her head enough to see she was in a large room with stairs off to the left side that led to a door.

A basement. She had to be tucked in a basement somewhere. That would explain the smell—rot and mildew mixed with earth and something harsh, more chemical. Damn, that still didn't explain why she couldn't move her arms. Dakota winced as she tilted her head up and she caught a glimpse of rope. A quick tug and nothing moved again. There was a slight burning down her arm, pins and needles that made her grit her teeth and try to pull even harder, which was pretty useless.

Her abductor had tied her down tight to some sort of anchor point in the floor.

That would explain why her arms and legs weren't obeying her brain—blood loss from being tied hand and foot to something behind and in front of her.

"You're awake." A male voice echoed throughout somewhere in the basement. Dakota couldn't see him, but the tone of his voice made her stomach sink like a stone as a chill twisted up her spine. She jackknifed forward as far as her bonds would let her move. "Now we can have some real fun. I'm not into somnophilia." Footsteps approached then the man who'd attacked her in the laundry room came into focus.

"Get the fuck away from me, asshole," Dakota said as she tried to writhe and yank herself out of the ropes binding her down. "Don't you dare touch me!"

"You don't have a fucking say in any of this, slut." The man's hollow laugh reverberated around the room and made her choke with fear.

Dakota started tugging on the tethers again when she saw movement in the corner of her eye. She turned her aching head and saw someone walking slowly in her direction. Fingers of ice started at the tip of her toes and worked their way up her spine when she realized it was Golden Retriever boy from the incident at Duffy's bar. He knelt down by her hip then bent over her so she could see his face: big grin and hollow, vacant eyes. His body heat pressed up tight against her waist, and Dakota tried to wiggle away but was unsuccessful.

"So, you do remember me? Good. I like that, baby."

Revulsion hollowed out her gut then seething anger followed as she flailed and wiggled in her restraints, trying to break free so she could claw his eyes out. Different scenarios went through her mind, but the one she homed in on was Cobra busting through the door, beating the shit out of the two creeps, then cuddling her in his arms as he walked up the stairs and took her out of this hell hole. *To safety. Oh ... Cobra.*

"What do you say, pretty girl?" Golden Retriever said against her ear.

"Fuck you." She spat at him and turned her head away.

At the very least, her loud noises might draw more attention to anyone else who was in the house. Maybe someone would take pity on her and stop this asshole from doing anything she would make sure he'd regret later. His hand hovered over her body as if he was deciding where to touch her first. Dakota continued to writhe like a hell cat, determined that if she fought hard enough, he wouldn't lay a hand on her at all.

His palm descended on her right breast through her tank top and he groaned with appreciation, kneading into her flesh. When he tweaked her nipple through her bra, Dakota thought she'd throw up. Her muscles ached, tiring quickly as he toyed with her breasts. How much longer would she be able to put up a fight before wearing herself out? It made more sense to bide her time in hopes that the fucker untied her to get a better angle and gave her the small chance of escape.

So Dakota squeezed her eyes shut, clenched her teeth, and pretended she was somewhere else.

His heavy palm connected with the side of her cheek and she gasped from the burning pain. She tasted blood where the inside of her mouth had scraped against her teeth. A painful cry slipped out of her lips despite her efforts to thwart it; the fucker was probably the type who got off on hurting a woman.

"You'll look at me, little slut. You hear me?"

"Yo, Sean! I told you not to go down there yet. Get your fuckin' ass up here. Now!" a nasally voice boomed from the top of the stairs. Heavy treads made the stairs off to her left creak and groan.

The asshole's mouth turned downward and his brows knitted as he glanced toward the staircase, but he didn't stop groping her—only slowed it down. He slid his fingers under the hem of her tank top and her flesh crawled.

"You better leave her the fuck alone," her abductor said.

"I'm going to get what I should've gotten back at Duffy's." Sean looked down at her. "Where's your fucking biker now? You sent him to kick our asses that day, so it's only fair that I take something he wants. Right, baby?"

"What the fuck did I tell you about touching her, asshole? That's not what she's here for right now, goddammit! Get the fuck upstairs." A heavy set, older man in a basketball jersey and sweats ambled into her line of sight and rubbed a hand over his thinning hair. "Shit! You hit her? What the fuck's wrong with you? I told you I need her intact to lure that fuckin' biker. Cobra's gonna see right away she's been smacked. Asshole!" The man punched Sean in the side of his head and he toppled over.

"She was mouthing off and trying to escape, Big Pat," the punk whined.

Big Pat looked over at Dakota's kidnapper. "Is that true, Chewy?"

The tall guy shook his head *no* then glanced back down at the phone in his hands.

Another punch to Sean's head, and Dakota couldn't help but smile inwardly.

Before the clean-cut asshole could say anything, Big Pat yanked him back by the collar and shoved him forward so that the punk lay sprawling on the concrete floor.

"I oughta shoot your ass. It's because of you and you fuckin' friend's bullshit that I have the Steel Devils on my ass in the first place. You're fuckin' dispensable, so you better do as I say or I'll make sure you just disappear. Now get the fuck upstairs!" Spittle flew out from the older man's mouth.

"What the fuck, Big Pat? Without me and my friends, you wouldn't even have a damn operation, and now you're acting all fucking *Godfather* on me? Give me a damn break. I was just playing around with the goods, wasn't nothing going to come of it."

"Bull fucking shit," Big Pat gritted and took a step toward Sean. The younger man scooted away and put up an arm as if to ward off a blow. "You've been a pain in my ass from the start, and you're more trouble than you're worth."

Dakota watched, her eyes glued to the scene playing out before her eyes. Big Pat cracked his knuckles, tilted his head to one side, and reached in the back of his sweatpants and pulled out a big ass hand gun. *Oh shit, he isn't—*

The shot rang out before Sean had any time to beg or say much of anything. Dakota saw the bullet hit him in the forehead and a spray of blood and brains burst from the back of his skull as his body landed with a thud on the floor.

A wave of nausea assaulted Dakota as thoughts kept stopping and starting. Her pulse pounded against her temples and she trembled over every inch of her body. Everything kept fading in and out as shock permeated her brain, but one realization broke through the clearing: she was a witness. There was no way Big Pat would allow her to ever testify against him. He's an idiot and she was a dead—

"You alive over there? You sound like you're hyperventilating." Big Pat gently kicked her leg and crouched down to eye level. "I need you to get your boyfriend on the phone and arrange a meeting."

Dakota swallowed and made a primal noise that was half-whimper, half-snarl.

Big Pat ran one ragged fingernail down the side of her face, scratching her. "Yep, that's just what you're gonna do if you want me to treat you good. And you do want that because I can be a mean SOB." He looked over at her attacker, who was still fussing with his phone. "Right, Chewy? This bitch better stay on my good side."

Chewy glanced up and his gaze skimmed over Dakota and he nodded. "Yeah, boss." He hung his head back down and stared at the phone.

Big Pat chuckled, but it wasn't jovial or lighthearted, it was downright sinister. "You're gonna get Cobra to come for you because he's the reason I'm in this fuckin' mess. I should add *you're* the reason all this shit started. You told him about the date rape drug, and he went snooping around, and now everything's a fuckin' mess. But it's not gonna be for long." The drug lord stood up, his hand still clutching the gun as he mock pointed it at the far side of the room and then checked the chamber. "You'll get him to meet you, and then we'll have everything nice and taken care of after our little chat."

"And if I don't?" Dakota asked through her teeth, her voice trembling as she fought to get out the defiant words. "You're going to kill me anyway, aren't you?"

Big Pat chuckled so his midsection jiggled, and he knelt back down, jamming the cold muzzle against her temple. Her whole body froze with a rush of dread. "Maybe … maybe not." His gaze brushed over her, lingering on her hips then her breasts. "There might be some hope for you … if I'm feeling generous. But the fastest way you can end up either dead or on the sex slave auction block is by fighting me. Choice is yours."

"I hear you," Dakota said in a soft voice. "How's Jake involved in all this?"

"He's my bitch. Jake's been on my payroll since he started working at the motel. He feeds me information and I give him what he needs to feel real good. He also does well enough that he can afford more trips to the strip bar and to his whores. Until recently, I'd been using the motel as a drop location, did some sweet deals there. But shit has been a little shadier since the Steel Devils got wind—thanks to your boyfriend, so I've had to keep my work on the down low. Which, let's be fuckin' honest, is a hassle and a half, don't you agree?" Big Pat pressed the gun even further into her temple with an appreciative noise, as if he was getting off on the mental picture. "Now, I'm going to give you until the count of three to make your choice on whether or not you're helping me out. I'm actually doing you a favor, baby girl. Cobra is one of the most vicious members of the MC, and if he tells you anything different, he's a lying sonofabitch who's trying to paint his truth to look a little more pussy friendly. He's a fuckin' hypocrite, and you can do so much better. Don't play the martyr for a cold bastard like him."

Dakota knew that Cobra wasn't the best man in the world. Sure he'd made mistakes like anyone else, but he wasn't who Big Pat said he was anymore. Maybe he had been a long time ago, but now, she knew his heart and knew *him*.

All of a sudden the card she'd found from Jenny didn't mean the same thing to her as it had earlier that morning before this nightmare had started. It was crazy that she was even thinking about all that now, especially with a gun to her head. But if it came down to her being dead in the next minute and a half, Dakota would go to her grave knowing that she trusted Cobra implicitly. In one moment of crystal clear clarity, she realized she *loved* him.

The very idea that Dakota had fallen in love with him over the course of their time together hit her over the head like a ton of bricks.

But it was so absolutely obvious. He was kind, generous, understanding, and sure, complicated as hell, which was the only way to describe his current lifestyle—but where it counted, he had been nothing but good. That trumped anything else this pig had to say about him.

"I'll make the call for you," Dakota said. Her muscles relaxed when Big Pat moved the gun away then rose to his feet.

"Smart decision."

The dirtbag didn't need to know her reason for agreeing to play into his hands. When she'd call Cobra he'd know something was up, and as soon as he realized who was holding her captive, all hell would break loose. There was one certainty that Dakota held close to her heart: Cobra would walk through fire to keep her safe, and he had a fuck ton of backup to help out.

Dakota may be inviting him into the lion's den, but Cobra could hold his own, and she had no doubt that his tactics would be as fatal as the fangs of the most venomous snake—the King Cobra.

CHAPTER TWENTY-FOUR

COBRA

COBRA PUSHED OPEN the motel room door and rushed in, tripping over his feet in his haste. His eyes darted around the room and landed on the unmade bed, and his gaze jumped to the bathroom door, but there wasn't any light under it. In several long strides, he was at the door, lightly knocking on it as he opened it. Nothing. Dakota wasn't in the room. Cobra dug out his cell phone and pressed the button to call the burner cell.

It kept ringing.

"Fuck." He stared at the screen until the call automatically disconnected.

Cobra tried again. Same result.

An icy feeling swept through all the small hairs on the back of his neck. He tried to shake the shroud of dread pushing down on him. A knot of muscles at the side of his jaw pulsed, and he tried calling her one more time. He put the phone on the table as his paranoia began kicking him in the ass. Dakota was in trouble. This wasn't about her being pissed at him or giving him some kind of drama. No, she wasn't answering her phone because she *couldn't*. Cobra hadn't heard from her since he'd left for work that morning. He wracked his brain trying to remember when he first tried to get a hold of her. It'd been around one in the afternoon. He'd taken off from work early to head over to Missoula to iron out the plans for torching Big Pat's warehouse.

She said she was gonna wash clothes. He marched over to the closet and noticed that some of his apparel was gone then he rushed over to the dresser and opened the drawers. A lot of them were empty, and he knew it sure as fuck didn't take hours to wash a few loads of clothes. Whatever had happened to her, she hadn't made it back from the laundry room.

Slamming the door behind him, Cobra hustled over to the laundry room. He pulled open the door and looked inside. Empty. His heart sank even though he didn't quite know what he was expecting to find. A part of him had hoped that Dakota had fallen and was just unable to get up, but the eerie silence in the room spooked the fuck out of him. He walked over to the washing machines and lifted the lids. The first one was empty but the second one still had clothes immersed in water. Cobra pulled out a T-shirt and a pair of shorts and his blood turned cold. The apprehension he'd been keeping at bay crashed through, leaving no room for suspicions anymore. Dakota had been kidnapped.

His head pounded like someone had just clobbered his skull with a tire iron. Cobra clenched his fists as rage burned through him like acid. "Fuck! Where are you, sweetheart?" Anguish tugged at his heart and pulled at his soul. How could he have been so reckless? He should've had a prospect watching her at all times. "Fuck!" He threw the clothes back into the machine then slammed down the lid.

After a few minutes, Cobra buried his emotions deep beneath the layers of detachment he'd built over the past twenty years. Cold, hard distance was needed to focus and find Dakota. Level-headedness was an asset, whereas feelings were lethal.

Scanning the room, his gaze landed on the corner of a card under one of the machines. Cobra bent down and picked up the card, staring at the familiar logo for Satin Dolls. He turned the card over. *Anytime, Jake. Ivory 40-28-36.*

Cobra bent and squeezed the card until it crumpled in his hand, then shoved it into his pocket. His hands curled into fists at his side as he stalked out of the room and up the stairs. The yellow neon Vacancy sign in the lobby window blinked sporadically. Jake sat behind the counter with his elbow on top of it, his head resting down into his hand when Cobra entered. The manager's head snapped up, and fear flashed across his face for a millisecond then he smiled a yellowed-toothy grin. The corner of his right eye was blood-red.

"What can I do for you?" His voice trembled slightly.

Without wasting any time, Cobra rushed toward the counter. Jake slid off the stool and tried to make a run for it, but the biker grabbed him by the neck. The manager gripped the outlaw's arm and tried to push it off him, but Cobra's grasp only tightened. He slammed Jake against the wall a few times, the shuddering sound resonated through the lobby.

"Where the fuck is she?" Cobra yelled as he gripped the man's throat.

"I don't know what you're talking about," Jake said, his eyes wild and pleading.

"Wrong fuckin' answer!" Cobra lashed out and landed a hard punch under the side of the manager's jaw. "Try again!"

"I don't know where she is. I swear." Clear fluid ran out of Jake's nose.

The next punch landed on the manager's ear. The third one right in the stomach. Jake sucked in air as he gasped and bowled over. Cobra yanked him upright by his hair then slammed him once again against the wall. He slipped his free hand into his cut and took out his fighting knife.

"I'm gonna ask you one more time then I'm gonna skin you alive before I cut your fuckin' throat." Cobra pushed the tip of the blade against Jake's cheek, pressing the skin inward until the flesh broke and blood oozed out. "Where the fuck is she?"

"Okay ... okay," Jake panted. "Put the knife down and I'll tell you."

Cobra pushed the blade in further. "You're not in any position to negotiate shit."

Tension crackled in the air between the two men.

"Okay. Big Pat's got her. I didn't wanna be a part of this shit, but he made me. I swear. He threatened me."

"I need a fuckin' address, and my patience is done." The knife went in deeper.

"5288 East Granite Street. It's his place—the big Victorian on the corner."

"When did he take her?"

"I dunno."

"Wrong answer, asshole." Cobra ran the knife across Jake's cheek, leaving a thin red line and dark trickles of blood running down the side of his neck.

"It … it was around noon."

"How many people are at the fucker's house?"

"Depends—five, sometimes more or less."

Cobra took the knife away and slipped it into the inside pocket of his cut. He yanked Jake away from the wall and dragged him toward the front door.

"Where're you taking me? You said that if I told you where she was you'd let me go."

"I don't remember that. The agreement was that I wouldn't skin you alive before I cut your throat." Cobra fished out the keys from the manager's shirt pocket then locked the door. "If you give me any trouble, I'll gut you like a fuckin' fish."

When they arrived at Cobra's room, he pushed Jake inside then locked the door. He threw the trembling manager on the bed before Cobra picked up his duffel bag and took out rope, zip locks, and duct tape.

"What're you gonna do?" Jake asked.

"Make sure you don't tip off the motherfucker." Cobra walked over to the bed.

Jake scrambled away and pressed his body close to the headboard. "I won't do that."

Cobra laughed dryly and grabbed the man's legs and yanked him to the edge of the bed. "Yeah, like I'm gonna believe you."

"You can. I swear."

He rolled Jake over, and trussed him up—arms, legs, hands, and feet bound together in a tight package.

"I can help you kill Big Pat," Jake said.

Cobra slapped a couple of strips of duct tape over his mouth then picked up the prisoner like a bag of potatoes and threw him down on the floor of the closet. He closed the door and put a chair under the knob for extra security then walked out into the night.

He took out his phone and tapped in Slinky's number.

"Yo, dude. Heard you guys kicked some fuckin' ass tonight."

"Yeah, but I got more shit to deal with. Big Pat's got my woman."

"Fuck."

"And I know where he's hiding her. We can take the fucker out and save my woman. I'm gonna need some backup on this one."

"Iron and Razor were telling me about what happened to your woman at Duffy's with those fuckin' punks. We've got your back, bro. When do you wanna roll?"

"Soon. Anyone still in Philipsburg or did they all head to Missoula?"

"Iron, Brute, and Breaker are still there. They're at the strip joint. I can get a few more brothers to come up and help out."

"Thanks for the offer, bro, but there isn't time. It'll take you at least an hour to get here. I'll connect with Breaker."

"We're with you in spirit, dude. Watch your back."

"Thanks."

Before Cobra could slide his phone back in his pocket, it rang. His heart pounded when he glanced at the screen—*Dakota*. He slid his thumb over the answer button and shoved the phone to his ear.

"Are you all right, sweetheart?"

"Cobra?"

"I'm here. What's going on, sweetheart?" He leaned against the outside wall and a shot of relief went down his spine. "What do you need? Do you need me to come get you?"

There was silence on the other end of the phone.

"Dakota?"

"I'm still here. I'm uh … I'm confused, about everything … about you and me … none of it makes any sense anymore." He heard a strange rustle in the background. "I need you to meet me."

Cobra wanted to tell her that he knew where she was, but he doubted that Dakota was calling him of her own free will. It was so fucking transparent that Big Pat was using her to lure him. *Damn amateurs.* "Sure. When?"

"Uh … tomorrow morning."

"You gonna be okay until then?"

"Yes. I'm staying with a friend."

"Okay. What time tomorrow?"

"Early, like at seven in the morning. Can you make it?"

"Yeah."

"Okay. So this is a for sure, because we *need* to meet at the park."

Dakota's voice sounded tinny and faraway, so he figured she may be on speaker phone. Cobra wanted to keep her on as long as possible so he could hear her voice.

"Okay, darlin', I'll come to the park like you want me to at seven in the morning. We can talk, and everything's gonna be just fine."

"I know." Dakota's quivering voice hit him square in the heart.

"We'll be back on track. Don't worry about anything."

"I won't," she whispered, and empathy thrummed through his veins.

"Is your friend there with you?"

"Uh-huh."

Cobra wanted to reach through the phone and pull her to him. He wanted to wrap his arms around her and keep her safe … forever.

"Can your friend hear you?"

"Not really. I know seven o'clock is early."

Good job, sweetheart—you're not on speaker phone but the bastard's with you. "I need you to listen to me. Be careful, don't piss off the fucker, and sit tight for me. I'm coming for you. You've gotta be strong for me. Can you do that, Dakota?"

"Of course." A small giggle.

That's my woman. "Good. Now you need to act like I bought this stupid phone call and tell the bastard that I'll be in the park tomorrow morning. But I'm coming for you. Just know that." His throat squeezed tight until his voice sounded like churning gravel. He nearly broke the cell, he was clutching it that hard. "I need you to be my strong, brave woman."

There was a muffled, strangled sob on the other end of the line. *Sonofabitch.* He was gonna rip off Big Pat's damn balls then tear out his fucking throat. A rage unlike anything he'd ever known consumed him.

"He hasn't …" Unable to say the words, not wanting to imagine the possibilities, he left the unsaid in the air between them hoping against hope that he wasn't too late.

"No, I'm okay." Dakota sniffled and whimpered. "Cobra, I love you—"

A wave of mixed emotions shot straight through him as whoever was with her must have ripped the phone away from her hand. He let out a long breath, swearing that each fucker who was in that house would pay for what they did to his woman.

Cobra still held the phone to his ear when it rang again.

"Dakota?"

"It's me," Breaker said. "Slinky called and said your woman's in trouble. Said that you know where we can find Big Fuck."

"Yeah. I got a plan how we can get into the fucker's house. Are you guys still at the strip club?"

"Yeah. I'm gonna reserve asking you when the fuck you got a woman until after we get her back."

Cobra smiled. "Agreed. I'll be over in twenty minutes."

"Just fill us in. We're ready to roll."

"Cool. Later." He stalked over to his bike, jumped on it, and switched on the engine then took a right out of the parking lot.

As Cobra rode over to Satin Dolls, guilt ate him alive from the inside out. If he had only had a prospect watching her. His instincts had gotten soft as shit since he'd gone nomad. Back in the day, he would've had a prospect on the job without even batting a fucking eye. Instead, Dakota was at risk, and he could've avoided it. Cobra slammed his fist on the handlebar and the bike swerved to the left. Wiping out wouldn't help Dakota. He shook his head, pushing his emotions away once again, and focused on the road.

Everything would be all right. It *had* to be.

CHAPTER TWENTY-FIVE

COBRA

COBRA PULLED UP into his usual space and looked up at the oversized red neon sign for the Satin Dolls Gentlemen's Club. The lot was pretty much filled, and he saw his brothers' bikes lined up on the southside of the building.

He turned off the engine and stared at the tan stucco exterior as a whippet of wind shifted through his cut. Thick clouds covered the night sky and in the not too far distance, Cobra heard the steady rumble of thunder. The scent of rain permeated the heavy air, and he hoped it wouldn't pour before they got to Big Pat's house.

He jumped off the Harley and walked inside the dimly lit club. Buckcherry's "Crazy Bitch" blared from the speakers as two naked women pranced around the stage, one of them wrapping her body around the pole. The scent of weed and strong booze curled around him and Cobra squinted as he looked for his friends.

"Hey, honey." Long fingernails scratched over his biceps. "It's been a while."

The strong smell of roses tickled his nostrils, and Cobra turned his head.

"Hey, Cheetah."

"Jenny's on her way. Can I get you a drink?" The woman leaned in close to him, her tits practically pressed against his chest.

Cobra stepped back. "A shot of Jack would be great."

"Will do." Cheetah brushed past him.

"Now, she's got a fine ass," Iron said.

Cobra glanced at the woman's swaying rounded globes and shrugged.

"Dude, you gotta admit, she's got some movement going there." Iron dragged his eyes to Cobra's.

"I guess. Where are Breaker and Brute?"

"Breaker's in the john, and Brute's getting a private dance with a real sweet number. He should be done real soon."

"Hiya, Cobra." Jenny gave his arm a squeeze.

"Jenny," he tugged her into a hug. "How've you been?"

"Okay. I was hoping you'd stop by."

He ran his hand over his face. "Yeah, sure. We should go somewhere private. I've got something I wanna ask you."

Jenny's eyes lit up. "Let's go to one of the rooms. I'll give you a special dance." She leaned in closer.

He gently pushed her away. "I got some business I wanna discuss with you. I don't have time for a dance."

"Here you go, honey," Cheetah said, handing Cobra his drink.

"Thanks." He placed a twenty on the tray. "Keep the change."

Iron snagged the woman's wrist. "I could use another drink, baby."

"You ready to go?" Jenny asked Cobra.

"Yeah." He turned to Iron. "I'll be back in a few. Sit tight."

"Have fun." Iron smacked him on the back.

Cobra weaved through the people and followed Jenny down a long hallway that smelled of many perfumes, cigars, and hair spray. He was familiar as hell with the club, and that's how he'd first met Jenny. For his taste, she was the prettiest dancer in the place, and after several private lap dances, Cobra had found that he enjoyed her company, so they'd hooked up for a while. It had been almost a year since he'd broken off their arrangement, but they remained friends, sometimes with benefits. Mostly, he'd been helping her out financially, since she was a single mother and stripping made her an easy target for lowlife scum, stalkers, and assholes who thought their money bought them more than a quick dance. Cobra knew that Jenny would jump at the chance to be back in a relationship with him, so he had to make sure he didn't give her the wrong impression.

"Here we go," she said, opening the door to the *Champagne Suite* room.

Cobra walked in and plopped down on the plush red couch and rubbed his palms down the legs of his jeans. All he could think about was Dakota and how time kept ticking away. He *had* to get to her.

"So how've you been, handsome?" Jenny flipped the lock then sashayed toward him. She wore a little pink plaid school uniform. She pulled down the tiny top and her huge tits popped out, the barbells in her nipples gleaming in the low light. "You look so tense, baby."

Before he could get a word out, Jenny crossed behind the couch and started rubbing his shoulders, her fake nails digging into the flesh of his back as he tried to process what he wanted to say while all the tension fell away from him.

"Jenny, it's good to see you …" He grunted and moaned, molding like clay into her professional hands. "Everything going okay here?"

"Aw, so my white knight really only came in for a business call?" Jenny pouted and he could hear the disappointment in her voice. Her fingers stopped massaging and she walked around the couch until she sat on the footstool across from him. "Everything's fine. I just miss you around here, handsome. You haven't stopped in for a while and I was getting worried."

"How's Abby?" he asked.

"Good. She's getting so big. You know she's almost six years old."

Cobra nodded. "You guys getting along okay? I mean, financially."

Jenny's head cocked to the side. "I don't want you to think that's the only reason—"

"I don't think anything. I know how tight things can be, and raising a daughter on your own can be real expensive."

"It's just that sometimes it's so damn dead in here, or the guys are so fuckin' cheap with the tips. I'm thinking of moving to Billings. I know a girl who makes more money in tips on a Tuesday night than I sometimes do on a Saturday. It's crazy."

"Yeah. You gotta do what you need to for you and Abby. I'll come by your place in a day or two to drop off some cash. I'd like to see Abby."

"She'd like that." Jenny reached over and squeezed his hand. "Thank you. I really do miss you."

He coughed and licked his lips, meeting her straight on stare.

"Do you want to have some fun? It's on the house, handsome." A flirty, secretive smile danced on her lips.

"Thanks, Jenny, but I've got a woman," Cobra said. "I just want to make sure you're doing okay."

Jenny looked down at the floor before glancing back at him, disappointment racing across her face. For a long moment, silence stretched between them, and then she put her hand on his knee. "You're really the sweetest, handsome." She lit up like a goddamn Christmas tree.

"No one's messing with you?" Cobra studied her to make sure she was giving him the whole truth up front.

"Everything's good. I swear." Jenny leaned in and kissed his cheek, slowly drawing back to look into his eyes. "If there's an issue at the club, Manny takes care of it, and if he doesn't then Randy does. It's all fine."

He narrowed his eyes and searched her delicate face. She grinned, flipping her long brunette hair from one shoulder to the other. "What's her name?"

"Dakota."

"I can tell she means a lot to you. Lucky girl." A small sigh escaped her lips. "Women know these things. Like right now you're trying your damnedest not to look below eye level, baby. And that means something big between you and me."

"Well ... yeah." Cobra shifted on the couch and sat back, folding his hands in his lap. "Am I keeping you from customers?"

"No, don't worry about it, baby. Catch me up on life."

"Another time. I got a favor to ask of you."

Her brown eyes sparkled. "I've been waiting a long time for you to ask me for something—ask away."

"My woman's in trouble and I gotta help her pronto. Do you know Big Pat?"

Jenny rolled her eyes. "All the girls know him. He comes in here several times a month. He's disgusting, but he tips real well. Yours truly is one of his favorites."

Cobra shook his head. "He ever hurt you?"

"No. We got call buttons in all the rooms, remember? Anyway, why are you asking about him, and what kind of trouble is your girl in?"

"He's holding her at his house, and I need a distraction so some of my friends and I can get in there."

"I've been to his place—the old Victorian mansion on Granite."

"Do you think you can go over there and say that Manny sent you as a gift to him? I'll have your back every step of the way. I just need you to occupy him until we get inside. I'll make sure nothing happens to you."

"Sure, I'll do it."

"Just kill some time, but I don't want you to think you gotta do shit with him. We'll be in before anything gets outta control."

"I trust you, baby. I can wear my room service outfit—he's got a thing for that."

"You sure you want to do this?"

"Hell, yeah. It sounds exciting, and with you and your buddies watching out for me, what have I got to lose?"

"We'll pay you for your missed hours at the club."

"It's on me. I'm just happy to finally be able to give back to you after all the times you've given to Abby and me."

"Thanks, babe."

Jenny crossed her arms over her breasts and shook her head. "I never thought I'd live to see the day that you fell in love. I have to say I wish it were with me."

With a non-committal grunt, Cobra stretched out his legs, crossing them at the ankles.

"You love her, idiot." Jenny tapped his knee and he narrowed his eyes. "You need to tell her. Women like to hear it—it's real important to us."

He dragged a hand down his face. *Fuck, Jenny makes it all seem so damn simple.* But maybe it was. Dakota's last words to him on the phone were that she loved him—simple and honest.

"Yeah, well, I'll deal with all that later. We gotta get going." Cobra pushed up from the couch. "Go get dressed and we'll meet you out back in five to go over the plans."

"Sure thing, baby."

He opened the door and Jenny scurried through it, then he ambled back into the main room to find his brothers.

I'm coming, sweetheart.

CHAPTER TWENTY-SIX

COBRA

The rain sprinkled over the men as they walked down the wet pavement. A cool, crisp breeze blew through the trees, and Cobra pulled up the collar of his leather jacket as the air rustled his hair and slipped around his neck.

Gnarled oak trees abounded in the neighborhood making them the perfect shield for the bikers as they waited for Jenny's arrival. The damp asphalt reflected the golden glow from the streetlights and the occasional appearance of the moon. The men crossed the street then stopped in their tracks in front of a fancy wrought iron gate in a gray stone wall. The house behind it was a large and imposing two-story Victorian, painted in mustard yellow with dark green trim. Grass and weeds grew between the cracks of the stone pathway leading up to the wide wrap-around porch, replete with ornamental spindles and brackets.

"This is it," Cobra said. "Jenny should be here soon."

"She gonna be able to let us know how many fuckers are in there?" Brute asked as he shoved his hands into his pockets.

"Yeah. She said she'll tell Big Fuck that she's got to let Manny know she got there." Cobra cupped his hands and blew into them.

"Does she know the asshole deals drugs?" Iron asked.

Cobra shook his head. "Nah. She's not into that scene. Jenny doesn't wanna know where some of the dancers get their stash. She always tells me that the less she knows the better. I gotta make sure nothing happens to her in there."

Cobra stared at the darkened windows and wondered which room Dakota was in. A few slivers of light filtered out from the sides of three windows on the main floor, but all the others were blackened. He stomped his feet in frustration: He needed to get inside, rescue Dakota, and punish the fuckers who'd taken her.

A low whine of a car drifted on the wind, and the four men quickly hid behind the large trees. The glow of headlights brightened the street as it approached, and the SUV drove past then parked halfway down the block.

"Jenny," Cobra said as he pushed away from the tree and started walking toward the parked vehicle. "I'll be back in a few."

As he walked past the other guys, he saw Iron light up a joint, and Cobra wished he'd have brought a couple along with him.

When he approached the SUV, he heard the click of the door unlocking. Cobra slid inside and smiled at Jenny, who reached over and gave him a quick hug. The scent of jasmine perfume curled around him, and he turned in his seat to face her.

"You're sure you're still okay with this? It could get dicey in there. You need to get out as soon as we give you the signal." Cobra put his hand on hers and looked down the street at the mansion on the corner. "You can back out."

"No, no." Jenny shook her head. "I'm here and I'm staying, handsome. I'll keep him occupied for as long as possible while you do what you need to do to get your girl."

Her small, hopeful smile made a dent in his apprehension. "If you can't text me the number of fuckers in the house, no worries. I don't want you taking unnecessary chances."

"Okay. If you don't get a text after a few minutes of me going inside then just listen until you hear the music and do what you need to do. I'll be careful—I promise."

Cobra inhaled deeply and blew out a long, steady breath. "I really appreciate this."

She bought his hand to her lips and kissed it. "I know."

He stared through the rain-slicked windshield at the Victorian. Between the dismal rain and overcast sky, the house gave off an ominous vibe. He glanced back at Jenny. "You ready to do this?"

She placed both hands on the steering wheel and nodded.

"Be careful," Cobra said as he exited the car.

He shoved his hands in his jacket pockets and bolted back to the oak tree.

"All good?" Brute asked.

"Yeah," Cobra replied. "I'm guessing this arrogant sonofabitch doesn't have much security."

Breaker pulled out his suppressor-ready Glock 17. "I'll be ready for whatever Big Fuck's got."

"You got a silencer gun?" Iron asked Cobra. He shook his head, and Iron reached into his jacket pocket and pulled out a Berretta M9A3. "Here you go. No sense in alerting the neighbors."

Cobra gripped the gun and lifted his chin. "Time to roll."

"I bet the asshole doesn't even know his operations are fuckin' toast," Brute said as they crossed the street.

"Just a matter of time before he gets the call. The wail of sirens broke the fuckin' sound barrier," Cobra said, and the men chuckled.

The bikers went from behind, several houses over, so that they crept as a unit from backyard to backyard; their boots barely made a sound through the soaked grass. They stuck to the shadows, ducking and weaving against the other houses' siding until they were in the back, pressed against the wood.

A few seconds later, the SUV pulled over to the curb in front of the house. Adrenaline pumped through Cobra as he watched Jenny close the car door and walk slowly up the pathway to the front porch. The way she teetered a bit on the wet pavement told him she was wearing her five inch stripper heels.

Cobra and Breaker moved quietly until they huddled beneath one of the windows near the porch, keeping to the darkness. When Jenny pressed the doorbell, Cobra heard the jingle shudder through the whole house. The front door jerked open and honey-colored light from the foyer spilled onto the porch, illuminating her. Jenny's brunette hair shone with raindrops and she wore a thick pink faux fur parka. Two guys came outside, their voices too muffled for Cobra to make out what they were saying, but he heard Jenny, clear as day, ask for Big Pat, saying the club owner had sent her as a gift since Big Pat had been such a good customer lately.

The two men walked back inside, and in less than a few seconds an older, heavy set man stood in the doorway, a large grin plastered on his face. Cobra recognized him as the dude he'd seen with Jake the night Dakota had gone for a swim.

The sound of Jenny's laughter pierced the quietness of the neighborhood. It sounded high-pitched, like a child's gleeful warble. Cobra darted his eyes around the area, but all was as it had been since they'd arrived. Jenny disappeared into the house, and the door closed, shutting out the light.

"She's in," Cobra whispered as he pressed closer to the wall. "Let's go around back."

Cobra and Breaker joined Iron and Brute and silence descended over the group until Cobra's phone pinged. He looked down and opened the text.

Jenny: *There r 4 in the house. Includes Big Pat. I'm good. Deleting this now.*

"Only four fuckers to put down," Cobra said, slipping the phone in his jeans back pocket.

"This is too damn easy—we're gonna get spoiled," Breaker said, and the men sniggered.

Cobra squinted in the rain, watching the street, and a few minutes later he heard the heavy bass growl of one of Jenny's favorite songs to strip to at the club. *The signal.*

There was no time like the present. Cobra glanced back at his friends, and Brute gave him a shit-eating grin.

Cobra nodded. "Showtime. Let the bodies hit the floor."

He made a quick motion with one hand, knowing the others would be right behind him. They crept up toward the back door, and Breaker took out a skeleton key and tried the lock. Nothing. He then took out a plastic card and slid it into the crack of the door where the lock was. After a few seconds, he turned the knob and the door opened. The men shuffled in to what looked like an enclosed back porch. Cobra walked over to a second door, and his eyes widened when it opened freely.

"Fuckin' dumbasses," he muttered under his breath then walked into the kitchen.

The hard hitting beats of "Pour Some Sugar on Me" blared through the house, and Cobra followed the music from one room to the next until he stopped short. In front of him was what looked like the living room, and he could see Jenny getting her swerve on all over Big Pat. She'd turned off all the lights in the room except for a low table lamp that only provided a little bit of mood lighting. Perfect for a quick sneak in and out.

Cobra walked backward a few paces then turned around and went back to the kitchen. "Jenny's doing her thing with the fucker."

"I can secure the rooms upstairs," Iron said.

"No, stand watch at this door," Cobra pointed to a green painted wood door. "I'm guessing it goes to the basement."

"I can help you go through the rooms on this floor or watch the staircase leading to the second floor," Brute said.

"Yeah, you do that, and Breaker and I will sweep through this floor."

The men took their positions, and Cobra and Breaker divided, each of them taking half of the first floor. Each time Cobra opened a door, his body perked up in anticipation of finding Dakota, but then disappointment wound through him when the room was empty. *Where are you, sweetheart?* At that moment, he didn't want to entertain the idea that Big Pat may have moved her to another location, so he just kept going on his quest to find his woman.

Through the wall of one of the rooms Cobra was in, he heard a small crash and a very human grunt. He rushed away and walked into a bedroom and saw Breaker holding a pillow over someone's face.

"You need help?" Cobra asked in a low voice as he watched the downed man's legs twitch and move.

Breaker shook his head. "Got this one. Now we only got three fuckers to deal with."

"We're almost done on this floor. I'm gonna go see Big Fuck and persuade him to tell me where the fuck Dakota is." Cobra rolled his neck then left the room. If Dakota wasn't somewhere on the property, he'd find out where she was then he'd nuke the damn place with everyone inside it. A purge of fire.

Cobra didn't hesitate, he stalked through the rooms back to the one where he'd seen Jenny and the old pervert. When he approached the living room, Big Pat sat on a plush ottoman with his back to Cobra. Jenny's tits were in the asshole's face as she wiggled and gyrated like a gymnast. Cobra dropped to his belly and slithered silently across the room until he was right behind Big Pat.

"Come on over here, slut. Let me touch your tits," the perv said thickly.

"In a minute, baby. I just want to get you all hot and excited," she said.

"You already have. Now get your fuckin' naked ass over here."

The moment Big Pat reached out his hand, Cobra struck. He yanked out his bowie knife, grabbed Big Pat by a hunk of his greasy hair, and shoved the blade against his throat. The pig gave a little squeal, his exhale like a giant puff of air with no sound. His fingers scrambled out in front of him. But there was nothing he could do and no one he could call when Jenny shifted back and threw her short black dress back on over her head.

"Thanks, babe." Cobra nodded toward the door. "I'll call you."

Jenny nodded, grabbed her bag, and scurried out of the room. Cobra waited until he heard the solid thump of the front door closing and the sound of the car's engine.

"I have money in my pockets," Big Pat said.

"I don't want your fuckin' money," Cobra said as he pressed the knife harder against the man's skin.

"Who are you?"

"Your seven a.m. appointment. I always like getting to places early." Cobra felt the asshole's throat move as he swallowed. "Yeah, now you know who the fuck I am."

"What do you want?" the perv whispered.

"You know *exactly* what the fuck I want, you sick sonofabitch. You're gonna tell me where you're keeping my woman."

"What's in it for me?"

"Dying a fast death or a long, tortuous one. You know, we can keep a guy alive for a few weeks before his body can't take it anymore. We're good at that … but I'm the expert." He nicked a piece of flesh on the man's throat.

Big Pat yelped. "I'll tell you where she is, and I'll go away and set up shop somewhere else. Far away. You can have the money and all the drugs I have at my warehouse. You're welcome to it all."

"You fuckin' used up your chances with us, motherfucker," Breaker said as he walked into the room. "You were warned in Lolo to stop dealing in Steel Devils' territory."

"And now you've set up shop here, and you kidnapped my woman. Pretty fuckin' stupid, asshole." Cobra cut the sniveling jerk again.

Big Pat gurgled and twisted on the ottoman. Cobra pushed the knife deeper into the man's flesh and he quickly went still, his large torso wrenching up and down with panicked breaths.

"You know, breaking in here is so fuckin' boring," Cobra said, and Breaker laughed. "This is a two-bit, sorry excuse for an operation you're running, and I should fuckin' gut you right now, but today's your lucky day, asshole."

Big Pat didn't say a word. Cobra spun the big oaf around and shifted the knife from the man's neck to right above his balls, the tip pointing down into the crotch of his pants.

"For the last time, tell me where you're keeping my woman."

"Oh fuck, man, I don't know what you're talking about. I don't fucking have her." Big Pat's voice went up and down, spewing out lies like a junkie trying to score his next hit. "It was all those fuckin' frat boys' idea. The ones who messed with her in the first place at Duffy's. I never accepted that. They were fuckin' pissed she got away, so they took her, and when I found out I reamed into 'em good, made 'em see the light. I don't know what they did with her though. I told them to let her go, and if they didn't, they'd have to answer to me. I'm just gettin' my shit together. Gettin' ready to get outta town, just like your club wanted me to. I swear, I fuckin' swear to you."

"Funny," Cobra growled, digging the knife in even harder so that he felt it pierce the guy's pants through the fabric. "I don't see any fuckin' moving boxes. Do you?"

"Uh, no, I …" Big Pat said, and Cobra could just picture the idiot's little brain running out of oxygen in his panic.

"Second floor's clear." Brute walked into the living room then shrugged. "You need me to do anything else?"

"Check for Dakota and come right back as soon as you find her." Cobra glanced over at Breaker. "I got this, dude. You can help Iron and Brute—we got two more assholes unaccounted for."

"You got it." Breaker followed Brute out of the room.

"You're running out of time to talk, asshole. If they come back with my woman's location, this isn't going to end well for you."

Big Pat made a noise in the back of his throat and Cobra saw his

Adam's apple bob.

"If you were going to do anything," the man puffed, wheezing out the last few words. "You'd have done it."

"I found her, brother." Iron's voice caught Cobra's attention and his head jerked up toward the foyer. "She's tied up in the basement. You want me to do the honors?"

"Fuck," Cobra mumbled under his breath. "No, don't touch her yet. She's been through enough and I don't want anyone who's a stranger going near her until I finish with this fucker. Were the other two there?"

"Yeah—Brute and Breaker are dealin' with 'em now."

Cobra licked his lips, hating the idea of leaving his baby tied up in the basement, uncomfortable and terrified while she waited for him. He breathed out a slow breath then jammed his free hand around the back of Big Pat's beefy neck.

"You piece of shit!" Cobra yelled as he threw the man halfway across the room.

Big Pat landed against a lampstand before sprawling into a heap as the lamp crashed on top of him. Before the asshole could draw a breath to say anything else, Cobra buried the steel toe of his boots into the jerk's ribcage again and again and again.

"What the fuck did you do to her?" Cobra yelled, delivering a kick to a different part of the loser's body with every word. "Fuckin' tell me. Now!"

"Okay, please," Big Pat sniveled. He was curled up on the ground like a little damn pussy as he tried to protect himself.

Fucking pathetic. "I don't stop until you tell me what the fuck you did to her."

"I gave her a dose of GHB to keep her quiet—that was it. Nothing else. I swear I never fuckin' touched a hair on her head, and I didn't let the others guys mess with her."

"This may be a surprise, but I don't fuckin' believe you." Cobra yanked the asshole's head back and spit in his face, racking his bowie knife so it cut through the man and grazed enough of his chest to draw blood.

"Goddammit, I swear. No offense, but your chick's not my type. I love big tits, and hers are too small, and her hips are—"

Cobra grabbed the bastard by the hair and rammed his fist repeatedly into Big Pat's face until blood covered his knuckles. The guy's head lulled in Cobra's hold, his neck like jelly.

"I didn't touch her," Big Pat moaned, his eyes rolling into the back of his head.

"I'm done with this shit," Cobra growled.

"Let me at him," Iron said. "You go get your woman. I've been wanting to waste this bastard since Lolo."

Cobra nodded and gave Big Pat one final kick. Iron whistled as he strolled over to Big Pat who was bleeding on the richly patterned Karastan rug as if this was any ordinary weekday night.

Cobra sheathed his blade and didn't waste time running to the basement door and bolting down the stairs to Dakota.

"Fuck," Cobra said as his gaze fell on his beautiful woman lying on the concrete floor against the far wall. "I'm so sorry, sweetheart. I'm so fuckin' sorry this happened to you."

For a second, all he could do was stand there and look at the terror etched across her face even as she slept in a drugged coma. His eyes skimmed over her: her tank top was pulled up on one side, she was barefoot, her arms and legs were swollen as hell. Cobra rushed over to her and started cutting at the ropes.

It wasn't until he had her arms free that he saw the corpse stuffed in the corner perpendicular to Dakota. It was the asshole who'd assaulted her at Duffy's. The hole in the middle of his forehead pleased Cobra to no end. He turned away and worked on cutting away the restraints around her legs.

Cobra's heart physically hurt to watch her squirm and wiggle out of his hold even in her sleep. Dakota was thirty shades of gone to the world and she was still trying to get away from who she thought might be her attackers. When he traced a slow hand down her cheek, she moaned and turned away.

"Goddammit!" Cobra closed his eyes and took a breath, not willing to pick her up until she knew she wasn't in any more danger. "Sweetheart, can you hear me? Do you hear me? It's Cobra. I'm here. I came for you just like I said I would. You're safe now, and nothing's gonna hurt you again. I'm taking you home now."

He whispered the words into her ear, and she must've heard and understood something because Dakota groaned back at him, her fingers spasming against her shorts. Good enough for him. They had to get out of there before someone called the badges. Cobra took a deep breath and shifted so that his arm went under her butt and another under her shoulders, lifting her up from the floor.

Dakota sank into his arms, small and weighing barely nothing, as her head curled into his chest and he kissed the top of it.

"Yes, that's it, sweetheart. I'm here—I've got you."

Cobra carefully climbed the stairs, every move forward making him feel as if he were slogging through mud as his head cleared from the shit that had gone down that night.

"You good?" Iron eased up to him looking down at Dakota in Cobra's arms.

"I need to take her away from here. You take care of that fucker?"

"Yep."

"You gonna get rid of the bodies?"

"That's the plan. I'll go get the truck then you can make her comfortable in the back cab while Brute, Breaker, and I wrap the bodies in tarp. We'll get rid of them on the drive back to Missoula." They'd come in the truck that the club parked at Gary's house. He was an old dude who used to be an active member of the MC but retired for health reasons a few years before.

Cobra turned around when he heard footfalls on the steps behind him. Breaker and Brute walked into the kitchen.

"Everyone's accounted for," Breaker said. "Big Fuck helped us out by offing one of his own." The men chuckled.

"I knew he had to be good for something," Brute said.

"You guys leave any of your blood?" Breaker asked Cobra and Iron.

"Nope. I offed the Big Fuck with a couple of bullets through the head," Iron replied.

"I already looked at my gloves—no cuts, so I'm good." Cobra pressed Dakota closer to him.

"Let me go get the truck. You just worry about your woman—we got this, bro." Iron slipped out the back door.

Soon they were all packed up in the cab, and the tightly wrapped bodies lay in the bed of the truck. The rain had stopped, and the streets were dark and quiet as they put distance between them and the Victorian.

It wasn't until Cobra was arranging Dakota's head in his lap that he remembered Jake in the closet back at the motel.

"The douchebag responsible for snitching to Big Fuck about Dakota's whereabouts is locked in the closet."

"Well shit, man, you kept a plaything for me? You shouldn't have. How fucking thoughtful of you." Iron smiled in the rearview mirror. "I'll take care of him and he won't be a problem, got it?"

"Sure."

True to his word, when Iron pulled into the motel's lot and shut off the engine, he and Brute walked straight into Cobra's room with a key he'd given them. No less than a minute later, Iron hauled the asshole manager into the back of his pickup, his hands and feet still bound together. Clearly, he was out like a light.

"Did he give you trouble?" Cobra asked.

"Didn't have a chance. Just knocked him in the head, and we'll take care of him when we get outta town," Brute answered.

"It felt good having you back on the team, brother," Iron said as he helped Cobra out of the cab.

"Same here." Cobra laughed wryly, shaking his head as he cradled Dakota to his heart. "Hold the door for me?"

"Sure," Brute said.

Cobra placed her gently on the bed and pushed a lock of blonde hair back from her eyes. Even in her sleep, drugged out of her mind, she still looked beautiful.

"That one means a lot to you, doesn't she?" Brute cleared his throat and stuck his hands in his pockets, rocking back on his heels.

"You have no idea, bro." Cobra sighed and couldn't tear his eyes away from her, swearing to himself he'd never let her out of his sight again.

"I hope you know what you're getting into here."

Cobra looked at him out of the corner of his eye before all his attention went back to Dakota.

"Man, I have no fuckin' clue. But as long as she's beside me, I'm good with not knowing shit, you get me?"

"Nah, dude." Brute laughed softly. "I don't fuckin' get it. I'm lovin' the single life too much, but I'm glad you're happy. Just let me know when she's gonna be your ol' lady, and we'll throw you a killer party."

Cobra grinned ear to ear at the idea of Dakota being his old lady—of her being *his*—period. Nothing in all his years had ever felt so right. Damn, so much bullshit had happened in his life, and if someone had told him this was the direction it was heading, he would've thought they were off their fucking rocker. *Never expected this, but it's fuckin' good. Yeah.*

"I'll let you know," Cobra said, his gaze still on Dakota.

"You think you'll ever come back full-time? We miss you—the club needs you."

He scrubbed the side of his face and turned to look at Brute. "Not sure I'll be full-time again, especially now with Dakota in my life. Grinder and the rest of the club know they can count on me if I'm in the area."

"You proved that tonight. You're the one who found out that Big Fuck was dealin' on our turf."

"Anytime, bro." Cobra gripped Brute's shoulder. "I'm always just a phone call away."

"We should get going," Breaker said as he walked into the room. "Give us your keys, dude, and I'll ride your bike back here. Then we gotta take off."

"I can get it later," Cobra said.

Breaker tilted his head toward Dakota. "You gotta take care of your woman."

Cobra nodded and tossed the keys to him. "Thanks, bro."

Breaker lifted his chin and ambled out of the room with Brute following behind him.

Cobra dragged a chair over to the bed then plopped down in it. He clasped one of Dakota's small hands in his own and kissed the back of it, closing his eyes and praying for the first time since he was a kid that she'd open her brown eyes and call him a stupid motherfucker for being so damn late in saving her ass.

CHAPTER TWENTY-SEVEN

DAKOTA

PUSHING HER WAY through a curtain of cobwebs, Dakota couldn't grasp what had happened. The only thing that seemed real was the searing pain in her head. Through the discomfort, she was becoming aware of a sound coming from somewhere in the depths of the blackness shrouding her. Voices, maybe? As hard as she tried to focus, Dakota couldn't hold on to a thought for more than a few seconds. And as she struggled to gather them, a hand caressed her cheek. She swallowed hard and tried to scream. No sound came out; her mouth and throat were dry as leaves in the winter. She needed water badly.

"Sweetheart, can you hear me?"

The voice sounded muffled and distant, as if it were echoing from the end of a long tunnel.

"It's okay—I'm here, darlin'." Another stroke against her cheek.

Cobra? Dakota gathered what strength she could muster and attempted to open her eyes. After several tries, they finally flickered open. Shapes formed in her line of sight, and then, as the drug-induced fog that had enveloped her brain began to lift, her gaze landed on him. Cobra's brows were knitted from worry, but his eyes shone with adoration, the color reminding her of the forest after it rains.

He leaned over and kissed her gently on the lips. "I was so fuckin' worried about you." Relief washed over his face as he kissed her again. "Do you want anything?"

Her arm felt as though it weighed a thousand pounds as Dakota lifted it and put it over his shoulder. "I need some water." Her voice sounded like a foghorn.

Cobra leapt to his feet and went over to the cooler and pulled out a bottle of water. "Do you want some aspirin or Tylenol?"

"Aspirin's good." Her throat felt like sandpaper, and when he came back with a glass of water, she curled her fingers around it and drank deeply.

"Let me get you some more," he said, taking the empty bottle from her. "I'm glad you finally opened your eyes, sweetheart."

"Everything's so fuzzy, but I'm starting to remember what happened. That fucking manager arranged all this. What's his name? Dammit ... I can't remember—my mind's a wall." She took another water bottle from him, closed her palm around the two white pills, then put them in her mouth and swallowed.

"The motherfucker's name's Jake."

"That's right." Dakota struggled to sit up and Cobra was by her side in less than a second, stuffing pillows behind her as he settled her against the headboard cushioned in a cloud of softness. She groaned and lifted her hand to her aching head. "Why the hell did he do that?"

"Don't try to figure it out, darlin'. He was a fuckin' bastard."

"*Was?*" Dakota's hand fell into her lap.

Cobra darted his eyes away then brought them back to hers. "I set him straight. He's not working here anymore, so you don't have to worry about him."

"But he's still a bastard."

He laughed then went over and sat on the bed next to her. "Yeah, the fucker's still a bastard."

"Why did that Big Pat guy want to hurt you?" The images from her ordeal were now coming back in full force.

Cobra shrugged. "Lotta guys got a problem with me. It goes with the territory of being in an outlaw club. Don't think about it. The important thing is that you're okay. You are, aren't you?"

"Yeah. I was pretty scared, but Big Pat wouldn't let anybody mess with me. Strange, huh? I mean, he's the one who was behind the kidnapping." Dakota shuddered and brought her knees up. "I still can't figure it out." She reached out and grasped Cobra's hand in hers. "Through the whole thing, I just knew you'd come for me."

Cobra pivoted and tugged her to him, embracing her tightly. "Fuck yeah, darlin'. I'll always have your back."

And Dakota believed it. Gone were any of her concerns that Cobra wasn't into their relationship as much as she was, and when he sealed his mouth to hers and gave her a kiss that trumped all other kisses in her life, she fought back the tears of happiness that threatened. His kiss was passionate, tender, and filled with yearning, and Dakota knew exactly where she stood with him the second Cobra pulled back from her and she saw his eyes brimming with emotion.

He turned away and cleared his throat.

Dakota laughed weakly, nearly coughing up a lung in the process. He jumped and patted her gently on the back as the fit subsided. It seemed strange after everything she'd been through, but she couldn't keep a smile off her face.

"Fuck. I don't think you're okay." Cobra made small, smooth circles with his palm on her back. His gaze seemed to survey her body from head to toe and back again, several times, as if searching for some kind of possible injury he could've missed in his assessment. "Do you need anything?"

"Really, I'm okay," Dakota managed to wrestle out from her scratchy throat. "Nothing hurts too bad. The drug is definitely starting to wear off. How long have I been out?"

She did a mental assessment of her body and realized that was mostly the truth. Where she'd been tied still burned, her muscles twitching with a dull, bone-deep ache, but that was nothing compared to what Cobra must have done to the sick and twisted fuckers who had taken her in the first place.

"All night and most of this morning."

"Wow. What happened last night at that house?"

"You sure you want to know the answer to that, sweetheart? You've been through a lot and you probably need to rest—"

"Cobra, I can handle it. Tell me."

Concern wavered behind his eyes as he took a deep breath and put his elbows on his thighs then clasped his hands under his chin.

"A few of my buddies and I went to rescue you."

"I know *that*, but how did you know where I was, and what happened to the guys who were in the house?" All of a sudden the image of Sean, bleeding with a hole in his head assaulted her. "Oh, fuck! I saw that old guy kill one of the guys who messed with me at the bar. The guy killed him right in front of me." She shivered. "It was awful. There was so much blood." Dakota's voice quivered.

Cobra scooted by her side in an instant, wrapping his arm around her shoulder. He held her securely to him, her face pressed to his chest. "I know, sweetheart. That must've been a horrible thing for you to see," he said.

"It was. The old guy got so mad at Sean for trying to touch me." Dakota felt Cobra stiffen, and a low growl sounded in the back of his throat.

"Did the fucker mess with you?" he whispered.

"He wanted to, but Big Pat got pissed. They exchanged words and then the old dude shot him."

"Sounds like Big Fuck did you a favor."

Dakota snuggled closer against him. "Yeah. So what happened to him?"

"Big Pat?"

"Yeah." Dakota knew Cobra was evading her questions about what had happened. All of a sudden, she wasn't too sure if she really wanted to know what had transpired in the house that night. *Maybe it's better to let it go.*

"Iron found you while I was talking to Big Pat. Iron kept an eye on things while I came downstairs and got you." Cobra swallowed so hard she could see the constriction in his throat. He swiped his palms down his jeans brought his lips to her right temple and kissed it. "Could you hear me while I was talking to you?"

"I think so. I heard something." She licked her dry lips and shifted on the bed, wincing from the pull of her weak, tired muscles. "So … what happened to Big Pat?"

"He won't bother you anymore."

That was all Cobra said on the subject. She had a damn good idea what he meant. Dakota had decided that she didn't want the details, but a strong sense of knowing that justice had been served washed over her.

"You went through something terrible so you might have nightmares for a while, but I'll be here. I'll always be here," he said.

Shock made her whole body numb for a beat while Dakota processed his words. *Always. He'll* always *be here.* That was a pretty big and important word to be throwing around, especially since Cobra was a nomad, and he hadn't yet told her how he felt about her. But as he stroked her hair, gently whispering "You'll always be safe with me" into her ear, she knew he meant it.

Then the images of her ordeal came stalking across her peace of mind. Apprehension grabbed her. As if sensing her disquiet, Cobra held her tighter, his hand reaching for hers.

"Oh shit. Am I going to have to testify at some kind of trial?" A shiver of fear made Dakota's teeth chatter and she nestled even harder into Cobra.

"No, darlin'. Don't even worry about it. Scum like those assholes never make it to trial. You won't have to think or worry about any of them again."

"Okay." She relaxed against him.

"We need to get out of here, sweetheart."

Dakota lifted her head, though it felt like a million pounds worth of effort.

"Leave? Why? Do we have to go on the run or something?"

"No." Cobra chuckled and tweaked the tip of her nose then brushed his lips across her forehead, making her knees go weak even though she was sitting down completely supported by him. "We're leaving this fuckin' shithole. You deserve better than to be here. I'm gonna get us a room in a good hotel—room service, mints on the fuckin' pillows, a mountain view ... the works. Does that sound good?"

"I can't afford anything—"

"You really think I'm such a dick that I'd make you pay for your own room? Everything's on me. You stay here and relax, and I'll pack our bags and pay the bill for this dump."

Considering Cobra was wearing his "don't argue" face, Dakota didn't bother pointing out her second thought, which was an insult to injury. She wondered if he made enough to afford such a nice room in the first place and if he did, why the hell had they been slumming it in this joint for so long?

"I can read your mind, you know." Cobra looked across the room from where he was stuffing his shit into a duffel bag. "I didn't stay anywhere worth a damn because it didn't matter to me. Having you in my life reminds me that there's more to life than the rough times."

A tingling heat spread across her chest and neck and she averted her gaze from him to the twisted sheets. Dakota was still trying to understand how everything that she'd ever wanted was now falling into her lap. At that moment, it seemed as if fate had finally cut her a break.

"Although, wherever we stay, wherever we go, you're never going out unarmed again. I'm gonna teach you how to shoot a gun, and then I'm getting you one."

"But—" Dakota sputtered then stopped when he held up his hand.

"At the *very* least, I'm getting you a fuckin' knife that's ten times bigger than the pocketknife you carry."

"Yes, sir," she said, slanting her hand against her forehead in a mock salute.

Cobra winked and pursed his lips, feigning a kiss in her direction. Dakota giggled. She'd never seen this playful side to him. In her joviality, she gathered her courage and cocked her head to the side. Ever since she'd found the business card from the gentlemen's club with the note from a woman named Jenny, she'd wondered about it.

Dakota straightened the sheet at her waist then crumpled the edge of it into a wrinkled ball. "Tell me about Satin Dolls." She fidgeted with the bed covers as she hung onto her surety that the man who'd saved her from that basement was the same man who wouldn't cheat on her with another woman. "I found Jenny's card and … I called the club."

Cobra went stock still, and she saw the muscles in his jaw tense as he stared at her. Well … damn, that wasn't a good reaction. Dakota held her breath, bracing herself for the worst. *Whatever happens, it's going to be okay. I'll figure out my life even if it's without him.* But God, she hoped it wasn't without him.

"She's a friend." Cobra's voice broke through her thoughts. He rubbed his chin and sat on the edge of their bed. "I've known her for quite a while. We used to be more than that—I'd shack up with her and Abby—that's her daughter, when I'd be in town. It wasn't anything too serious, at least not on my part. But it's been over a year now that we've just been friends."

"Have you had sex with her since you all just became friends?" Dakota shook her head. "No, don't answer that. I don't have the right to ask you that."

Cobra pressed his lips together. "Yeah, you do. We've slept together on and off during the past year, but I haven't been with her in a few months."

"So what was that card about?"

Cobra shrugged. "I've probably had it for a while. Jenny's always giving me cards, reminding me to call her when I come through. Now, I help her out if I'm in town and if shit goes down in the club. And when she needs cash. She's a single mother and things get tough. Abby's dad's a deadbeat and doesn't pay anything." He shrugged again. "I try to be there when she needs me."

"Life can be so hard. I can't imagine having to raise a kid all on your own. It's nice of you to help her and her daughter out."

His eyes bored into hers. "Don't think for one fuckin' minute that I fucked her while I was with you. There's no damn way I would've done that. I don't roll that way. Anyway, I wanted to be with you."

"So you haven't seen her since I've been staying with you?"

Dakota searched his serious face and his gaze never left hers. Cobra held out his hand.

"I've never lied to you, darlin', and I'm not gonna start now. I went by the club to talk to her and tell her I'd help her out. Nothing happened, and nothing will ever happen. I told her about you—that I got a woman."

She looked down at his open palm and blinked before she scanned his face looking for any trace of a lie or a gussied up half-truth. But there was nothing. Cobra had always been straight with her and to the point, and there was no reason to think he was lying now. Her mouth pressed tightly together as she stretched out her hand and clasped his.

"Thanks, darlin'." His words were soft, and his whole body seemed to exhale the second she touched him.

That was when Dakota knew he was telling her the truth.

"You know you could've told me about her. I kinda felt ambushed and hurt."

"I'm fuckin' sorry for that, but I never meant to hurt you. There's nothing going on with Jenny and me, so it didn't occur to me to bring her up." He brought her hand to his lips and kissed her knuckles. "Relationships aren't really my thing. Haven't been for a long ass time. I'd never intentionally hurt you."

Dakota tried to ignore her pounding heart, her racing blood, the growing heat and tingling between her legs.

"So do you know other strippers who might come between us later on?" she quipped, pinching his hand so he knew she was screwing with him.

"No, I don't." He slightly smirked. "But if it happens again, feel free to cut me up after the weapons training I'm going to give you. Deal?"

"Deal." A big smile spread across her face.

Cobra pushed up from the bed and went over to their bags and zipped them up. "I'm gonna close out then we'll take off. You think you can ride on the back of my bike?"

"With you as my support, I can do anything," she replied.

He stared intently at her then strode across the room. With a growl, he bent over her and crushed his mouth to hers. Her lips burned with the fierceness of his passion as he buried his fingers into her hair.

"Cobra," she murmured against his mouth as she pressed closer to him, breathing in his familiar scent.

"I'm fuckin' crazy about you, darlin'." His hand trailed over her shoulder and down her bare arm. He gently nipped her lips then kissed her neck. "You're so beautiful," he whispered in her ear.

"I'm so fucking crazy about you," she murmured.

His lips made a trail upward over her chin and to the side of her mouth. Dakota shivered in his arms, and she didn't want him to stop. The way her skin heated from his touch made her hunger for more.

"That feels good," Dakota said.

His mouth covered hers, and Cobra kissed her again, longer and deeper this time, the palm of his hand cupping the back of her neck. Then he pulled away and looked into her eyes.

"I want you, but I understand that you may not be ready."

A slight smile ghosted her lips and she relaxed into him. Dakota felt safe and warm with him, as though nothing could touch her as long as she was in his arms. Painful memories had become the staple in her life for too long. There was nothing she wanted more than to erase them from her mind and focus on being happy with Cobra.

"I don't want to let the bad stuff define who I am or what I can do. I'm not a victim. Inner strength is what has gotten me through some of the dark moments of my life. I want to be with you—that's it."

Cobra cupped her face between his hands and kissed her tenderly. When he pulled away, Dakota could see the desire brewing behind his smoldering look. A surge of excitement coursed through her.

"I want you real bad, but I don't want us to do anything in this dump. Let me pay up then we'll be off."

"I'll go with you."

He nodded then took her hand in his and they walked out of the room into the early afternoon heat.

LOCATED IN THE heart of Philipsburg, the Crestwood Hotel was an elegant yet cozy inn, which offered modern comfort in a historic building that dated back to 1885. Large pots of greens, vintage furniture, Native American rugs, and a distressed limestone fireplace decorated the lobby. Chandelier-like iron fixtures adorned the ceilings and an artisan mural depicting the history of Montana wrapped around the room. A few guests sat in large, cushy chairs, their heads buried in books, which lent to the causal and unhurried atmosphere.

"This is beautiful," Dakota whispered as Cobra waited for their room key. "I've never stayed at a place as nice as this."

"Only the best for you." Cobra winked and took the keycard from the front-desk clerk.

When they entered the room, the sweeping view of the Sapphire Mountains greeted them, and she rushed over and threw the French doors open then stepped out on the balcony.

"We got some fruit here," Cobra said from behind her.

She looked over her shoulder and saw him holding a wicker basket filled with pears, apples, bananas, and oranges.

"Looks good," she said then turned back to the spectacular view.

Dakota smiled when she heard footsteps and smelled the scent of his cologne and leather, a sensual blend that caused her pulse to race and sent sparks sizzling through her veins.

"You like it here?" Cobra said. His warm breath fanned over her shoulder.

"Very much," she replied softly.

"My sweet Dakota," he said in a low, gravelly voice as he pulled her against him, burying his head in the crook of her neck.

She moved her hand to cover his. "Thanks for everything—I really mean that."

"You're welcome, sweetheart." He nibbled at her ear.

Dakota giggled, pleasure trickling through her at his touch.

Cobra held her tighter for a long moment, then he buried his face in her hair and kissed the tender skin behind her ear. Her head fell back and she melted deeper into him as he continued from her neck to her collarbone.

A soft moan broke from Dakota's lips—it felt so good. She closed her eyes and let the sensations take over. All of a sudden Dakota felt her world shift and her lids snapped open when she realized he'd lifted her in his arms. With a sigh, she flung one of her arms around his neck and nestled her head on his shoulder.

They passed the two plush chairs, the sleek ceramic top dresser, the flat-screen television, and the glass-and-metal writing desk before Cobra lay her down on the fluffy, soft covers of the king-size bed. Bending over, he caught her mouth and kissed her deeply then pulled back to look at her.

Dakota stretched out her arms and reached for him, but he stared intently at her until his gaze slipped from her face and roamed over her body, lingering along the way. She swallowed and folded her hands on her stomach, pressing hard to keep the butterflies from bursting out.

Cobra kept his eyes on her as he slipped out of his cut and lifted his T-shirt over his head. The ink on his skin moved like a sea of colorful waves, mesmerizing her, and she was unable to look away.

"I'm surprised you don't have more tats on you. Most tattoo artists I know are covered in ink," he said as he kicked off his boots then unbuckled his belt.

"I'd like to get some more. I'm working on some real cool designs," she said, her gaze still fixed on the moving art all over his body.

"The bracelet of roses around your left ankle looks great, and I can guess what the shattered heart on the inside of your wrist is about, but why don't you tell me?"

"It's a reminder that love can hurt and break you in two," she replied.

"Still think that?"

Dakota stared as he pushed his black boxer briefs down his legs. When he straightened, his dick was thick and erect. "No … I don't," she said softly.

The mattress jiggled as Cobra climbed into the bed, and a rush of desire burned through her body. "That's good." He poked the side of her leg with his hardness then inched his hand over her shoulder and down over her breast, squeezing it lightly. "Do you feel how fuckin' hard you make me, darlin'? And just from that." His fingers brushed over her nipple and she gasped.

Cobra's mouth followed his hand, running his lips along the swells of her breast, where her skin met her tank top.

A rush of sensation shuddered through her. "Shit," she muttered.

"You like that?" he asked, sitting up.

"Yeah," she whispered.

Cobra slowly eased her top up until her belly was exposed then he leaned down and peppered kisses all over it before swirling his tongue inside her navel, making her stomach muscles quiver. Then he tugged her tank over her breasts and she pulled up a bit as he lifted it over her head.

"Fuck, you're gorgeous."

Cobra traced a finger down her throat to the tops of her breasts, and she clutched the edge of the bed covers. "So beautiful," he murmured, lightly brushing his digit over the thin fabric of her bra.

Small nips, feathery kisses, light flicks of the tongue. Cobra teased her over and over—languidly and deliciously, and when he slid the straps of her bra down her arms, Dakota cried out, her body a trembling mess of excitement.

"Cobra," she muttered. The heat in his dark green eyes connected with something feral, something wild inside her. "Please," she whispered.

He stroked her breasts in circles, grazing her nipples with each stroke until she thought she was going to lose her damn mind. When he pinched them both at the same time, she nearly shot off the bed.

"So responsive, sweetheart."

Then he was on her, sucking her stiff buds deep into his mouth, and she bucked from the sheer pleasure of it, nearly exploding right then and there.

"So fucking good," she groaned, burying her fingers in his hair and holding him close to her.

His hardness pushed into her thighs, the throbbing between her legs intensifying, and she shifted then rocked into the long length of him. With his teeth and tongue playing with her nipples, and his dick now pressing against her pulsing, damp core, Dakota was close to losing it.

As if sensing that, Cobra skimmed one of his hands down past her stomach until he reached the button on the front of her shorts. He popped it open, lowered the zipper then teased the smooth triangle of exposed skin. Releasing her nipple, he pulled back then slid his finger inside her.

"Fuck," she rasped, tugging on his hair. He pushed in another finger and curled the two of them and stroked. "Oh ... *damn!*" she cried out while clenching around him. Heat flared out from her core and spread to the rest of her body, and the steady pressure of his thumb on her clit was beyond fantastic.

Dakota clutched at him, desperate to have him inside her, to have them fused together as one in their lovemaking. Cobra bent down and captured her mouth, plunging his tongue in deep then matched it with the rhythm of his fingers thrusting in and out of her.

She placed both hands on his face and pushed him away. "I want to feel you inside me. I *need* that." The wild-eyed look she gave him must have hit home because he withdrew his digits then reached down and grabbed his jeans and fished through the pockets.

Dakota gripped his arm and stopped his hurried movements. "I'm clean and on the pill." She tugged him back to her.

"I'm clean too—do you trust that?"

"Fuck, Cobra, we're so beyond that. Of course I trust you."

"That's all I wanted to hear." Again his digits slipped inside her.

Her legs trembled. "Please," she whispered.

"Fuck, darlin', I like the sound of that. You're close to coming, aren't you?"

"Yes," she rasped.

"Try and hold it. It'll be better if you do, trust me." His low voice stroked her, making every inch of her skin tingle.

"I'll try but ... I just want you inside me."

Cobra held her gaze as he sat back on his knees. He slid his fingers out and lifted them to his mouth and slowly licked off her juices. Dakota couldn't breathe as she watched his movements, transfixed. He was so incredibly sexy, wonderful, loving, and ... well ... just *everything*.

Running his hands up her body, he squeezed her breasts and tweaked her nipples while he dipped his head down and bit her bottom lip, licking and teasing her with his tongue.

The tension that had been coiling tighter and tighter in her depths was at its breaking point. "I don't think I can hold out any longer," she moaned.

He pulled away and cool air replaced the heat from his body. Still staring at her, he lifted her legs and placed one on each of his shoulders then leaned into her.

"You do shit to me no woman has ever done, sweetheart."

The head of his cock pressed against her slick entrance, and she gasped.

"You look so fuckin' beautiful with your nipples tight and red from my mouth, your tits already showing my love bites, and … fuck, darlin' … your lips are all swollen and parted from my kisses. Fuck … just *fuck*!"

His words hit her from the tips of her taut buds to her soaked pussy, and before she could react, he plunged into her so hard that it took her breath away. She bunched the edges of the duvet in her hands as he thrust in and out of her.

"So damn good," he panted.

Cobra grasped her hips and shifted her so that when he surged deep and withdrew he hit her g-spot, which sent streaks of fire racing to every cell in her body. Her head thrashed back and forth on the pillow, and Dakota cried out as a rumbling groan burst from deep in Cobra's chest.

Suddenly, there she was, together with him and shooting over the edge of sanity. Gasping. Holding on to each other. Crying out their mutual release. At that moment, she felt a sense of union as if they were one body, one heart, one soul. The depth of it overwhelmed her, and she closed her eyes as the tears seeped out.

Cobra collapsed on top of her and his heavy breathing soothed her. She slipped her legs from his shoulders then wrapped her arms around him.

"Fuck, Dakota," he said in a low voice.

Afraid he'd hear the tears in her voice, she just kissed the side of his head. After a long while, he raised himself on one elbow and looked down at her. She wanted to shout "I love you" but bit her inner cheek instead. Cobra hadn't said the words to her, and he hadn't mentioned anything after she'd told him that on the phone the night before. The last thing Dakota wanted was to rock the boat with him, but it would be wonderful if he felt the same way about her as she did about him.

"What're you thinking?" Cobra asked as he traced the tip of his finger over the line across her forehead.

"That we're good together," she replied.

A warm smile spread over his lips as his eyes bored into hers. "We are." He brushed his thumb under the bottom of her lip. "You sure you're okay?"

She cuddled closer into him then bobbed her head. "Yeah. I'd be a damn mess if I were alone, but with you … I don't know … it's just real good."

"I know what you mean."

Dakota inhaled then let it out as she gathered up her courage. She pulled away a bit from him and started playing with his free hand. "Uh … what I told you on the phone about—"

Cobra placed his finger over her lips, silencing her. "We're on the same page. I love you too, sweetheart."

She looked up and met his gaze. "Really?"

"Really. Shit, I'm as surprised as you are. I never thought I could fall in love. What the fuck do you know?" He chuckled then swept his lips over hers.

"I never thought I could find a man who wouldn't try and control me. I always thought that's just what men do—they hurt a woman and try to break her spirit. Then I met you."

Cobra smoothed down her hair with his palm. "For me, women were only for pleasure or passing time. In the back of my mind I never trusted any of them, so I never gave anyone a chance, until you. I don't know what it is, darlin', but you slipped into my heart and my mind, and there's no fuckin' way I'm letting you out."

"I don't want to get out—*ever.*" *He loves me! I've never had a man tell me that. They always took from me.* Dakota kissed his hand. "Why do you love me?"

"You're an amazing, strong, smart, and resilient woman, and as a side note, you've got the sexiest ass I've ever seen." Cobra laughed and fondled her naked butt with a grin. "What's there not to love about you? You bring out the good shit that's been buried pretty damn deep inside me. You make me feel like there's hope and that I want to share my life with you. You're the best part of me, Dakota."

Her mind went blank at the same time that her heart swelled tight in her chest. The way she saw it: Cobra's love was a beautiful and wonderful gift—the best gift in the world. His love would iron out the bumps in her past and pave the way for a smoother and healthier future.

"What's going on in there?" Cobra tapped her skull with the side of his finger and kissed her forehead. "Do I need to retract everything so you don't run out of the room screaming? You started it."

Dakota laughed then smiled at him. "I was just thinking how lucky I am to have met you. It has to be fate. I mean, I just picked this town with my eyes closed and my finger hovering over a damn map. And then there you were, and my life has changed in ways I never thought could be possible. I didn't think what we have together existed at all. I just love you so much." Her lips trembled and she buried her face in the covers.

"It exists, darlin'. I love you too." With two fingers under her chin, Cobra tilted her head back. "You got any questions you wanna ask me?"

Her forehead screwed up in a frown and Dakota clenched her teeth, unsure if either of them should tread down this path. Once they started talking about it, they couldn't leave it alone, because it defined everything.

"What, uh, what are you going to do about the club? About being a nomad? The lifestyle ..." She paused, allowing his brain to fill in her questions.

"Yeah." Cobra drew her closer to him and stared over her shoulder. "The brothers want me to come back and be part of the club again on a full-time basis. And I know you got your job."

"None of those work with being a nomad," Dakota said softly, swallowing past the sudden tightness in her throat. "And love doesn't just change life or reality. It's fantastic, but it's not magic."

"Hey, none of that fuckin' pessimistic shit from you, got it?" He smiled and kissed her lightly on the lips. "Your love is worth everything to me—you need to know that. If we need to switch things up to make it work, then that's what the fuck we'll do. As long as we're together, we can figure it out. One thing you should know is that I'm not planning on going back full-time in the club."

She widened her eyes. "Is it because of me?"

"Nah. I made that decision when I went nomad. I like being able to help the club out when needed and see my brothers when I'm in the area, or at Sturgis. Going back full-time isn't for me anymore."

Dakota cupped the back of his neck and tugged him to her, and then she kissed him, long and hard, and with enough passion to set the bed on fire. "I'm not obsessed with my job. It's just another tattoo shop. There are thousands of them around the country."

"A nomad lifestyle is so fuckin' freeing, but it can be hard too. I just wanna make sure you know what you're getting into."

"We can talk about it some more, but I'm pretty sure I'm good with it. I can't see you settling down in one place with a nine to five job."

"Yeah, that would fuckin' suck, but I'm not against putting down some roots as long as there are still months spent on the road." Cobra raked his fingers through her hair. "We still gotta talk about it, but we got time. I planned on staying in town until the weather changed. The landscaping gig pays pretty well."

"The shop's not too bad either. I seem to be getting more referrals, which means I get a small commission on those clients."

He nodded. "We got time. As long as I can keep you safe and not like—"

"No, we're not talking about *that* anymore, Cobra. You have to know it wasn't your fault."

"If I had—"

"No," Dakota put her finger over his mouth. "It's over and I'm okay. You didn't do anything. I won't listen. You saved me." She kissed him on the chin. "End of story."

Cobra grunted and inclined his head forward just as her stomach growled. A smile broke across his face, softening all its hard angles. Dakota rolled off the bed and padded over to the fruit basket and rummaged through it.

"Strawberries! I didn't see those in there." She grabbed two then walked over and climbed onto the bed. Dakota bit into the fruit. Intense flavor exploded over her tongue. "That's so sweet and delicious. Try one." She brought it to his mouth and he bit into it, sending juices slipping down her fingers and wrist while she giggled and drew it back, popping the rest into her mouth.

"You're feisty." Cobra cocked his head.

"Blame the sugar high." She laughed then leaned toward him. He pulled her close and kissed her, the berry sweetness in his mouth mingling with her own sugary taste.

"Is that the only reason?" he said against her lips.

"And the ultimate high of loving you." She pulled away a bit. "I'm starving."

Cobra laughed and scooted back until he leaned up against the headboard. "You wanna go out?"

"No way. I want to order room service then cuddle next to you while we watch an action film. Remember—it's your choice since you watched two romantic comedies in a row."

"That sounds like a great plan. The menu's on the desk."

Dakota sprinted from the bed and snatched the menu then sat next to him while they perused the selections.

"Whatcha going to have?" she asked, her stomach growling again.

Cobra chuckled. "A burger, medium rare, and fries should do it."

"That's all?"

"Yeah, but order what you want."

"Okay. Let's see … nachos." She glanced at him. "We can share."

"That's it?"

"Not on your life. Chili cheese fries, a BLT with extra bacon, a dinner salad with blue cheese dressing, and a brownie." Dakota closed the menu. "That should do it."

Cobra had the biggest grin on his face as he reached for the telephone. "Where the fuck are you gonna put all of that?" Happiness danced in his green eyes.

"In my stomach," she joked and lightly punched his arm. "Anyway, we can share then keep the leftovers in the mini fridge in case we get hungry later."

Grabbing one of her arms, he yanked her to him and kissed her hard. "You're such a kook, but that's another reason I love you."

Warmth spread through her and she snuggled next to him as he cleared his throat then gave their order over the phone.

CHAPTER TWENTY-EIGHT

COBRA

Three weeks later
Boise, Idaho

COBRA PULLED HIS trucker hat down a little lower and his jaw clenched tight. This was the second night he'd staked out the swanky bar on the corner of West Broad Street. The intel he'd received from Razor reported that his target—Taylor Rubal—hung out at Cooper Lounge at least three or four times a week. Razor had called Cobra a few weeks ago and told him the fucker had moved from Idaho Falls to Boise. The asshole had taken an IT job with a big salary and lived in a pricey apartment building in a nice part of town.

Cobra had spent several of his days off trailing his prey, and he quickly found out that the overpriced apartment complex had a slew of security cameras that were fake as fuck. Relying on the cheapness of landlords always made Cobra's jobs easier. From his surveillance over the past two weeks, he knew Taylor rarely went out with friends, but seemed to usually take a chick home with him after the bar closed on Friday and Saturday nights, but never on the weeknights. That was the reason Cobra sat in Breaker's truck on that Wednesday night waiting for the perfect time to strike and devour his prey.

He poured another cup of coffee from the thermos and checked the time on his burner phone: 12:30 a.m. Taylor always left the bar before closing on weeknights. Cobra made a quick phone call to Breaker, who was waiting in Iron's pickup near the fucker's apartment. Breaker confirmed that they were ready to roll at Cobra's signal.

Cobra put the phone in the cup holder and leaned back against the seat. When Razor had told him he'd found the fucker who'd raped his woman, Cobra had wanted to jump on his bike and rush to Boise and beat the shit out of the asshole, but he held back, knowing that acting out of emotion led to dire consequences. He'd learned that when he'd come to the defense of Sharie years before in Vegas. That mistake had landed him in the fucking pen. So he waited, making the long trips to Boise to track his target's every move, all the while keeping the rage that consumed him in check. He told himself over and over that the time would come to unleash the fury, and ... the time had finally arrived.

When Breaker had reached out and told Cobra that he was going to help him out, Cobra had balked because his mission was personal, not club business. But Breaker wouldn't hear of it, and soon Iron, Brute, and Pee Wee joined Breaker in their quest to right a wrong that had been committed against one of their brothers' women. *That* was what the brotherhood was all about.

And when Cobra had asked Grinder if he could spare a prospect from time to time to watch his woman while he was on surveillance, Grinder hadn't even hesitated. Yeah ... his family always had his back. Loyalty, respect, and honor would *always* be the bond between him and his brothers, and he was a Steel Devil *forever*.

The buzz of the burner phone broke through his thoughts and Cobra brought it to his ear.

"Yo, just checking in to say your woman's good."

"Thanks, dude."

"I'll check in again in another hour."

"Later."

Cobra let out a long breath of relief and fixed his gaze at the front door of the bar. Dakota didn't know anything except he was on club business. Perhaps he'd tell her one day what he did to the man who'd taken away her innocence and fucked her up, but that would only be if the nightmares continued. Since they'd declared their love for one another, Dakota seemed calmer, happier, and less restless.

A burst of loud voices and laughter spilled from the bar as Taylor pushed open the door and walked out. Cobra watched him as he shoved his hands in the pockets of his pants and ambled down the street to a cobalt blue Mustang with bold white stripes painted on the hood, roof, and trunk. The minute the lights flashed on and the jerk opened the door, Cobra picked up the phone and called Breaker as he drove away. Both Breaker and Iron were inside the underground garage waiting for the target to pull into his parking space. Cobra found that it was easy as hell to slip into the garage when a car drove through the opened gates. Brute stood sentry on the inside, next to a pad that manually activated the opening. Cobra had instructed him that when Brute saw him approach, he was to open up the barrier so Cobra could gain access into the area.

He parked the truck just under a large tree with drooping branches, which provided a perfect cover for it in the shadows. Cobra's all-black attire helped him blend into the night as he jogged over to the garage. The mechanical clanking of the gate pierced the silence for a moment as he slipped in. He lifted his chin to Brute then rushed over to Taylor's parking space. Breaker and Iron bumped fists with him as they took their positions behind the thick and wide concrete columns around the fucker's location. Cobra hid behind the one right next to the asshole's assigned spot. The pillar had blue paint smeared on it, and Cobra figured the jerk had scraped it when he'd come home drunk. He'd witnessed the fucker driving drunk on several occasions during the past two weeks.

Adrenaline pumped through him when he saw the glare of headlights from the approaching Mustang. Music filtered through the half open windows, and Cobra saw Taylor's fingers flicking to the rhythm of the song as he swung a left and pulled into the spot. Cobra's body tensed as he reached in his waistband and pulled out his Glock 9mm.

The fucker turned off the engine and rolled up the window then got out of the car. The clang of his keys hitting the concrete ground bounced off the walls. Cobra slipped out from behind the column and silently walked over to the unsuspecting target. When Taylor straightened up, Cobra clipped him good and hard with the butt of his gun. The asshole groaned then crumpled to the floor.

Iron and Breaker strode over and in less than two minutes, they had the asshole tied up in the passenger's seat of the Mustang. Cobra threw the car keys up in the air and caught them in his hand.

"In case we get separated, you know where we're going," Cobra said as he opened the driver's door.

"Yeah," Breaker said.

They wanted to get out of the garage as fast as possible. Breaker and Iron slipped into the back seats and Cobra drove out to the street and dropped them off at the truck he'd parked under the large tree. Pee Wee and Brute were already in the other pickup, ready to go.

The curbside maple trees whispered in the summery breeze, and moths fluttered under the streetlights. The neighboring complexes were as quiet as their windows were dark. No dogs barked. No one walked the empty streets. The truck door closing and the low rumble of the Mustang's engine were the only sounds breaking the silence.

Cobra took a quick left down a dark street, and soon he and the others were out of the city heading to the mountains. They'd found a spot deep in the wilderness the week before, and if everything went according to plan, Cobra should be back in Philipsburg by noon, and the others would be in Missoula paying a visit to T-Roy's chop shop to get some money for Taylor's snazzy blue Mustang.

The sportscar drove up the winding mountain road, and the rear tires slid a bit as Cobra took the curves a little too fast. A low moan came from Taylor, and from the corner of his eyes, Cobra could see the asswipe shift in his seat then pull at the ropes.

"What the fuck's going on?" Taylor slowly straightened up and, as he looked over, Cobra could see his eyes were wide with fear. Another tug at the restraints.

Cobra clenched his jaw and turned his gaze back to the road.

"Who are you?" he asked.

Cobra glanced over for a moment, then a grim smile flickered across his face. "I'm the fuckin' angel of retribution."

Taylor's shoulders slumped, his face grew ashen, and his chin tucked down to his chest. "I think you have me mixed up with someone else. I don't know you, and I'm not involved in anything illegal. You have the wrong person."

Cobra gripped the steering wheel until his whitened knuckles ached. "Last I heard, rape's illegal."

"Rape?" His head snapped up then he shook it vigorously. "Yeah, you got the wrong guy. I never raped a woman. I never had to."

The damn fucker had the audacity to chuckle. Rage burned in Cobra's chest, spreading, growing hotter. He held the steering wheel even tighter, feeling like he could break it in two beneath his hands.

"You've got to be talking about someone else … I don't know you." The asshole's strained voice sliced through Cobra's anger, pushing his emotions back down deep inside, where they belonged.

"Dakota Krueger has a different take on what you did to her." Cobra's words were even and calm.

"Dakota? Did she tell you *that*? She lied to you, man. I don't know why, but she's always spread fucking lies about me. We were just kids doing kid shit together, nothing serious or anything, and she's always held it against me that I ended up dating another girl." Taylor struggled to pivot toward Cobra. "You know how it is, right? It was just kid stuff. I bet you messed around with a lot of women too."

"Don't fuckin' act like you know me. I never raped a woman. You did, and you're gonna pay for it. You can't do that shit and fuck up Dakota's life like you did and just walk away. I won't fuckin' let you."

Beads of sweat popped on Taylor's forehead, and it gave Cobra an immense amount of satisfaction. Before the night was over, the fucker would be drenched.

"Did Dakota pay you? I can give you more money. I make a lot at my job and—"

"Shut the fuck up!" Cobra punched the side of Taylor's face. "Dakota doesn't even know I'm here. We're done talking."

The jerk's head hung down, and they drove the rest of the way in silence. Cobra pulled off the main road and down a narrow one to the right until he stopped the vehicle and exited it. He stalked over to the passenger side, pulled open the door, and yanked Taylor out. A small pained noise came from the back of his throat.

"Please. I didn't do anything. I won't tell anyone about this."

Cobra punched him in the stomach and he bowled over. "I thought I told you to shut the fuck up. You don't listen too good, and that's why you're in this clusterfuck. Shoulda listened when Dakota told you to stop."

"Does she want me to apologize to her? I will. I can call her right now and tell her I didn't mean to hurt her. I swear I thought she was cool with it, but I'm willing to tell her I'm sorry."

Two sets of headlights lit up the darkness as the trucks pulled in behind the Mustang.

Taylor staggered backward his eyes wild and darting. He began to run away as if he realized for the first time that his death was imminent.

"You want me to get the fucker?" Breaker asked as he cracked his knuckles.

"Yeah—I'm sick of the piece of shit," Cobra answered.

The men waited in a circle, arms folded across their chests as Breaker walked slowly toward the man who'd just tripped over a fallen branch.

"I'm gonna switch out the plates on the Mustang while we're waiting," Pee Wee said.

"T-Roy's anxious to see it. We're gonna make some good money on this one," Iron said as he watched Pee Wee bend down by the vehicle.

"That's good." Cobra watched as Breaker grabbed the asshole by the back of the neck.

"No!" Taylor yelled.

"He gonna be missed?" Brute asked.

Cobra shrugged. "It's a new job in a new city and he doesn't have too many friends yet. I figure in a day or two, but we'll be long gone."

"We'll crush the burners at the junkyard. You gonna give us yours?" Iron asked Cobra.

"Yeah. I'll just check in with Skaggs to make sure my woman's good then it's all yours. I can't wait to get back on my bike—I fuckin' hate cages."

"I know what you mean," Iron replied. "Your baby's in the bed, all ready to go once we're done with this shit."

"It'll take a while for the fucker to be found. Lots of mountain lions in these parts," Brute said. "Don't think we need to clean up too much." He chuckled.

"All done," Pee Wee said as he joined the group.

"I swear I didn't mean to hurt her. I know she wouldn't want you to hurt me. I'm her brother's best friend, for fuck's sake." Taylor's voice echoed desperation and fear.

"Gag the motherfucker," Cobra gritted.

Pee Wee pulled out a roll of duct tape, tore off a piece, and slapped it across a struggling Taylor's mouth.

"The asshole just doesn't know when to shut the fuck up." Cobra drew forward until he was right next to the fucker's ear. "You're nothing but a pathetic piece of shit who preys on women. Well, that's gonna stop right here and now."

Cobra pushed Taylor to the ground, and the man tried to scramble away across the dirt when Breaker yanked him back by the hair.

"Hold him down." Moonlight glinted off the knife's blade as Cobra pulled it from his pocket. "Strip the fucker from the waist down then pin down his arms and legs."

Tears streamed down Taylor's cheeks as he tried to use his body weight to fend off the bikers, but it was futile. His body trembled and was covered in sweat, and Cobra thought the asshole would pass out before the biker even got started.

Cobra drew close then bent down on his knees, and with the knife in his hand, he ran the tip of the blade over the terrified man's cock.

"This is for Dakota, asshole."

CHAPTER TWENTY-NINE

DAKOTA

Two weeks later
Philipsburg, Montana

DAKOTA HUMMED AS she rummaged through the picnic basket she'd bought at the Dollar Store the day before. Several maple and birch trees provided ample shade in the small park located near the center of town. Wooden benches, a small pond, and a couple of dirt paths around the edges of the park made up the space. The east corner had a swing set, a slide, and a jungle gym for the children. Flower beds lent color to the expanse of grass.

A light breeze tousled her hair, and threads of sunlight filtering through the canopy of treetops warmed her skin. Dakota pulled out a bottle of water, twisted open the cap, and took a sip. She stretched out her legs in front of her and leaned back on her hands. It had been years since she'd gone on a picnic. When Dakota was a young girl, her family had gone on picnics at least once or twice a week during the short summer months, and she'd loved it. That had all changed after the day Taylor had raped her.

Dakota tilted her head back, welcoming the sun's rays on her face. At one time—not that very long ago, that day had been her constant companion, but since Cobra had come into her life, she thought less and less of it. *I've finally let it go.* It felt life-affirming and freeing to throw off the chains of the past, and her loving relationship with Cobra was the key that set her free. Never would she have imagined that one day she'd trust her heart and her life to a man.

Dakota had asked Cobra to meet her, and she'd bought his favorite sandwich—an Italian sub with extra pepperoni, salami, and hot peppers—a six-pack of Pabst Blue Ribbon, a jar of pimento stuffed green olives, and a bag of Doritos Fiery Habanero chips. Her honey loved it hot and spicy, and she tried to give it to him with food and in the bedroom. A thread of desire ran through her as she remembered how much fun they'd had that morning before they had to leave for work. A rush of heat spread through her as her heart swelled. Now that Cobra was in her life, Dakota couldn't imagine him not being there.

"Hey, sweetheart." His voice tingled over her.

Dakota straightened up and smiled. "Hey."

Cobra plopped down beside her on the blanket then leaned over and kissed her. "Have you been waiting long?"

"Not really. Did you get tied up at work?"

"Yeah. Jim was a no show, so that only left three of us to do a shitload of yards. Glad it's Friday." He glanced at the basket. "You got some beer in there?"

Giggling, she nodded and pulled out a can then handed it to him. "Drink fast because I bought a cheapo basket and it's not insulated."

"I can manage getting through the six pack before any of them get warm." He took a long gulp.

"I brought sandwiches too. Are you hungry?"

"Not yet."

Cobra pulled her to him and kissed her again. She slipped her tongue into his mouth, tasting beer and mint. "You taste good," she said against his lips.

"So do you, darlin'—all over. Fuck, I could taste you all day."

"Sounds like a plan for this weekend." Just then her stomach growled. "Shit," she muttered under her breath.

Cobra chuckled then flipped open the lid of the picnic basket. "Let's see what you got in here."

"An Italian sub for you from Ghinelli's Deli, and a sausage and pepper sub for me with extra provolone, of course."

He tweaked the tip of her nose. "You're so fuckin' cute." He pulled out one of the sandwiches wrapped in a red and white checkerboard pattern. "Is this yours?"

"Yeah—the green one is yours." Dakota undid the paper then dug into her sub. "So good," she said under her breath. She pulled out a small bag of Cheetos and the jar of olives.

"Watching you eat is making me hungry." Cobra took out his sandwich and unwrapped it.

"Did you used to go on picnics when you were a kid?" she asked, skewering an olive with a plastic fork.

"Nah. We'd go to the park sometimes when my old man was deployed, but mostly us kids thought of ways to stay away from the house as much as possible when the bastard was home." He took a big bite.

Whenever Cobra would talk about his father, sadness filled her heart.

"Don't," he said between mouthfuls.

"What?" Dakota put several olives on a paper plate and set it down in front of him.

"Feel sorry for me."

"I can't help it," she whispered. "My parents were always there for us."

"We can't choose our parents, sweetheart. You were lucky, I wasn't until now." He winked at her and she melted. "It's in the past. We've got our present and future, right?"

"Uh-huh." Dakota took a small bite and slowly chewed.

"Speaking of our present, we gotta talk about what we're gonna do."

She smoothed out the wrinkles on the blanket then pulled at a loose thread.

"Dakota, don't shut down on me. Tell me what's on your mind. I'm a big fucker, I can take it."

"I'm just trying to wrap my head around the whole nomad thing. So we just go wherever we feel like it?"

"Yeah—that's the nomad lifestyle, sweetheart." Cobra put his sandwich down and took another long pull of beer. "Can you live with that, being my old lady and heading out on the road all the time?"

"Your old lady?" What the hell was he talking about?

He laughed. "It means my special woman in biker lingo. It means we belong to each other. I'll honor and respect you and never stray. Mutual loyalty, respect, and love are essential."

"Oh, yeah, of course. I agree with all that. I just wasn't sure what you meant."

"The question is whether you can handle the lifestyle."

Dakota put her hand over his. "The way I see it is that my life and roots are with you. If you go places, I go too. I want to be with you no matter what. I actually can't wait for our adventure to begin with each other. The thought of seeing the country pressed against you on your bike is thrilling."

A big grin spread across his face. She squeezed his hand and he leaned toward her and crushed his mouth on hers for a long while then pulled back.

"I'm ready to head out after Labor Day. Thinking of going west to California or maybe southern Oregon. I fuckin' miss the Pacific. Are you down for that?"

Dakota knew this was the ultimate test between them. If she chose to go, her life would be forever changed in the best way. "I've never seen the ocean." She fixed her gaze on his. "I'm meant to be with you, and I'm not a one town kind of girl. Whenever we head out, I'm there with you on the back of your bike *always*."

Cobra cleared his throat and looked down. "You sure about this? It can get tough out on the road."

"Are you trying to talk me out of it?"

"Fuck no ... I just want you to be sure."

"I'm more than sure." And in case he didn't believe her, Dakota leaned over and grabbed either side of his face with both hands and stared into his eyes. "I love you. Don't forget it." She kissed him, slow and lingering as their tongues tangled. When she pulled away she had to catch her breath before they both started laughing at each other, stars in their eyes.

"We're ditching the fuckin' food. We'll put it in the fridge for later."

Dakota didn't have a chance to respond because Cobra yanked her to her feet and trotted them off across the park to his motorcycle. He stuffed the food and beer into one of the saddle bags and crammed the basket into the other one. The familiar vibration of the engine made her smile as she looped her arms around his waist. Cobra sped away and she felt the rush of wind at her face and an indescribable exhilaration.

He pulled the bike into a space near the front entrance to the hotel, and speed walked her to the elevator then down the hallway toward their room. By the time Cobra opened the door, he was already maneuvering her against the wall, slamming his body against hers as his hands wound in the back of her hair.

"Fuckin' hell, woman, I've gotta have you"

"Cobra," she whispered against his lips. "I'm yours—all of me."

He groaned and ground his hard dick against her while he pushed her legs apart and worked himself even closer.

"Say it again," he ordered, nipping her neck.

"I'm yours. *Always.*"

"I fuckin' love the sound of that, sweetheart."

"Yours … only yours," she whispered as his lips worked a magical line down the column of her throat making her skin dance and grow tight with goosebumps. "Bite me again."

"What, you're giving out the orders now?" Cobra pulled backward with a feigned scowl on his brow. Before Dakota could say anything else, he lifted both her legs until they wrapped around his waist.

She made a pleased noise in the back of her throat and rubbed her tiny skirt. "Not like I planned it that way or anything."

"Fuck, woman." Cobra bit her neck and walked her over to the bed then threw her on it.

Dakota gasped as he kneeled between her legs and pushed up her skirt, inch by inch with her fingers, his smoldering stare boring into her.

"Cobra," she rasped.

"Dakota," he rumbled low. A wolfish smile stretched across his face. "I'm gonna fuck you real good." When he lifted her skirt around her waist, his eyes widened and he groaned. "I didn't know you weren't wearing any panties in the park. Fuck."

"I took them off before I got there. I was going to tell you after we ate, but … here we are." Dakota played her fingers along her wetness. He stilled as he watched her from hooded eyes.

"You look so damn sexy, darlin'," he panted.

"I need you, Cobra. Oh shit …" she moaned as sensations bowed her spine and rolled through her body. "Now, please, *now*."

"It fuckin' does something to me when you beg me." Then he pounced on her, his right hand shoving down his jeans and boxers. "I love you so damn much, woman."

Cobra stole a quick, rough kiss, and then between one breath and the next, he slid inside her. Pleasure ripped through her and she clutched his shoulders while bucking against him.

"That's it, darlin'," he growled against her cheek, his fingers toying with her nipples through the gauze fabric of her top. "Fuck, I'm not gonna last too long. You feel so good around my cock."

As if her body understood him, her inner walls clenched tight as she rocked and writhed beneath him, every nerve ending in her body vibrating.

Cobra drew himself all the way out and shoved himself back in again, pounding into her until the headboard banged against the wall. He worked his hips in circles touching every hidden part of her from the inside until a cloud of euphoric release engulfed her.

"Cobra!" she screamed at the top of her lungs, not giving a rat's ass who heard her through the thin walls.

He thrust harder and deeper until he stiffened. Holding her gaze Cobra rasped, "Dakota," and then she felt the heat from him explode inside her. His dick kept twitching as her walls clamped around him, milking him dry. Dakota kissed his head and caressed him as he panted then collapsed on top of her, his chest heaving.

She ran her fingers through his hair, a big smile spreading across her face. *I'm his old lady. This is really happening.* It was like she'd woken up from a long, dark sleep and was ready to live again. The girl who was restless, broken, and scarred was sure of one thing—Cobra. For the first time in years, she'd found her way. Cobra was her light and she basked in it.

He rolled over on his side and snuggled her close to him. "I fuckin' love you so much," he said. "You're on my mind with every heartbeat, darlin'."

"I love you too. I've finally found the peace that's been alluding me since I started high school."

"We're a good team."

"The best ever," she whispered.

A loving silence fell between them, broken by the growl of her stomach. *Not again!* She buried her face into his chest.

Cobra grasped her chin, tilted her head up, and kissed her deeply. "Hungry?" He pinched the tip of her nose playfully.

"Starving."

"Then let's eat."

"Room service?" she asked.

"Unless you want me to drag my ass to the bike and bring up our lukewarm sandwiches and beer."

Dakota gave him a quick kiss then rolled out of bed. She tossed the menu to him. "I'll have a cheeseburger with chili cheese fries. Let's eat out on the balcony." She glanced at the sherbet-colored streaks in the darkening sky.

This is really my life.

She ambled back to the bed and climbed in and cuddled next to Cobra as he called in their order.

And this sexy, handsome, sweet man is mine.

Sometimes life was just perfect.

EPILOGUE

Three months later
Bodega Bay, California

THE OCEAN BREEZE tousled Dakota's long hair, and Cobra reached out and caught a few strands. The silken tendrils curled around his finger like a clinging vine. He breathed in the rich, briny smell of the sea and pressed Dakota closer to his chest until her body molded to his and his to hers. She leaned her head back against his shoulder then buried her bare feet into the sand. Gulls soared and swooped over the water, their raucous cries echoing above the breaking waves.

"Watching all those seagulls reminds me of Hitchcock's movie, *The Birds*," Dakota said. "It's kinda freaky, you know?"

Cobra chuckled and squeezed her tightly. "Not for me. I fuckin' love the sound, especially when the beach is empty like it is now. The tourists have gone home for the season and all you got is the sound of waves, the wind, and those fuckin' awesome birds."

Dakota tilted her head up and looked at him. "That's why you picked Bodega Bay to crash for the winter. You know this is the place where Hitchcock filmed the movie."

He dipped his head down and kissed the tip of her nose. "I know because you've told me that more than a few times."

She scowled at him. "Smartass."

He laughed then cupped her chin in his palm and kissed her deep and slow. "Love you, sweetheart," he whispered against her mouth.

"Me too. I'm so happy," she murmured.

"Yeah."

Dakota looked back at the water. "I'll never get tired of sitting with you on the sand watching the ocean. You were right—it's magical."

"Sharing it with you makes it even more special for me."

Smudges of coral, lavender, turquoise, and orange blended together in the sky as the sun began its descent into the depths of the horizon.

"This is my favorite part of the day at the beach. Time just seems to slow down and the fuckin' colors of the clouds just blow my damn mind. For me, it's always a Zen moment," Cobra said as he stared out at the water.

"It is beautiful. I've always loved sunsets, but the ones over the ocean are incredible," she said.

He watched her take out a paper bag and pull out a cellophane-wrapped piece of saltwater taffy.

She reached up and touched his lips with the candy. "Want one?"

"What flavor is it?" he asked.

"Pistachio. It's super good."

Cobra took it from her fingers, unwrapped it and popped it in his mouth.

"How do you like it?" Dakota asked as she took out another one and put it in her mouth.

"Pretty good. Damn, woman, since you've been working at the taffy shop, you've been bringing home bags of this stuff."

"I've got a confession to make—I'm obsessed with it," she groaned. "This is the worst job I could've taken. I can't stop trying all the flavors."

He rustled his hand along the top of her hair. "You're such a cute goofball. I guess it beats me bringing home fish from the cannery every day."

"True, but I do like it when you bring home crab and albacore. I never thought I'd love seafood so much."

When they'd arrived in Bodega Bay in early September, they stayed at a motel for a few days until Cobra met Rocky. The dude was a biker and he'd admired Cobra's purple Harley, so the two of them spent the next couple of hours talking about motorcycles. Rocky then told Cobra that he and his old lady had a houseboat in the marina where they lived six months of the year. The biker and his wife were from Texas, and they were planning to head back home to visit their four kids and he asked if Cobra would like to stay on the boat while they were away. The charge was the monthly slip fee, HOA, and utilities, all easily affordable based on what he and Dakota were bringing in from their jobs. So Cobra jumped at the chance, and when he'd come back to the motel later that day to tell Dakota, she couldn't pack fast enough.

The sky darkened and the wind picked up and he felt Dakota shiver in his arms. "Are you cold?"

"A little. It can get real chilly when the sun goes down."

"Yeah. Let's get going." He untangled his arms around her then pushed up. "Where do you wanna go for dinner? I've got a hankering for fish tacos."

Dakota got up, brushed the sand from her shorts, and leaned into him. "I'd rather stay home tonight—I'm beat." She stood on her tiptoes and brushed her mouth across his collarbone. "I can make you some real mean tacos."

"Fuck, darlin'." Cobra gently tugged her hair so her head tilted back then he kissed her. "You make the dinner and I'll provide the dessert." He winked and squeezed her ass.

She playfully smacked his chest then pulled away and slung her tote over her shoulder. He grabbed her hand and they made their way up the steep stairs to the parking lot.

The lights of the marina twinkled through the darkness, their reflection dancing and shimmering on the inky surface of the rippling water. The town's lights stretched out along the southeastern shore, its streetlights and lit restaurant windows glowed a dim, golden hue in the clear night air.

Above the clatter of pots and pans and the din of loud voices, sail ropes snapped against their masts and docked boats creaked as they swayed gently against their moorings. Cobra and Dakota's footsteps echoed hollowly up the aluminum dock as they hurried to the forty-four foot trawler they were renting.

The boat had a kitchen, a living space with a full-sized couch, two full bathrooms, a large bedroom and a small spare room. During the warm days and nights, they spent most of their time out on the mid-deck of the trawler, but on chilly nights, they cuddled on the couch in the living room in front of the space heater and watched movies on the thirty-two inch television.

After changing into sweatpants and a white T-shirt, Cobra joined Dakota out on the deck and handed her a glass of red wine. Since they'd been in Bodega Bay, they'd taken many small trips to Napa Valley exploring the lush countryside and vineyards. It was during one of their trips to a winery in Yountville that both he and Dakota discovered how much they enjoyed drinking red wine. Prior to coming to the area, Cobra never would've considered trying wine—he'd always been a beer and hard liquor sort of guy.

He sat down beside her and slipped his arm around her shoulders and she leaned into him. They sipped the wine and stared at the stars sparkling against the darkened sky.

"I made twenty sales today," Dakota said as she put her glass down on the small table in front of them.

Before they'd left Philipsburg for Bodega Bay, Dakota had designed a website to see if she could sell any of her tattoo designs. The site had a ton of information about the art of tattooing, whether a person should or shouldn't get a tattoo, a lot of funny anecdotes, and a hell of a lot of pictures along with her cutting edge designs. It seemed that her online business was starting to pick up, and a local journalist asked if he could do a story about her in the regional newspaper.

"That's great, darlin'." Cobra gently stroked her cheek with the back of his fingers.

"I'm so excited. I can't believe people want to buy stuff from me—

it's too cool." She brought the glass to her lips.

"You're a kickass artist. You got a real talent. The great thing is you can make money no matter where we are."

"I'd love to be able to make enough money so that's all I have to do. I could then start selling other related products and make a commission if someone buys them. The sky's the limit."

"It is—you can do whatever you put your mind to, sweetheart."

"Thanks for your support." Dakota looped her arm around his neck and kissed him.

"You'll always have it—you know that." Cobra took another drink of wine. "Fuck, this is real good. We gotta go back to that winery and pick up another case. My brothers would shit a brick if they saw me sipping wine." He chuckled.

Dakota joined in laughing. "Now I have something on you whenever we go to Missoula. I'd really like to see the clubhouse and meet all the guys."

"You will."

"And I'm ready to go back to the vineyard when you are. I love driving through all the rolling hills and winding roads through the countryside. It's so beautiful."

"Yeah. Maybe we can head over there next Tuesday." Cobra had worked it so he had the same days off as Dakota even though it meant he only worked four days a week instead of five. He didn't mind because the pay was good and it gave him more time with the woman who'd stolen his heart and blew his world apart in the best fucking way.

"I'm in. Oh … I talked to my mom today."

"Oh yeah? How's everything?"

Dakota nodded. "Good. You know, I really miss my parents. It's been over a year since I've seen them."

"We can make a stop in Pocatello when we head out in the late spring for the New England states."

"I'd love that! I'll call my mom and tell her tomorrow. She'll be so happy. I'm looking forward to seeing my sister and her new baby, and of course my brothers. Oh ... I forgot to tell you about Taylor—he's missing. It's the damnedest thing."

Cobra drained his glass then leaned over and poured some more wine in it. "Hmm ..."

"Luke told me. Taylor hasn't contacted my brother in over five months. His parents haven't heard from him either. It's strange. I wonder if he just decided to take off and start over."

"Probably pissed the fuck outta some dude by messing with his woman. Guys like that asshole usually end up paying for what they do. Now you don't have to worry about him anymore." Cobra shifted a little and plopped his feet up on the table, crossing his legs at the ankles.

"I could see that happening—he was such a creep. Since I fell in love with you, I haven't thought about him in a long time." She put her hand on his thigh and squeezed. "Do you ever miss your family? I don't mean your dad, but your sister and brother or ... your mom?"

"No fuckin' way on my mom, not too sure about my brother. According to my sister, he's a junkie and is part of the criminal justice revolving door system—in and out of court-ordered rehab when he's not in jail. I actually would like to see Sylvia now that we're in California. The new guy she's with seems like he's an okay dude which is a first for her. Last time I saw her she was just starting high school." He ran his hand through his hair. "Fuck ... that is a long time ago."

"Then it's time you saw her. It'll be great for both of you. Besides, I'd love to meet your sister and your nieces and nephews."

Cobra gave her a sidelong glance. "You sure about that?"

"Yes, why wouldn't I be?"

He shrugged and stared out at the water. "Just checking. We could take a few days off and go to Oceanside. It's about an eight or nine hour ride. Maybe we could go in two weeks. Check with your boss about taking the time off."

"I will. I'd love to see where you grew up. I can't wait to see you melt when you see your sister's kids," she said as she playfully poked him in the side.

In a movement so swift she didn't have time to react, he grabbed Dakota, pushed her down on the cushions of the love seat and started tickling her.

"You wanna see me crumble like a fuckin' pussy? he said.

"Yes, definitely." She giggled and squirmed.

Cobra tickled her ribs, her sides, and under her chin as Dakota squealed.

"You'd like that wouldn't you?" He smiled widely.

"Yes!" Dakota barely got the word out between her laughing and screeching.

He released her and stared down at her glittering eyes. "I love the way you laugh."

Dipping his head down, Cobra crushed his mouth against hers. Her lips clung to his, and she wrapped her arms around his neck and arched her back toward him. Desire burned and crackled inside him, and he slipped his hand under her back then pulled her tight against him and deepened the kiss.

A sweet moan from her mouth to his drove him fucking crazy as his tongue tangled with hers. He pressed against her harder until she gulped small breaths of air and still he wanted closer. He felt her tits against his chest, the nipples hard and tempting.

"I fuckin' love you," he said.

"Me too," she whispered.

For a second only their heavy breathing filled the air, and they were frozen in the moment, suspended in reality, existing only in each other's gazes.

Then Dakota traced her finger over his brows, down his nose, over his cheeks, and across his lips until he caught it in his mouth and sucked it lightly.

"You're my heart and my life," she murmured.

"And you're my fuckin' forever."

A small smile danced across her lips. "I like the sound of that."

He kissed her again then pulled back. "You're my old lady and that's serious, sweetheart. Our hearts are melded and you and me belong to each other."

"So are we engaged?" She smiled.

"More than that—we're fused together. And there isn't anything we can't love each other through. The good and the bad shit—it doesn't matter because we'll always be together."

"You're my soulmate forever plus one."

"Sounds perfect to me, darlin'."

At that moment, a low growl came from his woman's stomach and he laughed.

"I guess I should go in and make those fish tacos." She grinned.

Cobra stood and helped her up. She grabbed the wine bottle and walked down the steps into the kitchen. He closed the hatch and locked it then put his arm around her waist and snagged her to him.

"Let's have our dessert first." He nuzzled his face against hers.

Dakota licked her lips and took his hand then led him to their bedroom. Once there, Cobra wrestled her to the bed with his lips on hers as he pulled off her clothes. The room was dark except for the dim light from the stars streaming in through the two windows. There was a click as he switched on the bedside lamp and a warm yellow light suffused the room.

Cobra stepped back and sucked in a sharp breath as his gaze traveled over his woman: glowing skin, pert tits, erect pink nipples, small belly button, narrow waist, softly curved hips, shapely legs, toes, painted blue. Then his gaze swept back up and lingered at the smooth apex between her thighs before moving to her flushed face.

"You're so fuckin' beautiful."

His sexy, wonderful old lady completed him like nothing ever had in his life.

Locking his intense gaze on hers, he lifted his T-shirt over his head then pulled off his sweatpants, tossing it on top of his shirt on the floor. Cobra climbed on the bed and kissed her full lips hard then trailed his mouth down her throat, loving the way she shivered and moaned beneath his touch.

"I need you," she whispered. She grabbed his hair and pushed his head down farther, arching into him.

He gripped her wrist and pulled her hand away. "Put your arms above your head and keep them there."

"But—"

"No buts, sweetheart. I'm gonna get there when *I* want to." He winked at her. "We got all night." A grin spread across his face when she writhed and groaned on the mattress.

Crushing his mouth on hers, he kissed her deep and rough and hard. After a long while, he trailed his lips down her throat and kissed and licked her body as he slowly worked his way down to her hot sweet spot.

A whiskey neat. The rumble of the bike underneath him. The ocean waves crashing against the shore. His woman wet and ready for him. And the rest of their lives together.

Oh yeah ... life doesn't get any better than this.

Make sure you sign up for my newsletter so you can keep up with my new releases, special sales, free short stories, and other treats only available to newsletter readers. When you sign up, you will receive a FREE hot and steamy novella. Sign up at: http://eepurl.com/bACCL1

Notes from Chiah

As always, I have a team behind me making sure I shine and continue on my writing journey. It is their support, encouragement, and dedication that pushes me further in my writing journey. And then, it is my wonderful readers who have supported me, laughed, cried, and understood how these outlaw men live and love in their dark and gritty world. Without you—the readers—an author's words are just letters on a page. The emotions you take away from the words breathe life into the story.

Thank you to my amazing Personal Assistant Natalie Weston. I don't know what I'd do without you. Your patience, calmness, and insights are always appreciated. Thank you for stepping in when I'm holed up tapping away on the computer, oblivious to the world. You make my writing journey that much smoother. Thank you for ALWAYS being there for me! I'm so lucky on my team!

Thank you to my editor Lisa Cullinan, for all your insightful edits, comments, and suggestions that made this story a better one. You definitely made this book shine. As always, a HUGE thank you for your patience and flexibility with accepting my book in pieces. I never could have hit the Publish button without you. You're the best!

Thank you to my wonderful beta readers Natalie Weston, Liz Fabrizio, Darlene Perry, Clare Stevens, and Maryann Reed. You rock! Your enthusiasm and suggestions for Retribution: Nomad Biker Romance Series were spot on and helped me to put out a stronger, cleaner novel.

Thank you to the bloggers for your support in reading my book, sharing it, reviewing it, and getting my name out there. I so appreciate all your efforts. You all are so invaluable. I hope you know that. Without you, the indie author would be lost.

Thank you ARC readers you have helped make all my books so much stronger. I appreciate the effort and time you put in to reading, reviewing, and getting the word out about the books. I don't know what I'd do without you. I feel so lucky to have you behind me. And a big Thank You for your patience when I'm just on deadline.

Thank you to my Street Team. Thanks for your input, your support, and your hard work. I appreciate you more than you know. A HUGE hug to all of you! A big THANK YOU for pitching in there when some of the books are pretty close to the wire or at the wire. I am indebted to your patience and dedication.

Thank you to Carrie from Cheeky Covers. You are amazing! I can always count on you. You are the calm to my storm. You totally rock, and I love your artistic vision.

Thank you to my proofers who worked hard to get my novel back to me so I could hit the publish button on time. There are no words to describe how touched and grateful I am for your dedication and support. Also much thanks for your insight re: plot and characterization. I definitely took heed, and it made my story flow that much better.

Thank you to Ena and Amanda with Enticing Journeys Promotions who have helped garner attention for and visibility to my books. Couldn't do it without you!

Thank you to my awesome formatter, Paul Salvette at Beebee Books. You make my books look stellar. I appreciate how professional you are and how quickly you return my books to me. A huge thank you for doing rush orders and always returning a formatted book of which I am proud. Kudos!

Thank you to the readers who continue to support me and read my books. Without you, none of this would be possible. I appreciate your comments and reviews on my books, and I'm dedicated to giving you the best story that I can. I'm always thrilled when you enjoy a book as much as I have in writing it. You definitely make the hours of typing on the computer and the frustrations that come with the territory of writing books so worth it.

And a special thanks to every reader who has been with me since "Hawk's Property." Your support, loyalty, and dedication to my stories touch me in so many ways. You enable me to tell my stories, and I am forever grateful to you.

You all make it possible for writers to write because without you reading the books, we wouldn't exist. Thank you, thank you! ♥

Retribution: Nomad Biker Romance Series (Book 2)

Dear Readers,

Thank you for reading my book. This book is the second one in my new standalone series—Nomad Biker Romance. The book and series deal with those bikers who live a solitary life on the road, feeling the freedom of no boundaries. Each of the bikers in the series are loosely attached to MCs, but for various reasons, they've chosen to break away from the daily MC life and trade it in for a solo life on the road.

In the second book of the series, Cobra was once the Enforcer for the Steel Devils MC but broke away after doing a stint in prison. He wanted to get away from the violence, but he was not able to leave the Steel Devils MC entirely. A Nomad patch was on his back and he hit the open road on his Harley-Davidson. I hope you enjoyed the second book in my new series as much as I enjoyed writing Cobra and Dakota's story. This gritty and rough way of life is never easy, but being on the open road has its own kind of rewards. I hope you will look for the upcoming books in the series. Romance makes life so much more colorful, and a rough, sexy bad boy makes life a whole lot more interesting.

If you enjoyed the book, please consider leaving a review on Amazon. I read all of them and appreciate the time taken out of busy schedules to do that.

I love hearing from my fans, so if you have any comments or questions, please email me at chiahwilder@gmail.com or visit my facebook page.

To receive a **free copy of my novella**, *Summer Heat*, and to hear of **new releases**, **special sales**, **free short stories**, and **ARC opportunities**, please sign up for my **Newsletter** at http://eepurl.com/bACCL1.

Happy Reading,

Chiah

Animal's Reformation: Insurgents MC
Coming Early June 2019

A member of the Insurgents MC, Animal is a rough, free-loving biker. Hanging with his brothers, riding his customized Harley, and partying with the ladies are his idea of the ideal life.

Years ago, he made a stupid mistake with a woman he barely knew, but he pays the child support every month and sends cards and presents to his out-of-state daughter on her birthday and on holidays.

He doesn't want a steady woman, and he certainly isn't ready to settle down and have a family. Life is just too good now, and there are always so many women who want to come and play with this rugged biker.

Then one afternoon, the mother of his child struts into the clubhouse with his daughter in tow and tells him she's done. She walks away, leaving Animal and Lucy staring at each other.

What's he supposed to do? He knows about bikes and hard partying, not seven-year-old girls.

He has to change his ways, and his new hot next-door neighbor isn't helping to keep his libido in check. The way her long dark hair swings just above her sweet behind has him thinking all kinds of nasty thoughts, but she doesn't give him the time of day.

What's up with that?

Olivia Mooney is very aware of her neighbor's good looks and his

finely chiseled body, but she doesn't want to get involved. He doesn't realize it, but she's his daughter's tutor at school, and she can't get involved. She spends her nights thinking about him and chatting with an intriguing man on an after dark dating site.

Then a series of murders occur in the surrounding counties, and it looks like they are creeping closer to Pinewood Springs. At first the cops are stumped, but over time a pattern begins to emerge: the women all used an after dark dating site.

As fear and danger slink closer, Olivia is thrown into the arms of the sexy biker, forever changing their lives.

The Night Rebels MC series are standalone romance novels. This is Army's. This book contains violence, abuse, strong language, and steamy/graphic sexual scenes. It describes the life and actions of an outlaw motorcycle club. HEA. No cliffhangers. The book is intended for readers over the age of 18.

Forgiveness: Nomad Biker Romance
Already released February 2019

Flux once wore the Insurgents MC patch and his territory was Colorado. Now his bottom rocker reads Nomad.

The open road is Flux's therapy and facing a 1,500-pound bull in the rodeo ring is the way he blocks out the memories. One-night stands, booze and plenty of weed have done a damn good job at keeping his heart locked up.

Until he meets a sassy barrel rider.

The golden hair vixen runs rings around him faster than she rides her horse in the arena, and he can't keep away from her. For the first time since the unspeakable tragedy happened, something stirs inside him.

But he has a long iceberg of guilt that he doesn't want to get rid of. He's chosen to live with it as a reminder of what has happened. Couple that with a bunch of inner demons that don't play nice and he's nothing but a shell of who he once was.

Maggie Haves hasn't known anything except the discipline of practice. Touted as one of the best barrel riders to hit the rodeo circuit, Maggie doesn't have time for anything that will veer her off the pro rodeo trail.

Rugged, tatted and muscular Flux is a very big distraction. Not to mention complicated beyond belief.

Flux has lived on the wild side most of his life, whereas Maggie has always played it safe. She knows the biker is danger in leather, but she's drawn to him like a moth to a flame. Something about him keeps luring her, and she's willing to take a chance on love with this imperfect man even if it destroys her.

Will Maggie be the one to show Flux that he deserves to live again … and forgive himself, or will his demons devour her before he throws her away?

Can two unlikely people find love in the midst of so much darkness?

The Nomad Biker series are standalone romance novels. This is Flux's story. This book contains violence, abuse, strong language, and steamy/graphic sexual scenes. HEA. No cliffhangers. The book is intended for readers over the age of 18.

Forgiveness: Nomad Biker Romance

Other Books by Chiah Wilder

Insurgent MC Series:

Hawk's Property
Jax's Dilemma
Chas's Fervor
Axe's Fall
Banger's Ride
Jerry's Passion
Throttle's Seduction
Rock's Redemption
An Insurgent's Wedding
Outlaw Xmas
Wheelie's Challenge
Christmas Wish
Insurgents MC Romance Series: Insurgents Motorcycle Club Box Set (Books 1 – 4)
Insurgents MC Romance Series: Insurgents Motorcycle Club Box Set (Books 5 – 8)

Night Rebels MC Series:

STEEL
MUERTO
DIABLO
GOLDIE
PACO
SANGRE
ARMY

Nomad Biker Romance Series:

Forgiveness

Steamy Contemporary Romance:

My Sexy Boss

Find all my books at: amazon.com/author/chiahwilder

I love hearing from my readers. You can email me at chiahwilder@gmail.com.

Sign up for my newsletter to receive a FREE Novella, updates on new books, special sales, free short stories, and ARC opportunities at http://eepurl.com/bACCL1.

Visit me on facebook at facebook.com/AuthorChiahWilder

Made in the USA
Lexington, KY
08 June 2019